POSSESSION MIGHT BE NINE-TENTHS OF THE LAW— BUT NOT WHEN IT CAME TO CHRISTINA

MIGUEL CLEMENTE

Clever and conniving, he tested Christina to the point of no return—and lost in the end.

LAURINDA ALVAREZ

Her heart was in her mouth over Christina, and then her mouth was all over Christina's heart.

DIRK BOLAND

He was a British pathologist, but there was nothing dead about him, except his deadly desire for Christina.

KIM & LITA

They were Chinese travel agents who treated Christina to a trip around the world—without any of them leaving the hotel.

MARGOT WELLS

Titian-tressed, a legal dynamo, she loved nothing better than addressing herself to the briefs of Christina.

LILO

Her Polynesian tongue spoke a language that was immediately understood and appreciated by all who encountered it.

HWANG & CHUNG

They wrestled in Korea and pinned Christina to the mat and the mattress.

CHRISTINA WAS NOBODY'S FOOL—BUT SHE WAS EVERYBODY'S DELECTABLE DARLING.

Other books by

BLAKELY ST. JAMES

CHRISTINA'S ESCAPE
BLAKELY ST. JAMES

PLAYBOY
PAPERBACKS

CHRISTINA'S ESCAPE

Published simultaneously in the United States and Canada by Playboy Paperbacks, New York, New York. Printed in the United States of America. Library of Congress Catalog Card Number: 80-85110. First edition.

Books are available at quantity discounts for promotional and industrial use. For further information, write to Premium Sales, Playboy Paperbacks, 1633 Broadway, New York, New York 10019.

ISBN: 0-872-16820-4

First printing May 1981.

For Candy,
my sweet

CHAPTER ONE

Voilà!

Lying here on the terrace of my villa on the Costa del Sol, basking in the warm Mediterranean sun, it has just dawned on me that I have not made love to either man, woman, or child in almost twenty-four hours. Imagine one entire day in the life of Christina van Bell passing without once feeling the bliss of a devoted phallus or tongue in the nest of my crotch, or savoring the sweet succulence of a moist vulva against the profile of my face. Impossible, you say? Yes and I agree.

Before such a tragic statistic becomes a reality, I must do everything within my power to prevent it. I blame it all on Miguel Clemente, who swore he would be with me last night after almost a month in South America on business. Instead I had to drink the reunion champagne alone, forced to suppress my anticipatory passions with the carved ivory vibrator he had given me on the eve of his departure. It is not like me to wait for any man after a given hour, but he had been so positive and convincing regarding the time of his return besides being devastatingly handsome and charming that I had waited hours longer than I ordinarily would have. So long, in fact, that I was quite incapable of making other arrangements by the time it became obvious that something had delayed him.

Yesterday afternoon had been so merry with the arrival of a package from him. There were gold, silver, and emerald trinkets for me, but what really delighted me was a small, sealed jar containing a substance that resembled liquefied pearls. With it came a note: "My darling Christina To prove how much I love you and how faithful I have been to you in my absence, enclosed is a container filled with my entire month's total ejaculations (all hand-extracted). I must hurry back to you before I have a stroke from too many such strokes. See you as planned. Love always, Miguel."

I laugh again at his originality. He can be so clever and inventive just as he is in his lovemaking. Of course I did not in any way believe him. With his romantic resourcefulness, he probably paid a couple of young boys to masturbate into the jar until it was brimming with semen. I should hire a laboratory to conduct electropheresis tests on the sperm and so determine the blood type of the source. Even ingenious Miguel was unlikely to have thought of that possibility. But this is wishful whimsy since I am on the coast of Spain, far from such technology.

"Señorita?" a soft, musical voice inquired tentatively.

When I turned in response, I saw a stunning young girl in a peasant skirt and a billowy white blouse, smiling at me. Her hair had the luster of a panther's black coat, and lively dark eyes danced in her lovely face. "Yes?" I responded. I was sunbathing naked, and that seemed to make her hesitate in moving toward me.

"I am from the office of Señor Clemente," she explained. "He has requested that I offer you his apologies for the unavoidable delay in his arrival."

"Come closer," I invited her, sitting up on the chaise now to get a fuller view of her. "I'm not dangerous."

She smiled again, more shyly this time because everything that I am physically was now totally visible to her. "You are very beautiful," she said.

"Thank you," I responded. "You're an exceptionally lovely girl yourself."

Her eyes dropped in mild embarrassment. "I cannot compare," she said almost in a whisper.

"Sit down." I pointed to the cushioned chair next to me. "Now tell me what happened to him."

"Mechanical problems with his plane," she said in a quick summary. "They were forced to land in the Canary Islands, where he still remains."

"No one was hurt?" I asked.

"No," she reported. "Señor Clemente said to tell you the only pain he felt was the pain of missing his date with you."

"That rascal," I smiled. "He's tenacious."

She nodded, her eyes seemingly fixed on the slice that split my thighs. Little did she know that she had come in answer to a prayer and would save me from the dire fate of going a full swing around the clock without an act of intercourse.

"Do you live alone in this beautiful place?" she inquired with a degree of awe.

"I live alone, but I don't love alone," I replied blithely.

"That is quite easy to understand," she said, still being quite proper and businesslike.

"How about some champagne?" I suggested. "You've made this long trip to deliver a message; now you deserve to relax."

"Never at such an early hour," she reacted.

"Come on," I coaxed her. "Forget about the time. It's meaningless when you look out over the blue of the sea."

Her eyes followed mine as we gazed over the azure waters and the lacy, white embroidery of the waves on the shore. My imagination had begun to formulate a picture of her beneath her unrevealing apparel. By the time we looked into each other's eyes, my blood was simmering with desire for her based on that mental portrait.

"You haven't even told me your name," I purred, touching her for the first time. I could have sworn her pulse quickened at the contact, further accelerating my own heartbeat.

"Laurinda," she said softly.

"Christina," I introduced myself

She leaned over and kissed me delicately on the cheek. I needed no further stimulation. With a swift lunge I was upon her, adroitly finding the key hooks to removing her skirt and blouse She lay almost totally still, her mouth agape and her breathing shallow, as I skinned away everything hiding her body. Her breasts rose like fresh, olive-colored mountains. Beneath them, the bristly hairs of her cunt stood out like a triangular patch of sagebrush hiding the oasis of her vulva.

"Love me," she urged in a desperate voice.

Her eyes seemed to melt as our nipples touched and our cunts entangled. I slid my open lips over her trembling mouth and quickly engaged her tongue in a hot, frothy duel with mine. Our hands met briefly as each sought the other's pussy, fingering the slippery furrows in quest of the opposite clit.

"Aughhhhh," she groaned as her back arched with the impact of her first climax. I came almost immediately after she did, fucking her fully immersed middle finger as though it was the hardened cock of a randy schoolboy.

"Suck me!" she pleaded as I tore my tongue from her mouth to gasp for breath.

I went down on her instantly, spreading her legs apart as forcefully as I might break a wishbone. In the glistening blackness of her pussy hair, I found her tender cunt, crinkled like the meat of an English walnut. I sucked in the pungent juices as my tongue found its way to the hardened little digit of her clitoris. This I lashed savagely with my flailing tongue as she pressed the mask of her full cunt into my face.

"*Conjo!*" she screamed, the Spanish version of cunt. I bit her lightly for that, and instantly she came over my face, flooding it with the silvery juices of her love nest.

When she went down on me a short while later, I had a moment to evaluate her spectacular figure. How beautifully titted and curvily assed she was! The sight of her made the thrust of her tongue seem even deeper and more fulfilling inside me. I dug my fingers into the rich abundance of her jet black hair, bracing myself for the certain overlapping of multiple orgasms building within me. I was not disappointed.

"Laurinda!" I cried in magnificent anguish as the storm struck my senses. My legs locked about her head as tight as a vise while close to a dozen climaxes racked my body in quick succession.

We washed each other in the pool behind the villa, taking time to make love twice more before she had to go. "I will be back," she promised, "whenever Señor Clemente is away."

"I'll see that he's away often," I promised, "now that I've experienced what capable aides he leaves behind to substitute for him."

"I love you, Christina," she stated from the steps leading to her car.

I threw her a kiss and looked heavenward in gratitude. Someone up there must care about me. A full day had not been allowed to pass without a lovely reward for Christina.

CHAPTER TWO

After a leisurely breakfast of champagne and strawberries, I put on a pair of bikini shorts and a string bra, hopped into my Porsche, and drove up the coast from Marbella to Malaga. Miguel was due to land there in the early afternoon, and it was my intention to surprise him by replacing his chauffeur. Laurinda had helped me with that substitution by simply not telling his driver about the call she had received at the office, detailing their employer's plans.

The drive was sunny and pleasant, the breeze delicious as it flung back my long tresses like a flag waving behind me. I turned up the stereo and added rhythmic notes to the music created by the rushing air. What a buoyant mood I was in—frisky, frolicsome, full of fun and mischief. The lethargic attitude that had bogged me down for several days —before meeting Laurinda—had vanished, and in its place was my favorite facet of my own personality, the effervescent, devil-may-care, sybaritic Christina. I knew it was the one Miguel liked best, too.

Spain was such a marked change from the Riviera. It was so casual, subdued, and far less pretentious. I loved to come to the Costa del Sol when Monte Carlo, Nice, and St. Tropez began to get on my nerves as they had recently. And there was always Miguel as an added attraction—so courtly and distinguished, yet always mischievously erotic below the surface. To a large degree he combined all of the qualities I liked best in people—intelligence, passion, and a sense of humor in a body that was virilely handsome and physically powerful. The more I thought about him, the more I looked forward to our reunion in the next few hours.

Once again in my life—as it so often happened—the blond hair obsession of so many Spanish men got me a great deal of unwanted attention from the bolder males at the airport. I am not fluent in Spanish, but I know all the vulgarisms. And I heard most of them muttered as I walked by, references to me and my anatomy that I might consider provocatively flattering if only they came from the mouths of people I desired. As always I did my best to ignore them, even those who crassly clutched their crotches and made suggestive grunts. But I knew they would all be much more subdued and maybe even silent when they saw me exit with a man of the physique and good looks of Miguel Clemente.

However, an inquiry at the reservations counter sent me scurrying back through the terminal sans Miguel. A glance at my watch told me I was right on time, but I was in the wrong place. Private aircraft were handled at another set of hangars in another corner of the landing field. Damn! I had so wanted to surprise him the moment he stepped from his Lear jet, anticipating a routine greeting from his chauffeur or someone from the office.

My silver car must have looked like a bullet as I raced along a spur road to the correct terminal. I should have known all along that noncommercial craft would not use the same facilities as the international jumbo jets. A quick glance around the field as I neared the terminal gave me some hope. I didn't see any sign of the familiar Clemente logo on any of the planes on the ground.

There were the usual stares, but they were accompanied by approving smiles rather than coarse comments in this smaller terminal. It was a good thing because I was in no mood to tolerate any filthy propositions from random strangers—not when my plans were in danger of misfiring.

"*Por favor*," I said breathlessly to a man who seemed to be in charge at the flight scheduling desk, "has the Clemente plane arrived yet from the Canary Islands?"

He looked up and down unsmilingly and then consulted a clipboard on the desk beside him. "Miguel Clemente?" he asked.

"Yes," I responded eagerly, "he's the one."

"He is due momentarily," the man informed me. "Gate Three."

"*Gracias*," I gushed, cheered by the news that my plan seemed likely to work after all.

It was only a matter of minutes before the loudspeaker crackled with the announcement I awaited. "Clemente, Flight Seventeen, arriving Gate Three."

I watched as it landed as gracefully as a gull on a calm sea. The plane was flagged in to a spot only twenty feet or so from where I was standing. As soon as the engines were silenced, Miguel emerged, as eager and alert as he always seemed, even when everyone else was exhausted. I burst through the glass door and ran toward him, arms outstretched. The sight of me stopped him dead in his tracks.

"Christina!" he cried jubilantly. "Is this Malaga or heaven?"

"Miguel!" I shouted and threw myself into his arms. They closed around me in a strong yet tender embrace. A moment later his lips lavished kisses all over my face, ending in a sustained merger that brought applause from a handful of airport workers who were witnessing our reunion. That brought us both reluctantly back to reality. Miguel eased his hold on me, and I smiled at the workmen who had whistled and clapped good-naturedly at our impromptu exhibition.

"It's been a long time," I explained to no one in particular.

"How sweet of you to come for me," Miguel said as he guided me toward the hangar terminal.

"I wanted to surprise you—just as you surprised me with

that little container you sent me," I told him with a mischievous look.

He bit back a smile. "I wanted you to have a part of me," he said with mock solemnity, "a very real part of me in my absence."

"There were the makings of a whole army of little Miguels in that jar," I jibed.

Now he allowed a smile to surface on his face. "One is already more than enough," he declared.

Before I could respond, his pilot caught up to us, carrying several small pieces of luggage and a suit bag. "Señor," he addressed Miguel, "shall I take these to your home or will you be taking them with you?"

Miguel turned to me. "I don't think you are driving a truck or a limousine, are you, Christina?"

"My silver Porsche," I replied. "It's a little tight on luggage space."

"Carlos," he said to the slim, leather-jacketed man who was his long-time pilot, "you would be doing me a most gracious favor if you could drop them off at the villa—provided that does not interfere with any of your plans." That Miguel, always as considerate of his employees as he was of his social peers. It was a quality I thoroughly liked in a man, especially a man of his stature and success.

"Absolutely no problem at all, Señor Clemente," Carlos responded. "I am so happy to be back in Spain I would drive to Madrid if you asked me."

"*Gracias,* Carlos," Miguel dismissed him. "I will call you later regarding the week's schedule. With Christina here, there is a very good chance I won't be needing you for a few days."

"Whatever." He smiled and shrugged. A moment later he disappeared around a corner.

Miguel took care of the official details at the customs counter and filed his flight log with the proper department, then we were set to go. "Now," he said with a look of anticipation, "you, Christina, are my only concern."

He insisted on driving. Men do not sit in the passenger seat with a lady at the wheel unless they are ill or elderly, he declared. But I knew of his fondness for fast cars, and mine could quite literally fly. I offered only token resistance since I had further welcoming plans.

"You know what would be fun?" I suggested as we cleared the city traffic and headed for the coastal highway. "Let's drive naked—both of us."

He looked at me cryptically at first, then with visible delight. "As the British say," he responded, "that's a smashing idea."

He pulled the car to the side of the road, and we quickly shed our clothes. His cock rose almost immediately, providing another gearshift for the car. "Maybe we should do something about this before continuing," he said, studying the little mouth of his penis as it gaped up at him like a fish.

"Let's keep going," I replied, "or else we'll be getting back too late. Don't worry about that problem." I looked to his lap. "It'll be solved en route."

He glanced at me slyly. "That's a promise?" he asked.

"Cross my cunt and hope to die," I laughed. A second later I was whipped back in my seat by the speed of his takeoff. "You almost took my tits off," I chided him as we roared down the roadway.

"Never," he replied merrily, "they're tied on with your Fallopian tubes."

"Just be careful," I warned him. "You want me in one piece, don't you?"

"I want you in as many pieces as I can get you," he shot back.

We were both in buoyant spirits. It felt so marvelously free to be whizzing alongside the sparkling blue Mediterranean totally nude, the breezes whipped into a rush of wind by the speed of the car. I spread the lips of my pussy to allow the air to enter me. The funneled wind was like a transparent cock or tongue massaging my tender walls.

Miguel glanced over from time to time, his prick hardening perceptibly every time he saw my cunt.

"That's your red badge of courage," he indicated with a nod.

"That's my pink medal of honor," I corrected.

The sight of his aroused organ was beginning to intoxicate me. It rose like a church steeple against the flat of his belly, his balls hanging like bells in the tower. I reached over and shifted it the same way Miguel manipulated the car's gears.

"Put it in high," he urged.

"I'll put it where I want it," I replied, moving suddenly to devour its purplish corona. My lips slid over the apple-sized head, and I sucked in deeply.

"*Magnífico*," he gasped, his stomach growing taut with anticipation.

With my head rising and falling on his swollen cock, it seemed that we were traveling so fast we weren't even making contact with the highway. I did feel his thigh muscles tense, indicating that he was applying even more pressure to the accelerator. Since we were already going over 100 miles per hour when I began sucking him, the speed now had to be considerably higher. What would happen when he came? I knew how totally he succumbed to his orgasms and only hoped he could keep control of the car while his cock went out of control with climaxes.

"*Chupar! Chupar!*" he cried. "Suck! Suck!"

I began pumping the root of his prick furiously while my tongue slapped and my lips sucked the explosive head. The combination detonated him moments later, the thick cream of his cum spurting copiously into the cavern of my mouth so abundantly it oozed from the corners and dripped down my chin. The car had swerved slightly at the height of his orgasm, but he had managed to maintain control even as his cock was lubricating my mouth and throat. I lifted my head and watched the speedometer needle fall to a more respectable level around the 100 mph mark.

"You sure could have filled the jar with just that one load," I declared. "Are you sure that was a whole month's supply?"

"Don't interrogate me now, Christina," he pleaded. "I want to bask in the glory of that wonderful climax."

The speed at which we were traveling was hardly conducive to basking, but I did lie back and let the soft stream of wind seduce me for a while. There were fleeting looks from drivers and passengers in other cars, no doubt wondering whether their eyes were deceiving them. But they would never know for sure since the combination of our speed and their oncoming speed allowed them little more focus than a blur. It was fun, and I reveled in it.

"I can't continue concentrating on the road," Miguel complained, "with you naked beside me. I've got to pull over and make love to you."

"We'll have lots of time in Marbella," I reminded him. "Let's get there first."

"It's pure torture," he moaned. "I'm tempted to floor the car."

"This road is pretty well policed," I informed him, "especially in this sector."

"You're very negative, Christina," he chided me.

"I feel very positive," I replied. "Very."

"You look very positive," he noted, "but you react very negatively."

I laughed, and the wind carried my laughter away immediately. "The moment I dare to be logical," I responded with a mixture of mild annoyance and considerable amusement, "I'm considered negative. Men are impossible."

"You stole that," he kidded me. "That's a masculine line to be used in reference to the female gender."

"That line is bisexual," I argued.

"Ah." He seized my comment. "Then you agree—women are impossible."

"You're impossible." I narrowed the field. He loved to tease me, and I refused to give him any further opportunities.

"Hark!" he said, "is that a police siren I hear?"

I whipped around in my seat. "Put something on!" I urged.

"I already have a *hard*-on," he jested.

"Miguel, it is the highway police. We'll be arrested for indecent exposure or something," I stammered, trying my best to wriggle into my shorts. Bare breasts, at least, are defensible as Riviera fashion, but naked pussy is still a taboo along most of the Mediterranean coast.

He glanced back to confirm my observation. "I can't get my slacks on at this speed," he said, "and I can't slow down entirely or I'll be admitting guilt."

I threw his slacks over his cock and balls. "Tell them we were swimming and that you only have your trunks on," I suggested.

"Good idea," he said with a surprisingly unconcerned smile. "They won't look at me anyway if you let those gorgeous tits hang out like that."

"It's a calculated risk," I responded. Maybe we should have stopped as Miguel had wanted, but I would not admit that to him now.

Two policemen in brown leather coats and matching helmets pulled up alongside us on powerful twin motorcycles. The Porsche could have easily outrun them, I thought to myself, but that would only result in a road block farther ahead and far more serious charges than mere speeding. Their menacing looks faded, however, when they saw us up close.

"Señor Clemente," they greeted Miguel, "and Señorita van Bell. *Buenas tardes.*"

I smiled demurely as their eyes skimmed my semi-naked body. My picture had been in virtually every celebrity magazine on the continent so it did not really come as a surprise that they recognized me. Miguel was also quite well known as a playboy and as a multimillionaire. As they chattered on in lilting but lightning-fast Spanish, laughing intermittently, I knew almost from the start that we would escape with nothing more than a mild warning. Whatever Miguel was telling them, it must have involved me because they looked over at me repeatedly throughout the conversation. After a few minutes they remounted their cycles and with casual waves of their hands roared off down the ribbon of highway.

"Masterful diplomacy," I congratulated Miguel as he snapped the ignition and dug the tires into the pavement with a screech.

"You didn't understand what I told them?" he questioned.

"You're a native," I reminded him. "You talk like a machine gun, which is way beyond my elementary Spanish."

"It's better that you didn't," he said with a sly laugh.

"Tell me," I insisted, my curiosity piqued.

"You won't get angry with me?" he bartered.

"I don't get angry about anything that can get us out of a speeding charge especially in these tough Spanish courts," I responded.

He looked over at me, a devilish gleam in his eyes. "I simply told them I had lost my head because you had promised me a blow job the moment we got home," he snickered.

I reached over and pounded my fist against his crotch. "There's your blow," I snapped in mock anger. And then we laughed ourselves silly the rest of the trip to Marbella. He had spoken the words, but it was my mouth that had saved the day.

CHAPTER THREE

After a week of making love under both the sun and the moon, Miguel rather mysteriously requested a favor. Not an amatory one   those he got without special solicitation but a business one.

"I have to dispatch one of my most trusted aides to Zurich with an important package of documents," he related with deceptive casualness one evening as we were enjoying cocktails before dinner on his terrace. "I would feel much more secure if you accompanied her there and then met me later in Paris."

My heart leaped. Could he mean Laurinda? "You mean I'd be acting as some kind of bodyguard?" I hedged.

He smiled reassuringly. "Yours is the body that needs guarding," he replied smoothly. "But then hers is not exactly asymmetrical either."

"Who is this mystery creature?" I inquired with as much nonchalance as my eagerness would allow.

"I'm sure you've met her somewhere along the way in our relationship, Christina," he said. "You're an appreciator of beauty in both sexes, and Laurinda is most certainly an admirable specimen."

I hid my features in my glass momentarily. Miguel was a clever man. Perhaps he had extracted a confession from

Laurinda about our memorable first meeting. "The name is vaguely familiar," I admitted after a pause. He nodded as though confirming it.

"A classic Latin beauty," he verified. "Laurinda Alvarez. I don't know what I'd do without her."

"In a business sense." I supplied a qualification.

"Strictly," he responded immediately, his gaze knotting with mine.

I let a cynical smile unravel slowly on my face. He studied it and chose not to challenge it. "What do you say, Christina?" he asked instead. "Would you do it for me?"

"A woman who will lick a man's anus," I replied with mock eloquence, "will do just about anything for him."

He responded by zipping down his fly, dipping his swelling cock into his cocktail, and then presenting it to my lips. "You asked me over for cocktails," I remarked as I grabbed it by the base. "I take it that means your cock and my tail."

Miguel chuckled lightly. "*Que tiene de postre?*" he responded.

"This is your dessert," I reported as my mouth widened to accept the breadth of his thick prick.

"You will like Laurinda," he assured me, moving in and out of my oral cavity as though it was my vagina. The mention of her name again inspired me to a frenzy of dedicated sucking. I squeezed his testicles with one hand and pumped the trunk of his cock with the other. This one is for Laurinda, I said silently, my mouth too filled with juicy flesh to emit any sounds beyond grunts. It didn't take long before his cream overflowed the rim of his cock, squirting about my palate in loose lumps. I swallowed it and licked off the residue, handing his cock back to him in gleaming condition.

"You love cum, don't you?" he stated more than asked.

"Only when it's fresh," I replied. "Coming from jars, it loses something."

"Let me eat you," he suggested, kneeling before me like a sucking supplicant.

I pulled up my loose-fitting beach dress and spread my legs in welcome. "You're a man of compassion," I purred.

"I come with a passion," he said just before wedging his handsome profile into the velvety pleats of my cunt.

I had a marvelous, healthy orgasm as a result of his talented tongue and would have had more if we hadn't been interrupted by Miguel's houseboy. He appeared unfazed by the sight of his boss performing cunnilingus. "Important telephone call, Señor," he announced quickly, disappearing into the shadows from which he had emerged.

Miguel withdrew from me instantly. He was a man who normally kept his business and pleasure separate, but when they did happen to intersect, business came first. "Excuse me, Christina," he said easily, as if he were rising from the dinner table, "it must be Laurinda."

I felt a surge of warmth in my still spread pussy at the mention of her name. Fingering my clit as Miguel started to go inside, I told him, "Tell her I'll be going to Zurich with her."

He turned and smiled. "You are a princess," he said.

While he was gone, I brought myself to a shattering sequence of climaxes solely on the strength of the thought of reuniting with Laurinda. A vision of her gorgeous black-furred cunt looming before my face was enough to inspire a monument to orgasm.

From the moment of the phone call, everything accelerated with blinding speed. The leisurely days abruptly telescoped into a frantic schedule that included a midnight race to the airport in Malaga, a last-minute booking aboard a flight not for Zurich but Lucerne, and then a wild, predawn dash through the lake-strewn countryside to reach Zurich before the banks closed. Almost from the start I had suspected it was money   cash   that was involved, and from the way Laurinda guarded the attaché case she carried, I was certain of it. So many of my friends did the same thing in Europe   it was the only way to circumvent the merciless taxes that prevailed almost everywhere on the continent.

"Isn't this hell, having a mission instead of an emission?" Laurinda laughed in the midst of it all.

"I'm not leaving you until we get together," I pledged, "even if that means missing Miguel in Paris."

She reached over and squeezed my hand. "He'll wait," she assured me. "Just tell him we ran into some difficulties. He expects that anyhow."

"I have a friend with a lovely chalet overlooking Lake Zurich," I told her. "Let's go and spend a few days there just the two of us."

She smiled ruefully. "I wish I could," she lamented, "but I can't be away for more than two days and we've used this one already."

"Then we'll make it one complete, no-sleep twenty-four hours together," I proposed. "How about that?"

Her eyes shone. "I love it," she said with conviction.

With that promise I could endure the tedious routine of international banking. I waited for what seemed like more hours than it probably actually was in a cathedrallike bank in downtown Zurich while Laurinda did whatever it was she had been sent to do inside the massive-doored offices of the bank executives. She looked exquisitely lovely yet vulnerable in such an imposing setting. But I knew Miguel was shrewd and would not entrust her with anything so obviously important unless she was entirely competent and trustworthy.

A huge lobby clock tolled at fifteen-minute intervals. Each of those quarter-hours passed with the weight of a full hour for me. At the ninth tolling of the bells, Laurinda finally emerged. Two and one-quarter hours I had waited. I didn't think I could wait that long, even for an orgy with the royal family of Britain.

"Christina, you poor darling," Laurinda said the moment we were close enough to converse. "I'm sorry it took so long."

"It's sweet of you to be concerned," I responded. "If I'd known, I would have brought along some time accelerators."

"This is a tough country for that sort of stuff," she cautioned.

"They all are," I replied. "I've been getting away with it for years, though."

"You're a celebrity," she said. "They don't search you like they do me."

"Let's get out of this monstrosity," I suggested, sweeping my arm to indict the whole interior of the bank. "I feel like I'm either in prison or in church."

"You're right," she agreed, "let's get out of here."

I held her back momentarily at the entrance. "What about your briefcase?" I asked.

Her laughter was lilting   a good indication that everything had gone all right inside and the weight had been lifted from her pretty shoulders. "It was part of the package," she said with an air of dismissal.

"Proceed," I responded with a laugh of my own. Her mood was definitely lightened. She even went through the revolving doors twice just for the silly fun of it. I stood waiting on the sidewalk as she emerged almost skipping. The businesslike natives scurrying about regarded us with something akin to disdain. "We're not supposed to enjoy ourselves," I pointed out, "not in Zurich. *You vill be businesslike or ve take avay your papers.*"

Laurinda giggled at my mock German accent. "Bankers are impossible people," she confided. "I wonder sometimes if any of them have ever had an orgasm."

"Only when they get a large deposit," I jested.

"Then my man Heinrich must have just come all over his underwear," she confessed. I did not probe any further, and she did not elaborate. It was really none of my business—and besides I didn't really care. What mattered now was that we faced the prospect of a whole day and night together tucked away in a cozy chalet. That was one thing I had accomplished during my long wait in the bank. I had reached my friend in Paris and arranged to borrow his lakeside villa overnight. The housekeeper would be expecting us, then she would leave us alone until luncheon the following day. Perfect except for the brevity of it.

Laurinda called Miguel and informed him that all had gone well. Pleading exhaustion for both of us, she said we intended to stay overnight in a hotel, then she would return to Malaga the following evening while I continued on to Paris to meet him. I did not talk to him, but Laúrinda said he found that arrangement suitable and that he was elated over her successful transaction. "We're on our own, love," she declared merrily after the call.

Together we arranged for a limousine to deliver us to the chalet. It was always fully stocked with food and liquor so there was no need to waste time gathering supplies. We were both excited by the prospect of being alone together in a strange, remote place. I looked at her longingly as the pretty Swiss coutryside rolled by like a Technicolor film on all sides.

"Mmmmmmm," she purred, licking her lips. There was a look of intensely erotic expectation lighting her face, giving it a sensual patina I hadn't seen before.

"Don't turn me on yet," I whispered to her, "or the driver'll be forced to stop and let me cool down the only way possible."

"Which is?" she teased.

"By diving head first into that beautiful river of yours," I retorted breathlessly.

"What about me?" She continued to pursue the subject. "Do you think it's easy for me to be within easy grabbing distance and not finger your silky pussy and suck on those succulent tits?"

"Ba-beeee." I bit the word to emphasize the pressure she was putting on my libido. "Keep it up and I'll say fuck what the driver thinks and just start eating everything you've got."

Laurinda was writhing now, her short skirt bunching up under her derrière, exposing the creamy flesh of her thighs all the way to the edges of her plump and furry pussy. She slipped her middle finger into the center of her lacy bikini panties and depressed it, outlining her central vulva slice. I watched as she circled about the tip, touching the peak of her hidden clitoris. Almost instinctively I sought out my own hardened cunt-cock *simpatico* with her. Sitting there side by side on the limo's broad back seat, we quietly brought ourselves to climax with a desperate effort to avoid a cannibalistic public display. Thank God our chauffeur had begun the slight climb to the chalet off the main road. It would only be a matter of minutes, and then we could become as primitive and savage with each other as we desired.

"You will return for us tomorrow at four P.M.?" I reminded the driver. It was obvious from the stains in the crotch of his uniform that he had witnessed at least part of our masturbatory rites in his rearview mirror and now felt sheepish about his peeping Tomism.

"Yes, madame," he confirmed quickly. "Promptly at four P.M." With that he roared off, scattering pebbles in his haste to evacuate. Had he been friendlier, Laurinda and I might have treated him to a round of fellatio, but now I was just glad that he was gone.

"He was jerking off inside his pants," she noted when we were inside. I complimented her on her observational prowess.

"You don't miss anything, do you?" I laughed.

"Not when it comes to sex," she agreed.

The housekeeper was a motherly old woman with the proud, scrubbed features of someone who has worked hard all her life and would have had it no other way. She oohed and ahhed over us, telling us how beautiful we both were, and then insisted that we evaluate photographs of her daughters and grandchildren. The interlude of polite lying that followed served to cool us both down to some degree— at least temporarily. When the housekeeper finally left, promising to return to prepare us lunch at noon the following day, we both sighed with relief and stripped immediately.

"All I want of you," Laurinda said in her sultriest voice, "is everything."

We came together as though magnetized, generously exposed to each other by nature so that we could realize the completeness of our attraction. I pushed the mound of my cunt against hers and slid my hands over her lovely, smooth ass. Our tits came together, the nipples kissing as we undulated in classic fuck rhythm.

"Let's sixty-nine," I suggested, slipping my tongue wetly into her ear for emphasis.

"I want to suck every drop of sweet syrup from your beautiful cunt," she replied hoarsely, her voice thick with emotion.

A moment later we were on a bed, tenderly, hungrily kissing every inch of lower body flesh on the other, delaying our tongues' inevitable glide to the serpentine crack that was the prize of every woman. I dallied for a time in the small coral lake of her navel, flicking its tiny mounds and ridges with the tip of my mouth organ. Laurinda meanwhile was writing invisible words with her tongue on the thighs that served as her passageway to my simmering delta.

"I love you," she groaned before submerging herself in the slick, juicy valley of my cunt.

The first touch of her tongue was like a flame put to the wick of a dynamite keg. A spasm of sweet shock contracted me momentarily, causing me to cry out in delicious pain. We were like felines together, communicating our joys audibly as well as physically. It was not precisely an orgasm but something unique, like the advance herald shortly before a mighty display. I was inspired. Without any further preliminaries, I plunged my face into the breathing mouth of her cunt, licking everything within touch. Her clit hung like a pink stalactite from the densely bushed roof of her coral love cave. I sucked it as though it was a miniature strawberry ice cream cone, pulling it forcibly between my lips from time to time. The steady beat of my tongue on its durable yet exquisitely tender membranes made Laurinda open and close her pussy like an accordion performing "Flight of the Bumblebee."

"Aughhh!" she grunted from time to time as a climax rippled over the length of her body.

"Ooooh!" I joined in repeatedly as the early waves of orgasm surfed through me.

She had the face of an angel and the cunt of a sorceress, I thought to myself as I drank in the exotic liqueur of her magic hole. We were both producing juices copiously, flooding each other's faces with the exclusive extract of two marvelously vital vulvas. As if in unison by some prearranged formula, we both began exploring the anal tracks of the other simultaneously. She had confessed to me at our first meeting that she had a special fondness for sucking sphincters—assholes in the vernacular—and now we shared our mutual indulgence in the delicacy.

Somewhere along in our succulent lapping, a riptide began to build within me. I had come and come throughout our feverish interlocking, but still I knew that somewhere inside me lurked an enormous orgasmic force capable of transporting me to what seemed like the brink of death and the border of heaven. With little more warning, it struck suddenly and violently, jackknifing my body and all but choking my breath. The impact forced me to evacuate Laurinda's well in a desperate search for breath. I sprawled beside her, arms akimbo, sucking in air with all the frenzied dedication I had been sucking her cunt with moments earlier. The afterwaves of the orgasm continued to corrugate my anatomy as I lay with eyes clenched shut, absorbing their electric impulses. I had come with all the glory of a born-again Christina. And like someone who has just seen the light, I did not want to let it go.

"Are you all right?" Laurinda asked, hovering over me.

"Heaven . . ." I managed to relate.

She leaned down and kissed me fully, tenderly brushing back my long, golden hair to make an icon of my face.

"You are too beautiful to believe," she whispered softly.

I could remember nothing else after that until the watery, predawn light awakened me. Had we let precious hours elapse wasted in slumber? I rolled over and looked at Laurinda sleeping as sweetly and innocently as a child beside me. Poor thing. She was as exhausted as I, and so perhaps it was not a waste after all. We still had the entire morning to enjoy each other.

I knelt by the side of the bed and parted her legs. Slowly and gently, I made my way up the lovely canyon of her thighs and nestled my nose and mouth in the warmly moist labyrinth of her radiant vagina. She would awaken soon, that I knew, and I was determined to make it a memorable introduction to a new day.

CHAPTER FOUR

Miguel wanted me to join him in the bathtub of our luxurious suite. "Paris was made for passion," he insisted.

"Is that all you ever think about?" I chided him good naturedly. I was as high as Jupiter on some of the best cocaine I had had in months.

"Yes," he replied.

"Keep it up and you'll start to look like a pussy," I warned.

"Keeping it up *can* be a problem," he complained with a smirk.

"There you go again."

"I'd rather *come* again," he shot back.

I stood in the doorway of the large bathroom, shaking my head in amused resignation.

"Haven't you ever seen the brain of a man?" he questioned from his foamy throne. "It looks like it's made up of hundreds of little cunts."

"You're impossible," I sighed. He looked so much like a little boy, sitting on the floor of the oversized tub surrounded by soap bubbles.

"Come, let me see the source of life just one more time," he pleaded, "before I go down for the third time."

"You went down for the hundredth time before you were ten years old," I scoffed.

"Please?" he begged.

I was only teasing him. Now I began taunting him, slowly pulling aside the flimsy robe I had been wearing. I spread my legs and clutched my entire cunt as though it was a set of cock and balls. His eyes gleamed, and he stroked himself dramatically as he watched my striptease performance. I let the robe slip from my shoulders and gather about my feet, leaving me naked. Stepping out from the circle it created, I eased over to the commode and lowered myself onto its plushly cushioned seat. Lying back with my legs unscissored to the fullest extent, I peeled back the folds of my cunt flesh with my fingers to expose the dewy, pink center.

"Enjoy yourself," I purred, "you masturbating masochist."

His cum shot up in a plume of pearly white spray, creating something that resembled a fleur-de-lis, before disappearing in the surf of bubbles atop the water.

"You're inspirational," he said when the orgasm had subsided. "You ought to start your own religion."

"Fuckism?" I suggested.

"Call it anything you want," he responded, "but make yourself the deity."

I had gotten myself hot in the process of motivating him to climax. "I'm coming in the water with you," I announced, slipping over the rim of the tub and into the tepid water before he could react.

"*Coming* is the proper verb," he said in welcoming me.

I moved my arms about searchingly under the water. "Where's that arrogant prick of yours?" I asked playfully.

"Fish for it," he replied. "Use your tongue as a hook."

"I don't need a hook," I pouted. "I have the bait and the trap set right between my legs."

He slid himself toward me. "Just for that," he said, "I'm going to fuck the hell out of you."

"Do it!" I challenged him.

His cock at once became a submarine, hiding in the cove of my cunt. I leaned back, propping myself on my hands in order to lift my tits above water. Miguel got the message, and as he pumped my pussy with fluid force, his head bowed, allowing his tongue to lick the nipples of my breasts and suck the mounds of butterscotch flesh surrounding them. You see, I was tanned everywhere except the inside of my cunt, and that I wanted to remain forever pink.

"Your cunt feels like satin," he noted as I joined more fervently in the action.

"Fuck it," I urged, riding up and down on his cock like a flag being raised and lowered on a flagpole.

"You like my cock?" he inquired in a voice that was huskier than it had been earlier.

"I love it," I assured him. It was no idle compliment. He had a dreamy, creamy prick—smooth and sleek and crowned with a pale red corona that resembled a delicious candied apple. I could fuck it and suck it for hours without becoming the least bit bored.

Like every man, a compliment to his cock was like Adrenalin for his libido. My confession of adoration spurred him on to a wave-making fury of fucking. Neither of us could take such a pace for long without achieving the results we sought with such singular dedication.

"Pull out," I gasped as I felt the warning click of his cock trigger. I wanted to see the cum spurt up in the water, and since I had expressed that desire in the past, he knew the reason for my request. He yanked himself out just in time. The cum fled from his cock in little white clouds that turned into kites with tails as they floated upward in the clear water. I saw it only fleetingly as an orgasm exploded inside me like fireworks, creating a kaleidoscope of lush colors rendered even more breathtaking by the accompaniment of body-tingling shocks that seemed to electrify my entire system.

We got down to matters other than amatory ones after a mutual exchange of fellatio and cunnilingus on the living room rug. Miguel was eminently virile and potent, but even he could not hope to keep pace with a fully aroused Christina. No man could.

In order to reduce the temptations, we both got fully dressed for a change. I had a new Oscar de la Renta I had been wanting to wear out, so Miguel quickly suggested that we go to dinner somewhere formal rather than sticking to the hotel's restaurants.

"You look absolutely ravishing," he said when I modeled my outfit for him.

"I should," I declared. "You ravished the hell out of me!"

He laughed appreciatively. "I can't decide whether you look best with clothes on or with them off," he said. "You're so beautiful both ways."

"It's more fun with them off," I said.

I had chosen a Hapsburg military jacket of white wool and embroidered in black. Under it was a lovely, revealing blouse decorated with tucks and fagoting. The paisley sash over a flowing cotton skirt was the special touch that had endeared the outfit to me the moment I saw it. It gave me a marvelously feminine feeling to be dressed up after weeks and weeks in jeans and T-shirts. I liked being a tomboy at times, but being a girl-girl was still the best.

Miguel was handsomely attired in a soft, gray silk suit and a melon-colored shirt. His shoes were exquisite, made for him exclusively by a royal Spanish bootmaker. Miguel had promised to take me to him to fashion several pairs of spike-heeled boots I had designed for myself. I reminded him of that promise again now as I admired his foot attire.

"Miguel never forgets his promises," he assured me, "especially to lovely ladies."

"Yes," I agreed, "but who knows how many lovely ladies there are in the life of Miguel Clemente?"

He pretended to be wounded. "To think that I sent you all that I could for a month in a little package and you still do not trust me," he sighed.

"You came that much just today," I scoffed, kidding him.

He took it lightly. "You increase my production capacity

many times over," he told me. "If there was another woman
— and I'm not suggesting there is — she would get only one
drop for every pint reserved for you, Christina."

"You little *diablo*," I jibed. "As the Indians in America
say, 'Spanish man speak with forked tongue.'"

"Interesting," he nodded, "and to think that all the while
I thought that was said of the American man."

"Don't believe everything you're taught," I countered
with a wink.

"I could teach you a few things," he said with a smile.

"I'll bet," I agreed.

We were both in good moods, ready for an evening in
Paris. Miguel then asked me to accompany him to London
the following day, something he hadn't mentioned before.

"Does Laurinda know about it?" I inquired when he first
mentioned it.

"She knows everything I do," he replied.

"Does the same apply to her as far as you're concerned?"
I asked.

He looked directly into my eyes. "Absolutely," he said.

I did not pursue that matter further. Instead I immediately changed the subject to food. "I'm starving tonight," I
confessed. "How I'd love a luscious pink chateaubriand
with truffles and buckets of champagne!"

"You've set the menu," he responded. "Let's go get it."

We were off to Maxim's without another word about
Laurinda. I was still dubious that he really knew the truth
about us. But it scarcely mattered. He was certainly not the
only man in my life, and she was not the only woman. Nor
did I delude myself into believing that I alone satisfied the
appetites of a dashing *millonario* like Miguel Clemente.

"Come to London with me," he requested again during
dinner. "I have some business to attend to, but I will also
have some time to enjoy with you."

"I have a town house there," I reminded him. "You should
have asked me to use it."

"Thank you very much, darling," he said with sincerity,

"but I prefer to conduct business from the Dorchester. It is my address in London."

I shrugged. "Anytime you want to use it," I repeated the offer, "just call my lawyers and they'll arrange it."

He nodded his gratitude this time instead of voicing it. I knew I had the same standing invitation at any of his homes around the world. And even though neither of us ever seemed to take the other up on the offer, it was mutually appreciated as a warm and generous gesture.

The subject did not come up again until we were sipping our after-dinner Benedictine-and-brandies. "You still haven't answered me," he reminded me quietly.

I swept my eyelashes upward and pretended to be surprised. The champagne had made me want to exaggerate all my movements and responses. "Whatever could you be talking about?" I inquired airily.

His eyes narrowed momentarily, and an expression of mild irritation briefly clouded his face. "Why are you being so evasive?" he asked.

"Evasive?" I responded. "To be evasive one has to know what is being evaded, doesn't one?"

"Dammit, Christina," he snapped, "you're toying with me, and I don't like it."

"Toying?" I continued being coy, taking perverse delight in his exasperation. I attributed it all to the bubbles in the golden wine I had consumed with gusto during dinner. Champagne always had one of two reactions on me   either it made me carefree and giddy, which was usually the case, or it made me playfully obstinate. It was Miguel's misfortune that I was in the latter mood.

"What happened to you in Zurich?" he suddenly changed tack. "When you left Malaga, you were sweet and exuberant now a couple of days later you're stubborn and bitchy."

"*Me*? *Bitchy*?" I cried as though pained. "You never called me that before."

"I have never encountered you that way before," he defended himself.

"This is a very circular dialogue," I sniffed, "and now all of a sudden it's getting personal."

He threw his head back in vexation, rolling his eyes for emphasis. It was all I could do to keep from laughing at his performance. A moment later he leaned forward, hunching intimately over the table. "Okay," he said with a deep breath, "let's go back to square one. Did you enjoy dinner?"

"Yes. Very much."

"Good. Now number two. Is there anything else you would like before I ask for the check?"

"No, thank you," I replied demurely.

"Very well. Three   will you accompany me to London tomorrow?"

"You're going to London?" I responded, feigning surprise.

"You're putting me on, that I know," he retorted, searching my features for a sign that I was teasing. "Please answer the questions."

"I've answered all your questions," I told him with a look of utter innocence.

He threw down his napkin forcefully upon the table. If it had been metal or stone, it very likely would have gone through the top. "The questions are over," he declared in a suppressed but heated voice. "You're going to London with me."

I looked over at him like a little girl facing her father. "I never said I wasn't," I whimpered softly.

CHAPTER FIVE

It never occurred to me to inquire about the source of anyone else's wealth, so naturally I had no idea how Miguel had acquired his fortune or how he maintained it. He never spoke of it either, dismissing the whole subject in the same lighthearted way I regarded my fortune.

However, now and then he proposed some eccentric ideas that made me wonder exactly what he was up to, such as his suggestion the day after we arrived in London.

"Take a ride with me to Bristol," he said nonchalantly. "We'll stay the night and be back in London by tomorrow night."

"Bristol?" I exclaimed, making a face. "What would you possibly want to go there for?"

"I have to see someone," he said without elaborating. "You'll enjoy it. I have a Rolls at our disposal, complete with bar and all your favorite cassette recordings."

"We just got here," I said. "I haven't even checked out my own house."

"You can do that another day," he responded. "Please?"

"Why don't I go see my lawyers and meet you back here tomorrow?" I counterproposed.

He shook his head in disapproval. "You're with me," he said flatly.

"Miguel, I said I'd come to London with you. There was no mention of Bristol or anyplace else."

"It's only a little over a hundred miles away," he persisted "That practically makes it a suburb."

I scoffed, adding a hollow laugh for emphasis. "You're getting trickier and trickier," I told him. "One of these days I'm not going to believe you at all anymore."

"That's not fair," he snapped. "You'd think I was asking you to swim the channel or something. It's only a small side trip, Christina."

"I love London," I replied.

"You weren't here the day before yesterday," he argued "and I guarantee you will be back here tomorrow. What more could you ask?"

"To stay here today," I answered stubbornly.

"I'll get the maid to help you pack a few things," he said ignoring my continued obstinacy. "You won't need much just something a little chic for dinner perhaps."

"I can do my own packing," I objected, "*if* I decide to pack."

"You're being bitchy again," he accused me. "Last night you were all passion, and this morning you're all prickly "

"There's only one prick around here," I couldn't resist saying. I wasn't really in a bad mood I just resented his taking it for granted that I would accompany him to any dull place he felt like going.

"The car's waiting," he said, ignoring my dig. "Please hurry up."

"You're rubbing my fur the wrong way," I warned him

"Poor little pussycat," he suddenly changed his approach He embraced me in a gentle hug. "You're such a darling, I'd be lost without you."

"Now you're stroking it the right way," I said.

"You'll go, won't you sweetheart?" he pleaded softly

I let my resistance melt. "Yes, damn you," I replied Miguel was jubilant.

"We'll have a party en route," he declared, "champagne

caviar, pâté de fois gras, artichokes   whatever your beautiful heart desires."

"Glacé of sperm a la Clemente," I suggested in jest.

"*Mucho, mucho*," he agreed, laughing.

The car was an elegant silver Rolls-Royce with a uniformed chauffeur who reminded me of the English actor Robert Morley. I thought he was a bit plump for his chosen occupation, but he managed to squeeze in behind the wheel with minimal difficulty. The car had a closed-off section separating the driver from the passengers, and the partition had a convenient opaque shade if more privacy was desired. I was sure it would come in handy somewhere along the way.

"Bristol," I repeated aloud as though in disbelief that I was actually headed there.

"It's a historic city," Miguel assured me.

"I'm sure it is," I said with a teeny trace of sarcasm. "When I lie awake nights dreaming of my next exotic adventure, Bristol comes to mind immediately."

"You should see it once," he said, "everyone should go everywhere at least once. Otherwise how would you know you're not missing something?"

"Harvey's Bristol Cream," I recited for no particular reason.

"We'll have dinner at Harvey's," Miguel proposed.

"There is such a place?" I asked in mild surprise.

"Of course," he responded. "That's where the sherry got its name."

"I like it occasionally," I said. "But right now I feel like sampling the champagne."

"Excellent suggestion," he agreed. Two magnums were chilling in tall silver buckets beside us. Miguel skillfully peeled back the foil, unwound the wire cork protector, and then popped the cork. A plume of mist snaked from the end of the bottle as the bubbles began their dance.

"Mmmmmm, that's good." I smacked my lips softly after my first sip.

Miguel held his glass up to the window light. "Excellent sparkle," he observed.

We nibbled on canapes and drank the vintage champagne as the car moved easily and steadily through the English countryside. Miles outside London we passed through a village called Maidenhead.

"I'm no longer eligible to be a citizen here," I noted with a laugh.

"Did you get an honorable discharge?" he jested.

"Honorable, dishonorable   it all depends upon how you look at it," I replied.

"I'd like to look at it   right now," he said with a lust-honed voice.

"Then draw the curtain," I told him. Quickly he pulled the shade, cutting off the driver's view of the passenger compartment.

"I haven't done it in a moving car since I was a teen-ager," Miguel confessed.

"Done what?" I asked coyly. His cock had already made a spire in his pants. He fumbled about and freed the swollen shaft, waving it toward me.

"Fucked," he replied, swallowing hard.

The sight of his aroused prick carbonated my blood and sent it rushing to my crotch. I was instantly in heat   ready, willing, and eminently able to handle his throbbing organ. Pulling my skirt up to my waist, I squirmed out of the minute panties I was wearing and aimed the split beaver pelt of my cunt directly at the head of his prick. "Come and fuck me, you bastard," I said in a sultry tone.

Miguel literally pounced upon me in the back seat, plunging his cock into me all the way up to his balls. The champagne bubbles I had consumed seemed to burst inside me as he pumped to and fro along the slippery ravine of my pussy. It was a dreamy feeling, floating along the highway horizontally while being driven up and down vertically at the receiving end of a savage cock.

"Empty your balls in me," I urged as he bit along my neck

and stuck his tongue in my ears. He was quite a boudoir athlete, and now he was proving that he could effectively take his act on the road.

"Ride it like a whore," he rasped. I lifted off the seat and pushed my mound of Venus forcefully against his attacking prick. His testicles slapped the lower edges of my cunt as he accelerated the tempo to meet my own writhing rhythm.

Abruptly the car screeched to a halt, almost impaling me permanently on his cock. The spindle effect triggered first his orgasm and then mine, leaving us awash in our libidinous juices. "What's wrong?" Miguel gasped into the intercom.

"A cow crossing the road, sir," the driver's voice crackled back.

"First time a cow ever made me come," Miguel said to me. It struck me as very funny, and in the course of my laughter we disengaged ourselves.

"I can't fuck a laughing woman," he complained as he withdrew. "It will give me a complex."

"That's enough for now anyhow," I said. "Let's have some more bubbly."

He zipped up his fly and leaned back in the seat. "For a moment I thought I was going to go right through you and come out the other side," he noted.

"It was fun, wasn't it?" I commented.

"Any time I'm inside you is fun," he said, pouring me another glass of champagne. "Here's to your incredible, edible, glorious snatch."

I lifted my glass to toast. "And here's to your splendid, distended, rampaging prick," I countered.

We both drank in tribute to the genitalia of the other—as good an excuse as any for enjoying the sparkling wine.

"Should I let the driver in on what's been happening directly behind him?" Miguel inquired.

"He missed the best part," I noted.

Miguel winked. "We want him to keep his eyes on the road, don't we?" he asked as he opened the shade separating us. "Never know when another cow might pop up in front of us."

"And make you pop your milk," I added.

"It was good," he agreed. "It skimmed off the heavy cream."

There were times when I enjoyed reflecting on a particularly impressive orgasm— or one experienced under unusual circumstances. This one, precipitated as it was in the back seat of a Rolls-Royce by a meandering cow, definitely qualified as unusual.

We were both fairly buzzed by the time we reached Bristol. "One thing, Miguel," I cautioned as we rolled along the roads bordering on the River Avon, "I have no interest in doing any sightseeing. Just let me spread out in the hotel, and I'll occupy myself while you do whatever it is you have to in this godforsaken place."

"It's not that bad, Christina," he argued. "You should give it a chance."

"I give chances to males and females," I retorted. "Cities are on their own."

"You're jaded," he accused me.

"And diamonded and emeralded, too," I pointed out haughtily.

Miguel shook his head. "Too much of everything," he mused. "You could be split up into a dozen women, and there'd still be enough to make every one of them rich and beautiful."

"But they'd be like dolls," I said airily, "no pussies on them."

"Why?" he played along.

"I have just enough cunt for one," I declared. "If it was divided into twelve parts, there wouldn't be enough room in each to get the head of a pin inside."

Miguel cocked his head. "I guess we won't be splitting you up then after all," he concluded. "Anyway, I wouldn't like to see a single hair removed from that luscious mound between your legs."

I turned away as the car glided to a stop in front of our hotel, a place called the Avon Gorge Hotel. It was high up on something named Sion Hill, overlooking a great river gorge and a large suspension bridge. It hardly rivaled the spectacular views I was accustomed to elsewhere on the continent, but I had to admit it was nicer than I had anticipated for this port town.

"Remember," I said as we got out, "no sightseeing."

"Not even to see the white tigers at the Bristol Zoo?" he teased me.

"Only if you promise me a coat made out of one of them," I responded.

The chauffeur and a doorman carried in the few bags we had with us. It still puzzled me why Miguel had to come to such an unexciting place, but since we were already here and it was too late to change matters, I accepted my fate. One night of it would not do me in.

Our suite included a well-stocked bar, which Miguel had thoughtfully ordered to please me. Now I knew I would be able to endure the twenty-four hours somehow or other.

"Time to get stoned," I announced when the bellboy had gone.

"You're already half-calcified," he said with what I regarded as a tinge of sarcasm.

"You think so?" I challenged him. "Just wait until you leave. And if you find me in bed with any friends, kindly do not disturb."

His features sharpened and his eyes narrowed. "Don't start playing games with me, Christina," he warned.

"I do as I please," I declared, pouring myself an inch of cognac in a snifter and downing it in a single gulp.

"That's not being intelligent," he said coolly.

"I agreed to accompany you here," I announced with newly roiled hostility, "but nothing was said about my activities while we're here. I'll do whatever I want, do you understand? In fact, I'm going down to the hotel bar right now to see what's interesting around here. There just might be a diamond-in-the-rough in this gray-faced burg."

Miguel stepped over to block the doorway. "Christina, you've been drinking," he cautioned, "Don't make an exhibition of yourself."

I laughed with forced gaiety. "I'm always an exhibition," I proclaimed, "and I always have an audience. Let me out of here."

"I don't want you picking up anyone," he said flatly. "You're with me, and that's exclusive."

I pushed his arm aside and grabbed the door handle. "Don't get possessive with me, Miguel," I warned him. "I don't like it—and I won't tolerate it."

"Christina!" he cried out as I forced the door open and stumbled into the corridor. "I'll be down with you as soon as I make a phone call."

"Take your time," I said blithely as the lift arrived and opened it jaws to swallow me. "I'll find companionship even if it's only the bartender."

I chortled to myself, picturing his frustration. I could indeed be a bitch when I so chose. Miguel was getting too sure of himself with regard to me, and I was determined now to correct that cocky attitude.

The bar was not crowded, but I decided to take a small table rather than run the gamut of traveling salesmen and the like making their obligatory passes at a lone female at the bar. No sooner had I seated myself than a sandy-haired man in his mid-thirties approached me.

"Could it be possible," he inquired in an engaging manner, "that this is Christina van Bell herself—in Bristol?"

I flashed one of my dazzling smiles at him. "If it isn't," I replied, "I'm traveling under false pretenses."

"Pardon my asking," he said, wrapping both hands around the glass he was carrying, "but whatever brings such a beauteous and celebrated personality to our city?"

"I've always liked Bristol," I lied. "What's so extraordinary about anyone coming here for a visit?"

"On behalf of my home town, I'm flattered," he responded, "but aside from the Old Vic, this is hardly a theatrical center."

"I'm not only interested in the theater and show business," I told him. "I have many varied interests."

"That is intriguing," he said genuinely. "Somehow I'd always imagined that enormously attractive women like you were involved in glitter and glamour to the exclusion of everything else."

I sized him up—good physique, pleasant appearance, and a rather boyishly winsome manner—and decided to invite him to join me. "Won't you sit down?" I suggested. "It's awkward carrying on a conversation with one person seated and the other standing."

"Thank you," he said quickly, dropping into the chair opposite me. "I consider it a great privilege."

"You may live to regret those words," I laughed. "Other men have."

"Never," he said emphatically. "Surely you must be expecting someone."

This was an opportunity to teach Miguel a lesson, and I seized it. "Not really," I told him. "My appointments are for tomorrow."

His face lit up brightly. "Perhaps you'd have dinner with me?" he proposed.

I smiled coyly. "Perhaps after I learn your name," I reminded him.

He flushed momentarily with embarrassment. "I'm terribly sorry. I completely forgot to introduce myself—the excitement of recognizing you just robbed me of my manners. I'm Dirk Boland."

"A pleasure meeting you, Dirk," I said, giving him my hand. He took it and brushed it with his lips.

"I feel as though I'm in the presence of royalty," he declared convincingly.

"You're very flattering," I told him.

A waiter interrupted us to hand me a message from the

front desk. Miguel had called down and asked them to tell me he would be delayed about twenty minutes. I tipped the waiter, then tore up the note.

"Anything important?" Dirk asked.

"Nothing," I said with a quick smile of dismissal. "Now about that dinner invitation . . ."

"Oh, yes," he responded instantly, "would you do me the honor of joining me?"

"Only if we go to Harvey's," I said, recalling the place where Miguel had proposed to take me until he decided I was too intoxicated to go. Dirk obviously did not agree with his appraisal of my condition.

"Exactly where I'd planned to take you," he reacted with enthusiasm.

"Let's be off then," I urged. By the time we finished our drinks, we had just about enough time to clear the hotel before Miguel showed up. I was absolutely delighted with the prospect of standing him up. If only I could be there to see the look on his face when the waiter told him I'd gone off with another gentleman.

Dirk treated me as though I were a princess who had stepped out of a story book to fulfill his impossible romantic fantasy. He kept looking at me, smiling with delight and touching me from time to time as if to make sure I was real. I rather enjoyed his boyish enchantment with me, and I made a pledge to myself to reward him amply later for his unabashed joy in being my escort.

"I think it's the best place in Bristol," he said en route to the restaurant in the cab. "I love the veal with Lyonnaise sauce, and of course the Bristol cream sherry."

"You've made my selection," I told him. "That's what I'm going to have."

He seemed pleased. "You needn't order that on my say-so," he said.

"Always listen to the natives, I say. I learned that long ago."

"From what I've read about you," he reported, "you're native to many, many places."

"I do tend to get around," I agreed with a small laugh.

"It must be an exciting life," he contemplated. "I seldom go anywhere but London—and that's usually on business."

"You haven't told me what business you're in," I reminded him.

"It seems so plebian compared with your glamorous life," he said almost apologetically.

"Nonsense," I encouraged him. "You're a charming man. I wouldn't be going out with you if you weren't. Charming men always have interesting professions, whatever they might be."

He grinned in gratitude. "Thanks for being so kind," he said. "I'm a pathologist on the Bristol coroner's staff."

"A dead-end job," I jested.

"We deal strictly in people who have no future," he laughed in agreement.

"I think that's very fascinating," I told him, "but I'd rather we didn't discuss specifics during dinner."

"Definitely not," he said. "It's a dead issue as far as I'm concerned."

I liked his sense of humor about his rather grim but vital profession. "I'll pass on the formaldehyde cocktails before dinner," I kidded him as we entered the restaurant. He poked me playfully as the maitre d' approached.

"Two, doctor?" he greeted Dirk. Obviously he was no stranger to the place. Eyeballs shifted all around us as we were ushered into the dining room.

It was an attractive place with white-painted brick walls and an atmosphere of refined congeniality. "It's cute," I declared when we were seated.

"You have the most charming way of putting things," he reacted. "Now that was a double formaldehyde on the rocks you requested, wasn't it?"

I stuck out the tip of my tongue. "Brute," I japed. We

had progressed rapidly to an easy informality after Dirk's rather self-conscious initial approach. I felt as though I had known him considerably longer than an hour, thanks to the relaxing balm of champagne and cognac.

"We'll just have dinner here," Dirk proposed, "then I'll take you on a tour of Bristol's fabulous night life."

"No sightseeing," I pleaded.

"We'll be lucky if we can see our way home by then," he said with a sly smile.

Dinner went along famously. The veal with Lyonnaise sauce was as good as he had described it, and we drank our share of the house sherry. I had become progressively more risqué in my responses to Dirk's questions, which had resulted in increasingly more suggestive reactions from him. He had been hesitant at first to risk destroying such a rewarding but still tentative relationship by coming on too strong, but I managed to convey my feelings with mounting explicitness.

"Do you have a place of your own?" I questioned him.

"I have a flat in Clifton," he replied. "In fact it's only a few blocks from the Avon Gorge where you're staying."

"Let's skip the grand tour," I told him, "and confine it to mutual exploration of each other."

He looked at me warily, still reluctant to make a full commitment. I could tell he feared that I might only be taunting him, perhaps to amuse myself by denying him at the crucial moment after he had revealed his animal side. Some women did do that, but I was not one of them.

"I'll take you there for a drink if you like," he suggested. "But it's nothing fancy, Christina."

"I'm interested in you," I emphasized, "not your surroundings."

His eyes never left me. "I'll get the check," he said, sliding one lip over the other in thought. It's not too good to be true, I felt like telling him, it *is* true. Stop doubting it and start enjoying it. But my sensible side overruled, and I sat quietly, waiting to leave.

He was shy at first, uncertain how to begin the ritual of seduction. I excused myself on the pretense of having to go to the bathroom. Once there I hastily skinned off my soignée satin evening suit, keeping only my spike-heeled silver shoes on for anatomical effect. Casually I sauntered back into the parlor and confronted him naked.

"What do you like best?" I questioned him in a throaty voice. "What do you really like best of all?"

He stared at me in disbelief momentarily. "That is the loveliest body I've ever seen," he finally managed to utter.

"It's alive, doctor," I purred. "Why don't you take off your clothes and examine it?"

He tore at his jacket and trousers as though they were on fire, literally ripping them from his body. The head of his cock peeked out from the slit in his boxer shorts, standing rigidly at attention as though guarding the treasure of the balls below it.

"Let's fuck," I said in a voice honed with heat.

He pulled down his shorts and stepped gingerly out of them, his long prick almost touching his chin as he bent over. I waited for him with come-hither eyes and a coltish stance, my honey hair spilling over my shoulders and onto my tits. He ran his hand over his cock as though seeking reassurance that it would not fail him in the fulfillment of a fantasy.

"Kiss it first," I instructed him, pinning back the outer lips of my cunt to expose the tender pink meat of its interior. Obediently he knelt before me and administered a succulent kiss. "Now let's fuck," I said firmly, enjoying taking the lead in this horizontal dance.

He was almost surgical in his approach as I lay in wait on the couch near the door, opening the woundlike laceration of my pussy with long, slender fingers, then guiding his sharply angled cock into it with smooth precision. "I just entered the Gates of Paradise," he declared as the full measure of his organ sank into the velvety kiss of my labia.

"You just entered the hottest hole on earth," I disagreed. "Fuck the hell out of it, you pathological sonofabitch." The words were meant to ignite me as well as him and they succeeded admirably. He began tilling the furrows of my cunt with wild fervor, plowing deep for a place to plant his seed. The smoothness was now gone from his technique; he was fogged by a frantic desire to come and nothing else.

"Shoot it, you bastard," I groaned, bucking like a wild mare under him. Tiny jewels of perspiration dropped from his face onto mine as he pumped fiercely. I dug my fingers into the breadth of his back and tightened my legs around his buttocks as a series of orgasms ripped through me. Then with the kick of a .45 revolver, his cock fired. White jelly bullets landed silently against the walls of my pussy and collected like snowdrops in the hair of my cunt. He hovered over me and milked all he could from the swollen head of his brick-red cock.

"Extraordinary," he gasped, barely able to enunciate.

"Suck it," I demanded.

"My cum is all over it," he protested between breaths.

"Suck it," I repeated.

He looked at me intently and saw the lust simmering within me. Without another word, he genuflected and donned the damp mask of my cunt. The sight of him in his own ejaculations brought me to a quick set of climaxes that increased in intensity with each thrust of his tempered tongue. I was insatiable, coming repeatedly yet still hungry for more and more. As fate would have it, we were interrupted by a firm knock on the door. It startled Dirk.

"Who in hell could that be?" he wondered aloud.

I lay back, masturbating to replace his sweet tongue. "Who cares?" I groaned. "Just don't answer."

There was concern written all over his features. "I have to," he said. "It could be the morgue or the coroner's office."

"The morgue?" I said with a tinge of disgust. "Your cock just died?"

He did not smile. Instead he solemnly pulled on his pants and went to the door, opening it a crack. "Yes?" he asked.

The rest remains a blur to me. All of a sudden Dirk was on the floor, being pummeled madly. In the initial shock of the assault, I failed to look closely at who was delivering this rain of fists upon him. But then as I crouched in a corner, screaming and clutching my clothes before me in a vain effort to hide my nudity, I saw who the madman was.

It was Miguel.

CHAPTER SIX

He was like a maniac. I had never seen him that way before. There was blood all over his sleek body, all over his elegant clothes. I ran out of Dirk's place while they were still going at each other like wild animals in a death duel.

Someone I don't even remember who took me to the hotel, where I grabbed my belongings and fled to Temple Mead Station. The fact that it had been there since 1840 was somehow vaguely reassuring. History was on my side for a change. The fleet intercity train 125 mph most of the way would get me into London's Paddington Station in an hour. It almost did. One hour and eleven minutes was still good enough to beat Miguel and the Rolls, and that was all that mattered.

I didn't want to go anywhere where he might find me. That eliminated the town house and the Dorchester. I toyed with the idea of flying out of London immediately, but I was too upset and exhausted for that. Instead I chose an obscure hotel in Soho and donned one of my darkest wigs to hide my identity.

The Latin in Miguel had finally surfaced. He was disturbingly jealous and unacceptably possessive. Whatever kind thoughts I had had about him were now riddled with doubts about his stability. I searched my memory banks for recollections of previous bad behavior. Surprisingly I couldn't think of a single major incident in which he had performed so drastically before. At that point I truthfully had no idea whatsoever of the pressure he was under.

I called my pet lawyer the moment the train pulled into London. "I can't believe the change in Miguel," I related to him.

Kindly, venerable Winston Garrett was sympathetic and cautionary. "Be careful," he warned. "I've heard rumors that he's in serious trouble."

Since he seldom uttered a bad word about anyone, my curiosity was piqued. "Trouble?" I echoed. "What kind of trouble?"

"Financial," he replied succinctly.

It was difficult to believe, considering the lifestyle he led. But then it might be that very lifestyle that was contributing to the problem   whatever it was. I set up an appointment to see him at the law firm, then abruptly changed it to a restaurant instead.

"Miguel is crafty," I noted, "he might stake out your offices, expecting me to turn to you. Let's make it The Giraffe instead."

"That's fine with me," he responded. "Say one o'clock tomorrow afternoon?"

"Good," I confirmed. "I'll be incognito, so look the women over carefully."

He chuckled pleasantly, "Christina, my dear," he said, "you'd be unmistakable even shrouded head-to-foot."

I felt better after our brief conversation. There was something solid and comfortable about this fine, older man. He simply radiated intelligence and compassion   along with a little dash of mischief to keep him interesting.

We met at The Giraffe the next day under nervous circumstances. Someone had called my suite and left no message, according to the desk. Winnie denied making any calls, and there was no one else who knew where I was.

"I hope you took the precaution of checking out before coming here," he greeted me.

"I did," I assured him. "My bags are already en route to the airport."

"Good girl," he said paternally.

"I must confess I'm not very hungry, Winnie," I told him once we were seated at a far table. He had apparently notified the maitre d' in advance that we wanted the least conspicuous spot in the restaurant. It certainly was that   I could hardly see the entrance through the ferns and palm fronds obscuring our table.

"Have your favorite then," he suggested. "Champagne and strawberries. They import them here."

I smiled in gratitude. "You're always so considerate," I said, taking his plump hand in mine for a moment.

"Be careful," he kidded. "I'm not yet immune to the touch of a beautiful young lady."

"Good," I retorted. "I wouldn't want to be represented by a candidate for the knife of Dirk Boland."

He lifted his eyes. "Where have I heard that name before?" he questioned.

"He's the pathologist Miguel beat up in Bristol," I explained.

"Right," he nodded in confirmation.

"Were you able to find out anything about him?" I asked. "His condition, I mean."

"Not really," he said with a look of concern, "but I understand he doesn't intend to press charges."

"Why?" I inquired in surprise. "From what I saw, it was a pretty brutal beating he took."

"Apparently your friend Clemente was able to convince him that he was your husband," he confided. "The doctor assumes he deserved it for seducing another man's wife and getting caught."

"That's ridiculous!" I responded indignantly. "I can't let Miguel get away with that."

Winston reached over and patted my hand. "Calm down, my dear," he urged. "You'd be playing right into his hands if you make any effort at all to intervene."

"But I like Dirk," I confessed. "I don't want to see him suffer under Miguel's deception."

"Perhaps you can relate that to him some other time," he advised me. "Right now I want you to vanish for a while."

I bit my lip and gulped down a mouthful of champagne. Winnie was right, of course. But it galled me to think that Miguel had saved his own skin by lying about his relationship with me. A doctor on the coroner's staff surely had to have some clout with the police in the city. The thought of Miguel doing time behind bars for malicious assault became a pleasing picture to me all of a sudden.

"I suppose you're right," I agreed reluctantly. "But I'm going to write Dirk and explain the situation just for my own satisfaction."

"Later," Winston said. "No postmarks from anywhere for the time being. Agreed?"

I sighed deeply. "Yes, counselor," I replied, a trifle sardonically.

"How are the strawberries?" he asked, his point having been made.

"Juicy."

"They look good," he observed.

"I think I'll go to Singapore," I said, skipping off the subject of strawberries. They were really quite tasteless, but I wouldn't tell Winnie that.

"Good choice," he said in approval. "I was afraid you were going to say Monaco or somewhere on the Riviera."

"Which reminds me," I responded, "can you arrange to have my villa in Marbella closed down? Miguel lives nearby and he'll surely have someone spotting the place for the next few weeks."

"I'll send one of our junior attorneys over tomorrow," he replied. "The keys are with the groundskeeper, aren't they?"

"Yes," I confirmed, "and the maid has a set, too. She comes in several times a week when I'm not there to keep things in order."

"No problem," he assured me. "Remove it from your list of concerns."

I quickly ran my hand over my forehead. "Erased," I said with a fleeting smile.

We chatted about various other legal matters for the remainder of our lunch, then Winston instructed his driver to take me to Heathrow. "Wait until Miss van Bell is aboard the aircraft and it has taken off," he instructed him. We dropped him off at his offices after I gave him a warm embrace.

"Call me the moment you're settled, Christina," he said with mock sternness. "I want no one else to know where you are until this situation cools down."

"Yes, master," I kidded him. And then I was off—incognito and in confusion, but not in despair. What name had I used at the hotel? Nicole Stevens. Unfortunately I could not use it on the flight because it was international. My name on the passenger manifest had to match the one on my passport. So in transit I would be Christina van Bell. But in Singapore I would once again become the sultry, brunet Nicole Stevens. It wouldn't be the first alias I had assumed in my peripatetic career. Nor the last.

Singapore was hot and sticky, which simply meant it hadn't changed since the last time I'd been there. No one, least of all Miguel Clemente, would expect Christina van Bell—or Nicole Stevens—to select it as a hideaway. There were too many other places in the world where the climate was more soothing and appealing, which was precisely why I had picked it as an escape spot. Miguel would never find me here.

I checked into a suite at the Shangri-La under my pseudonym. "Welcome to Singapore, Miss Stevens." The manager went out of his way to greet me. My plunging necklines always seemed to have a special effect on hotel executives at every place I ever stayed. At times I actually thought the desk clerk had a secret alert button connected to the manager's office. Every time I checked in anywhere, the bosses seemed to be flushed out of their walnut offices like quail by bird dogs.

"Thank you so much," I said with sugary sweetness in spite of my thoughts. I intended to have a ball as Nicole since anything I did would not tarnish the image of Christina van Bell. It was like granting myself a license to be licentious.

"I am sure you will find your accommodations most satisfactory," he continued. "If there is anything that is not to your liking, please call upon me personally and I will see that it's corrected."

I smiled seductively. "*Merci*," I purred, flicking out the vowel with the tip of my tongue.

Before I could make it through the lobby to the elevators, I was approached by several men to whom I could readily adjust when it came to compromising positions. For the time being there appeared to be no need to venture beyond the hotel to search for temporary partners. I felt at home already.

"Follow me, please," the Chinese bellhop said in musical English.

"I'm right behind you," I assured him. He glanced back to confirm my position, but his eyes focused immediately on my décolletage. One nipple had managed to peek out, and I made no effort to restrain it.

"Oh, my," I heard him mutter to himself as we boarded the elevator. I smiled in amusement. It was always fun to be titillating, but somehow even more so with a cute little Oriental man.

The suite was attractive, appropriately in a Chinese decor. I felt myself developing a lusty appetite for something Oriental, male or female.

"Are there many Chinese people currently registered at the hotel?" I inquired as he hung up my wardrobe bags.

"Oh, yes," he said, nodding, "many, many."

"Europeans, too?" I asked for no particular reason.

"Yes, madame," he replied. "And Malays, Indians, Australians, even Americans."

"A real United Nations," I chattered on.

"Singapore a crossroads, they say," he reported with a toothy smile. "Little bit of everything."

I studied him for a moment, then decided against seducing him. It was not only that he was on duty, but also that he was too small and friendly to be erotically stimulating. I would go down to one of the bars after showering and examine the situation in my own inimitable way. As a blonde it would be overwhelming, but as a brunet I would blend in better, giving me time to evaluate my prospects before becoming a mental pincushion for dozens of eager pricks.

"Winnie, this is Nicole," I reported to London over the phone. "I'm at the Shangri-La. The flight was so-so. The weather here is unbearable, but I'm headed down to the bar to find a friend or two for some fun and games."

He laughed at the succinctness of my summation. "Enjoy yourself," he said cheerily, "but whatever you do, do it anonymously."

"I can't disguise certain essential parts of myself," I reminded him. "I'm going to be a brunet with a chestnut base."

He chuckled at my contrived dilemma. "When you get to that point," he said, "no questions will be asked."

"I love you," I said blithely in conclusion. "I'll call you again tomorrow."

"Don't forget."

Not many minutes later I was gyrating sensuously on the floor of the hotel's disco, The Lost Horizon, motivated by a very healthy snort of pristine cocaine that I had smuggled in a capsule in my vagina. That made it pussy-pure, and what could be better than that?

"What a beautiful set of udders," I heard a male voice beside me say. I glanced over and saw an absolutely divine-looking Oriental couple dancing next to me. The girl took her companion's observation of me without a trace of jealousy. In fact she smiled enticingly when I looked her way.

"I won them in a raffle," I japed.

"You ought to display them at the Raffles," the handsome young Chinese boy suggested. I got what he meant. The hotel of Kipling and Maugham was not far from the Shangri-La.

"Is that where you two are staying?" I questioned, continuing to dance as we conversed.

"No." The girl answered this time. "We are staying here."

"So am I," I informed them, "so why shouldn't I display them at the Shangri-La?" With that I pulled my blouse open and released both tits for full view. They both stopped dancing and simply stared.

"Like Venus," the girl said in admiration. "So perfect."

Her friend bent down and planted a kiss on each nipple, hardening them instantly. "Why don't you come up to my suite and have a drink?" I suggested.

They did not even bother to consult each other. "We accept," he declared with a grin. She nodded emphatically.

"When opportunity knocks," she said with a tinkly laugh, "Confucius say, don't knock it—take it."

I had some problem getting past half-a-dozen men who insisted on fondling my breasts as we moved toward the exit. It wasn't until I was in the hotel corridor that I was able to return my tits to their skimpy hiding place.

"My name's Nicole." I introduced myself. My two friends were a delight, so fresh and appealing. I was flying and getting hornier by the second.

"I'm Kim," the young man said with a dazzling smile, "and this is Lita."

"Are you from here?" I asked just to keep my tongue and mind occupied until we got to the rooms.

"No," he replied. "I'm with a travel agency out of Honolulu. So is Lita, but not the same one. What do you do, Nicole?"

I looked at him with my sultriest expression. "I do everything but jump out windows," I said as provocatively as I had ever uttered a line.

We wasted no time once we were inside the suite. They were like a pair of professional acrobats in the way they coordinated their bodies, positioning themselves for lurid and dramatic sex. Meanwhile I was no slouch either when it came to erotic athletics. My most difficult decision was whether to go for the cock or the cunt first. I decided to get both by going down on Lita while presenting my wet pussy, backside up, to Kim's smoking prick. They fell into the arrangement as if it had been choreographed and rehearsed to perfection.

"Lick me, babeee," Lita urged, spreading her pussy so that it all but totally encompassed my face. Her cunt blossomed from her crotch like the petals of a morning flower, soft-lipped and dewy. I sucked like a thirsty woman at an oasis, nibbling at the velvety lips and drumming a frantic tempo on her clit with my tongue.

"Put it up her ass," I heard Lita tell Kim. He was already stoking the fire in my cunt with feverish enthusiasm. The transition from my love canal to my alimentary canal was smooth and heady. I began coming from the moment we started our triple-header, and now that it was fully under way, I popped repeatedly, sending my body into uncontrollable spasms. The only remedy was more and more fucking and sucking.

"She's a beautiful bitch, honey," the girl commented to the hard-humping Kim. "I'm gonna suck her cunt all night." The declaration excited everybody. Her pussy contracted with orgasm, then flowered once more to accept further attention from my mouth.

"I'm coming," Kim gasped.

"Shoot it up her ass," Lita urged as she came again herself. This time he ignored her request, pulling out at the crucial moment. He came all over my ass and back like sticky confetti. His cum was strewn over me as though in celebration of a glorious climax. Naturally I had a sympathetic reaction to this rain of semen, coming so violently I almost choked for breath.

We went through every conceivable variation of every conceivable position during the hours that followed, finally winding up with Lita and I engrossed in a rapturous sixty-nine while Kim sandwiched his cock between our two bodies and fucked our tits for a spurting, hot climax. All that activity, combined with the snorting, the drinking, and some jet lag, finally did me in. When I awakened hours later, it was mid-morning and the two of them were gone. A note was pinned to the sheet near my head.

"Nicole," it said, "we helped ourselves to your succulent body while you slept. It was almost as delicious as when you are awake and participating   but not quite. We're in Room 711. Call when you're ready for more. Luscious love, Kim and Lita."

I reached down and felt my crotch. It was flooded with a mixture of cum and cunt juices. Slowly and deliberately I toyed with the hair and the flesh until it was aroused once again. Then with the adroitness of long experience, I teased my clit into tender firmness. They were quite a team, those two. My appetite for Chinese food was, if anything, even more pronounced than it was the night before. Recalling what we had experienced so passionately together, I plucked myself to a marvelously delayed and then an extraordinarily prolonged orgasm. It was really the only way to start a new day   in Singapore or anywhere else.

CHAPTER SEVEN

Winston called *me* on my second day. He sounded vaguely upset, though he always managed to control his emotions quite admirably. "I'm being hounded by some woman named Laurinda Alvarez," he reported. "She insists it's of vital importance to get in touch with you. Do you know who she is?"

I was taken aback for a moment. "Yes," I murmured. "As Christina van Bell I know who she is."

"She's not connected with Clemente, is she?" he inquired.

"In a sense," I replied, not really wishing to indict her.

"Well, for God's sake, don't respond to her," he advised. "Don't trust anybody for the moment, Christina."

"I'm listening," I said with uncertainty. "I don't keep you on retainer just to ignore your advice."

"Remember that," he said emphatically. "Now tell me how everything else is going."

"I had a marvelous first night," I reported. "I met a fascinating Chinese couple from Honolulu."

"Good," he replied without particular enthusiasm. "Just be careful."

"Thanks for your concern, Win," I responded. "I'll do my best."

After hanging up, I thought long about the possible motivations for Laurinda's attempts to locate me. I truly doubted that she knew anything about what had happened with Miguel in Bristol. But I could not be sure. I decided to go downstairs for brunch and mull it over. There was no denying that I still had a strong feeling for her inside me. It made true objectivity difficult for me.

"There she is," I heard a man at the bar say out loud as I entered, "the lady with the lovely jugs."

I ignored him, but I did feel the eyes of the whole crowd focus on me as I took a stool at the end. It was my own fault. I had done a semistrip in the hotel's disco, and no doubt a good portion of my audience for that exhibition was now in the barroom.

"A Rob Roy," I instructed the bartender, standing poised before me. "Very dry."

"With pleasure," he responded, making a little bow with his head. I was dressed a bit more discreetly than usual, not particularly anxious to attract multiple propositions. The call from Winnie had changed my mood. I had to think things out, and that meant keeping my mind open and my legs closed.

"Very pensive today," the man next to me ventured.

I nodded coolly. "I have a lot on my mind," I explained.

"You have a lot of everything," he quipped.

I turned away without responding, clouding my face with a pout. Thankfully he took the hint.

"Would you like a twist in that?" the bartender inquired. His hands hovered over my glass, ready to strangle a piece of lemon peel.

"Please," I replied. The garroting of the citrus was swift and deft, creating a slight, fragrant mist over the surface of my cocktail. I lifted it to my lips and inhaled the pleasant aroma before sipping. I considered skipping brunch and just mellowing my way into the afternoon. Despite the air conditioning, the humidity made wearing a wig decidedly uncomfortable. It had only been a matter of days, yet I was already longing to free my long, golden tresses and become

Christina again. I could never be Nicole forever, no matter how abandoned she might be.

"Is anyone sitting here?" A distinguished-looking man in his early forties interrupted my meditations.

I gave him my instant size-up, and he passed the test. "No," I replied after a pause, "help yourself."

"I didn't want to interrupt your thoughts," he apologized in his rich baritone. "You seemed deep in contemplation." He slipped onto the stool quickly and gracefully.

"I was," I responded with a smile. "I was trying to decide whether to have another one of these or switch to something else."

"That *is* serious." He played along. "I'm having a dry Gibson myself   if that's any help to you."

"With the little onions?" I inquired, peering innocently into his clear blue eyes.

"That's the one," he confirmed. "Back home we call them 'Loudmouth Soup.' "

I laughed. "That needs no explanation," I said lightly, "but 'back home' does. Where could that be?"

He replied with a brief chorus of "New York, New York." There was something quietly joyous about him that I liked. It was obvious he enjoyed life and was out to live it   not necessarily flamboyantly but fully.

"Love that city," I declared with enthusiasm.

"I'm glad to hear it," he responded. "There are some people who don't, you know."

"They must be dead from the ankles up," I said.

He smiled in agreement, revealing cute dimples in his cheeks. "Would you join me for a drink?" he asked.

"I might," I replied coyly, "once I know what to call my benefactor."

His smile expanded into a grin. "Lane Symington," he said, extending his hand.

"Chris   " I caught myself just in time. "Nicole Stevens," I corrected myself.

"Pretty name," he said, "but no name could ever be as pretty as you yourself."

"That calls for a Gibson," I responded, "with *two* onions."

"So be it," he declared, signaling to the bartender. "Two very dry Gibsons with a pair of onions in each, please."

When the drinks arrived, we toasted to our meeting. "Do you know Singapore?" he asked after our initial sips.

"Not well," I admitted. "Do you?"

"I come here often," he explained. "I'm in the shipping business."

"It's quite a port, I understand."

"Third busiest harbor in the world," he told me. "Only Rotterdam and Yokohama do more volume."

"I'd fail that in a quiz," I said.

"So would most people," he noted. "Nicole, would you like to take a little trip around the city? I'd be delighted to show you around."

"I'm not much for sightseeing," I warned him.

"Nothing like a guided tour," he said. "Just a few peeks to get the flavor of Singapore."

"Maybe after I've had a few of these," I responded, fingering my glass.

"Are you traveling alone?" he inquired. "Or is that too personal a question?"

"Alone," I confirmed. "By choice, of course."

"Of course," he agreed readily. "With your beauty and charm that goes without saying."

We drifted onto other matters, hardly any of it very personal or memorable, just enjoying the ease of this new relationship. His manner was friendly and nonthreatening, a personality that was almost immediately likable. And three Gibsons in rather quick succession smoothed the way even more.

"I feel like skipping the hotel brunch and just noshing at some of those food stalls along the streets," I decided suddenly.

"Great," he said. "Let's do it."

He settled the check hastily before I could change my mind. I had noticed the food stands all over the roads on my way in. Somehow they must have made an impression without my realizing it. Their pungent fragrances had lingered in my subconscious until now. Suddenly I was ravenously hungry.

Lane took me to a place called Newton Circus. There I was absolutely piggish, devouring *satay* chunks of mutton, beef, and chicken barbecued and dipped in a spicy peanut sauce. I also sampled *mee goreng* and *nasi goreng* fried noodles and fried rice. Thoughtfully Lane had brought along wine, which we used to wash down everything, including the delicious *murtabak*, a crepe fried with eggs and onions and dipped in curry gravy. Nicole Stevens was not just a sex maniac but a culinary glutton as well. Christina van Bell would never make such an obvious pig of herself. Whatever I was for the moment, it seemed to amuse and delight Lane.

"Let's walk off a few of those calories," he suggested. "That way I can force-feed you a bit of local color."

"I feel like I'm going to explode," I laughed. "That's the most I've eaten in one gastronomical orgy in ages."

"I'm glad you enjoyed it," he said genuinely.

We strolled hand-in-hand up Cross Street to Club Street, over to Ann Siang Hill, and then out to South Bridge Road. It was intriguing and picturesque with two- and three-story shophouses lining the roads, cluttered with Chinese signs hawking laundry and Oriental tiles and woodcarvings. From there we went to the Hindu temple of Sri Mariamman.

"I've had it," I sighed to Lane after leaving the temple. "Let's go back to the hotel."

"I'll get us a trishaw," he said, scanning the crowded roadway for one of the bicycle-powered rickshaws. It took a few minutes to find an available one. We rode, giggling merrily, through the pedestrian-packed streets back to the hotel, feeling marvelously giddy and fancy free. All I needed now for complete contentment was a good, invigorating oral massage and a nice, fervent fuck. That both were imminent was obvious.

Since I had a suite while he was staying in a single room, we elected to go to my quarters. My cunt was buzzing like a beehive, ready to receive the sweet nectar of a cock or tongue. He stripped me, and I did the same for him the moment we were inside the door. With a hum of anticipation, he swept his gaze over my body and then knelt to kiss my natural rose. I fell to the edge of the bed and spread my legs toward the ceiling, clutching my ankles to unpleat the folds of my pussy as much as possible. His tongue ferreted about the soft ridges and tiny caves with the darting deftness of a lizard. It was heavenly. He ate me like the winner of a cunt-lapping contest. I came with a low moan and then a shriek as the initial orgasm was overwhelmed by the waves of succeeding climaxes.

"I've got to fuck you now, baby," he grunted as I lay there, still shaken from the overlapping of multiple orgasms.

I grabbed his balls as he mounted me. They were like two shelled eggs, firm and smooth, dangling loosely below his rigid prick. His cock seemed to be bandaged in skin, wrapped tautly to protect the stem that held the blossom of his head.

"Do it," I encouraged him. "Fuck the living hell out of me."

He rammed the full angle of his chubby cock into my slippery hole as his mouth moved from tit to tit like the shuttle of a loom. The force of his entries and withdrawals drove me deeper into the bed. I grabbed him about the neck so as not to slide beyond the reach of his rampaging organ. The rhythm was too addictive, too tantalizingly pleasurable to risk missing a single stroke.

"You've got a bitch of a fuck cunt," he spewed out just before pulling out to enjoy the spectacle of his own orgasm.

I watched, too, as he came with volcanic force, his hot, white lava spurting over the mountains of my tits and running in cloudy rivulets over my rib cage and down the length of my torso. It was all I needed to set me off again. With eyes squeezed shut, I dug my fingers into the sheets and let the tidal wave surge through my interior. What an enervating brace of climaxes they were! I was limp from the whiplash of lust that had so marvelously punished my body.

Lane showered and suggested we go down to the disco. "I've got to make a phone call first," I told him. "You go and I'll meet you there."

"Okay," he agreed. "I should go to my room and change clothes anyhow. Let's make it in an hour."

"Perfect," I replied.

At the door he paused briefly. "If you'll pardon my vulgarity," he said with a smile, "you are one sensational piece of ass."

"You're no slouch in the sack either," I responded in kind.

He winked and pulled the door closed behind him. This was really the first chance I had had all day to think about what Winnie had told me. I lay back and pondered my situation for a short time. Should I or shouldn't I? Winnie, of course, was positively opposed. But Laurinda was my friend, my lover. She wouldn't double-cross me   not just to please her employer. Anyway she was beautiful enough to get a job anywhere.

To hell with the consequences, I decided. I would call her. After all, I was far, far away from the Costa del Sol. And if necessary, I could disappear on a moment's notice. Before I could change my mind, I picked up the phone and asked for the overseas operator.

"Laurinda Alvarez," I told her, "Malaga, Spain. I don't have the number, but she's with Miguel Clemente Enterprises there."

I took a deep breath and waited as the hotel operator

contacted information in Malaga. As if by magic, a vision of her appeared in front of me, naked and beautiful. I took the receiver of the telephone and rubbed it against my cunt. Even the mental image of her aroused me intensely. I came just as I heard the operator reporting the number to me.

"I'm sorry," I apologized to her for the delay, "I'm afraid I was momentarily distracted. Yes, please do put the call through at this time."

The next voice I heard was Laurinda's.

CHAPTER EIGHT

Kim and Lita begged me to come to Honolulu with them, and Lane Symington pleaded that I accompany him back to New York. But where did I go despite some inner trepidation? Of all unlikely places, I went to Trieste to tryst with Laurinda.

She had been so insistent, so beguilingly convincing that I could not refuse her. There was no mention of what had happened in Bristol. But I extracted an absolute promise from her that no one, especially Miguel, be told of our reunion. She swore to that, assuring me that being with me was her sole objective. That was why we decided upon Trieste as a sort of middle ground where no one would expect to find either of us. Of course it was much closer to her, but then I wanted to get back to Europe after a week in humid, muggy Singapore.

I left with promises to my new Chinese friends to visit them in Hawaii and also a pledge to call Lane when I was in Manhattan. It did not fully satisfy any of them, but the more I thought of Laurinda's silky curves and her comehither mouth, the more determined I became to take off. What's more, I intended to do it as Christina van Bell, leaving Nicole Stevens behind in Singapore. For that reason I politely refused all offers to accompany me to the airport. It was better that they remember me as Nicole and meet me as Christina at some future time.

I had managed to buy some excellent hashish in a forbidding-looking waterfront cafe the day before leaving. There was coke available, too, but I shied away from it, uncertain of the laws in Trieste. Laurinda would undoubtedly have a small cache of it anyhow, knowing how ardently romantic it made me.

No direct flights were available, which annoyed me, but I could understand it. Singapore-to-Trieste did not exactly sound like a regular, full-passenger run. Instead I had to fly to Rome and then transfer to a flight up the Italian coast. The hash would help me endure it, I consoled myself.

I felt emancipated out from under the dark wig, my hair once again flowing over my shoulders like pure honey. Somehow the threat of Miguel's wrath did not seem nearly so frightening and inescapable as I boarded the plane for Rome. He was not really a violent person, but he was a jealous and vengeful man. I was sure he had quieted down by now. However, that did not make me any more anxious to see him.

Ignoring Winnie's advice once again, I had stopped at the airport souvenir shop and bought a picture postcard to send to Dirk Boland. Since I was leaving Singapore and had no plans to return at any time in the foreseeable future, what harm could it do to correct a lie that had no doubt mentally wounded poor Dirk? None, I reasoned. I took my seat in the first-class section and recalled the brief message I had scribbled on the card.

"Dearest Dirk, Have never been   and never will be married to Miguel or anyone else. Hope you're healing handsomely. Love, Christina."

I felt good about having done it. If he now wanted to press charges against Miguel, that was all right with me. But I doubted he would. Too much time had elapsed, and too much international police and paper work was involved. He had taken a beating for behaving like a man and that was a shame. I turned my thoughts elsewhere, not wanting to rile myself up all over again.

The hash was heavenly. There were only two men and me in the front section, and neither of them objected. Nor did the flight attendant, who confessed she loved the stuff as much as I did. However, her job kept her from accepting my offer of a toke. The fellows preferred taking the martini route. Nevertheless, after an hour in the air, all three of us had reached the same plateau. The rest of the trip was a hazy, rainbow blur. I hardly remembered making the transfer in Rome to a domestic flight or landing at Trieste's airport at Ronchi del Leigonari twenty miles outside of town. Thank God Laurinda was there with a limo and a driver just as I had requested.

"Chris, darling!" she cried out as I emerged hesitantly from the jet. There was no mistaking her stunning figure in the small crowd gathered at the foot of the mobile steps.

"Laurie!" I shouted back, almost tripping in my haste to get down the stairs.

We whirled round and round as we embraced, almost merging into one solid hunk of flesh. I kissed her repeatedly all over her face, and she did the same to me. How wonderful she felt, how vibrant and alive, how delectable and desirable! Any doubts I might have had about the wisdom of meeting her now vanished in the passion of our physical togetherness.

"Naughty girl," she feigned a reprimand, "running off by yourself without even telling me."

"I had to get away," I explained in apology. "I was all mixed up."

She laughed gaily. "Well, you sure unscrambled yourself in a hurry," she noted. "You look positively edible."

"Look who's talking," I responded. "I could take a bite out of you right here and now you look so delicious."

"Come on, let's get your bags and stop talking about it," she urged.

"Let the driver claim them," I suggested. "He's just stand-

ing there watching us as though we were insane or something." He was a huskily built young man, silent and un-
smiling. I wondered fleetingly why chauffeur services em-
ployed such unfriendly types for a business that was as
much public relations as it was driving.

"I'll do it," Laurinda volunteered "He won't understand
what I'm talking about."

I thought that was curious, but I let it pass. It was so
exciting being with Laurinda again I didn't want any clouds
of doubt or suspicion diluting the sunniness of the occasion.
"I'll go with you," I said. "I don't want you running off on
me."

We both giggled over that. But the merrier we became, it
seemed, the gloomier our driver looked. "What nationality
is he?" I asked Laurinda, aware of the polyglot population
of Trieste.

"I'm not sure," she replied, "but I think he's Czechoslo-
vakian."

"Aha!" I responded gleefully, "somebody's given us a bad
Czech."

Laurinda shook her head from side-to-side, smiling
broadly. "Christina, you're incorrigible," she sighed.

We were both determined not to let the sullen disposition
of our chauffeur spoil our fun. Without any inhibitions we
spent the half-hour trip to the city hugging and kissing and
feeling each other up. I came just from my proximity to her,
and when she managed to finger my clit now and then in her
gropings, I enjoyed major orgasms. Even the sight of us
frolicking in the back seat had no outward effect on the man
at the wheel. There was more warmth in an ice sculpture.
To hell with him, I thought to myself.

"Where are we staying, baby doll?" I asked as the car
entered the bustling city traffic.

"I'm not exactly a connoisseur of the local hostelries,"
she replied in deliberately affected prose, "but I understand
the best temporary residence available is the Savoia Excel-
sior Palace on Riva del Mandracchio."

"What a mouthful," I commented kiddingly. "I hope it wasn't recommended by the same individual who touted this limousine service."

"What's wrong with the limo?" she challenged.

"Nothing is wrong with the car," I replied, "it's just the robot in the driver's seat."

She waved her hand in dismissal. "Ignore him," she recommended. "Pretend he's an accessory."

"The hood?" I whispered in jest. There was a gangster quality about him now that I thought about it.

"I told you, you're incorrigible," she responded, poking my ribs.

"Wait until I get you on a mattress," I threatened. "I'm going to get into you in every way but incorrigibly."

"Promises, promises," she taunted me.

"You'll eat those words," I warned playfully.

"I'll eat more than that," she purred.

The touching, fondling, and caressing were heated enough. With dialogue added we were both ignited. "Let's get to that damned mouthful-of-a-name hotel before I explode," I urged.

"I think that's it up ahead," she said hopefully.

"It is," I confirmed. "I can see the name on the marquee."

"Hallelujah!" she said in a throaty tone.

This time we did leave the bags to the driver and the doorman, racing up the steps to the lobby to register. I feigned a female emergency to speed up the registration process. It worked, getting us our suite in half the normal time. Naturally I did not spell out the specific nature of my distress—dangerously inflammatory lace panties. Immediately after the door closed, they were removed so that the wound inside could be treated with the most effective therapy yet devised—a long, wet tongue applied rapidly and repeatedly to the raw flesh of the torrid cunt.

"I've dreamed about this moment," Laurie confessed as she wriggled out of her clothes and knelt before me. Despite its heat, my cunt was like a sponge, soft and absorbent, as it welcomed the imprint of her face.

"Suck me, darling," I begged her.

"Mmmmmmm," she moaned in agreement. Her hands grasped the cheeks of my derrière, pulling the meat of my vulva even closer to her animated features. The soft, insistent stiletto thrusts of her tongue were already working wonders on my nervous system. Little, pleasurable shock-bursts exploded like shooting stars throughout the area of my crotch. I moved my own tongue, imitating hers, licking out at the atmosphere to express the multiple joys inside me.

"Baby, honey, darling, sweetheart," I muttered in ecstasy, "lick me, love . . . don't stop . . ."

It goes without saying that I came without hesitation not once but many times flooding her face with the sweet syrup of my pussy.

"Let's get on the bed," she said in a voice choked with the juices of unbridled passion.

"I want to eat you," I announced in a throaty tone. "I want to fuck you."

We deep-throated each other as we moved to the bedroom, playing with each other's tits and cunts along the way. Once there we collapsed in an undulating heap atop the silken bedspread, our respective faces sunk beyond recognition in the fevered pussy of the other. Lost in lust, we sucked like unweaned babies on the tits of their mothers, sending pulsating currents through both our bodies clitoral climaxes that strummed our bodies like twin guitars. It might have gone on forever if it weren't for the interruption of a knock at the door. Laurinda sat up, looking strangely startled.

"Who could it be?" I asked, far less surprised than her. "Someone on the hotel staff, that's all. Nobody else knows we're here."

She eyed me oddly, hardly moving. The knock was repeated, more sharply this time. "Don't answer," she said to me.

"But why?" I questioned. "We can't just pick up where we left off, so we might as well find out who it is."

"Don't, Chris," she pleaded, grabbing my arm to restrain me.

I stared at her with a puzzled expression. "You're acting weird all of a sudden," I told her. "This doesn't make any sense   ducking a knock on the door. Ten to one it's a maid or a bellhop."

"Let's just be together for a while," she said with a strange sense of urgency.

"I thought that was why we were meeting," I reminded her. "We've only been in Trieste an hour, and you're acting like it's the end of the world."

"I'm superstitious," she confessed. "That's a bad sign, an ill omen."

"What? A knock on a hotel room door?" I scoffed. I looked searchingly at her. Such an angelic yet sensual face, such an alluringly curved body. I doubted that I could ever get enough of her, even if we spent the next decade together. Whatever her motivation, I did as she requested, remaining stretched out naked on the cool but now damp sheets. "Whoever it was seems to have gone," I noted.

"Wait a little longer," she cautioned.

"Laurinda," I asked with my eyes momentarily closed, "is there something you're not telling me?"

"About what?" she responded.

"About anything," I replied.

"Let's fuck," she said, grabbing a handful of my cunt.

I pushed her hand away and pouted. "You didn't answer me," I told her firmly.

"It's an unanswerable question," she hedged.

"Why?"

"It's too general," she said. "Nobody tells anybody *everything*."

"I do," I said.

"*Everything?*" she quizzed skeptically.

"Everything that relates to my relationship with another person," I clarified.

"This is silly, Christina." She tried to change the subject. "We should be enjoying each other's bodies instead of playing verbal ring-around-the-rosie."

I refused to relent. "Who did you think that might be at the door?" I asked pointedly. "Who could possibly know where we are unless you told someone?"

"I didn't tell anyone," she replied softly.

"Well then, who do you suppose it might be? Certainly not Miguel, I hope." That possibility had occurred to me at just that moment. It sent a quick chill through my bones.

"He's in South America again," she informed me.

I was relieved to hear that even though I did not let on. "Then who do you think it might be? The police . . . a robber . . . a rapist?" I persisted.

"I told you it was just superstition . . . or maybe a premonition, that's all," she insisted.

I shook my head dubiously. "You're not convincing me," I said with a trace of futility.

She put her head down in the valley of my thighs like a penitent little girl. We had been going around in circles long enough on this issue. For that reason, I just lay back and let her tongue slither into my love nest. Moments later I was too enthralled with coming to care who or what might have been at the door. All that mattered now was who was at *my* door and what a welcome little lapper she was, sucking like a supplicant at the shrine of everlasting eroticism.

CHAPTER NINE

Laurinda seemed somewhat less paranoid the following day as we made our way about the city. But I did catch her looking over her shoulder several times as we lunched and shopped and drank and drank at nearly a dozen of the many restaurants and beer gardens scattered all over the center of the metropolis.

"Did we have to have that same gruesome driver?" I questioned when the limousine showed up with the very chauffeur who had picked us up at the airport.

"That's the way they do things here," she explained off-handedly. "We get the car with him included for the duration of our stay."

"I don't like him," I complained.

"Then ignore him," she advised.

"He keeps staring at me," I told her.

"If I were him, I'd do the same thing," she assured me.

I shrugged but with a scowl to underline my displeasure. "Let's lose him somewhere," I suggested. "We could duck out the back way in one of these places and catch a cab."

She looked at me with an odd mixture of emotions on her face. "Don't be silly, Chris." She dismissed the idea. "Come on, let's try that sidewalk cafe across the street. We'll sample every wine they've got."

"You're on." I accepted the challenge, little realizing how

many different vintages were available. To name just a few, I can recall the red meriot and refosco, gray pinot and white tokay, traminer and Prosecco. I was sailing by the time we left the place, although the reappearance of our driver did have something of a sobering effect on me. He seemed unamused by our drunken state, delivering us back to the hotel in silence as we giggled like schoolgirls in the back seat.

It was only much later, when I awoke in darkness, sprawled out on a couch in our suite still fully clothed, that I recalled he had carried me to our rooms while Laurinda was engaged in a puzzling, staccato dialogue with him. I remembered that she had addressed him familiarly as "Jan" and that Miguel's name was mentioned several times in their discussion. They must have assumed I was totally unconscious, I reasoned, since before this she had never given the slightest indication that she knew any more about him than I did. And that was virtually nothing.

In the haze of a formidable hangover, I tried my best to piece together some sort of explanation for it all. I stumbled to my feet and checked the bedroom. Laurinda was there, naked and sleeping peacefully. It was obvious that I had done much more of the previous afternoon's drinking than she had. Now it was me who was getting paranoid. Could it have been arranged that way deliberately? Ever since that unanswered knock on the door, she had seemed a trifle mysterious to say the least.

I poured some hair of the dog into a tumbler and sank into a settee by a window. Looking out at the lights of the city, I came to a sudden decision. I had to get out of Trieste, preferably right away before she awakened and convinced me otherwise. Intuitively I knew something was amiss. Earlier I had tried calling Winston Garrett only to have the hotel operator insist repeatedly that all the available lines to London were in use. At any rate he would be upset to hear that I had made the trip against his best advice. I knew now that he had been right, and it was up to me and me alone to correct my mistake as expeditiously as possible.

I moved about catlike in the silty darkness, gathering my clothes without concern for packing them properly. For a moment I considered leaving them all behind, but then decided that would be ridiculous. There was no reason to suspect I was in any kind of mortal danger, and well, Laurinda was still a friend of mine. I could always explain a sudden departure, but not if it looked like a desperate escape. If only I hadn't drunk so much, this spur-of-the-moment evacuation would have been so much easier to accomplish.

On a sheet of hotel stationery, I scrawled a quick note. "Had to go. Will call. Love, Chris." I left it on the desk, and then slowly eased the door open.

My heart stopped. Sitting on a folding chair in the hall, his narrow eyes glaring, was our chauffeur. "Wha . . . what are you doing here?" I half-stammered, half-shrieked.

He pulled my wardrobe bag out of my hands. "Get back inside," he ordered gruffly, "you're not going anywhere."

"Give me my bag!" I cried out.

"Shut up," he rasped, pushing me back into the suite and quickly locking the door behind him.

"What's going on?" I demanded. "You have no right to stop me from doing anything, anything at all."

The commotion aroused Laurinda, who came stumbling into the sitting room, rubbing her eyes. "What's going on?" she asked as though in a semistupor.

"She tried to escape," the man named Jan explained

"Escape!?" I reacted hysterically, "I'm free to go anywhere I goddam please, and no gorilla like this is going to stop me."

"Calm down," Laurinda pleaded, a look of anguish clouding her attractive features. "Jan, get out of here. I'll talk to you outside later. I want to be alone with Christina for the time being."

"She tried to slip out while you were sleeping," he insisted.

"I understand," she retorted. "Just leave us alone, please."

"Tell that to the boss," he grumbled as he unlocked the door and stepped outside.

I was sobbing uncontrollably as Laurinda slipped down beside me on the sofa. "What are you doing to me?" I cried out between sobs. "Why? Why? Why?"

"Poor baby," she said sympathetically. "I feel terrible about this, believe me."

"Who is that sonofabitch?" I blurted out, my cheeks awash with tears. "What right has he got to push me around?"

"I wish I had an easy explanation," she said, biting her lip in frustration.

"Just tell me whether I'm a prisoner or not," I demanded. "Can I walk out that door, take a cab to the airport, and fly out of this miserable city or not?"

Laurinda looked away. "No," she said after a long pause, "you cannot."

I pushed her away from me. "Why not?" I asked with hostile crispness. The tears stopped abruptly now that the gauntlet had been thrown down. Nobody took Christina van Bell captive without a fight.

Her eyes lowered. "Miguel is having you held for ransom," she announced softly.

"I don't believe it," I responded incredulously. "Why me?"

"You have the money he needs," she explained simply. "He's broke."

I was stunned. Absolutely stunned. I tried to talk, but somehow the words dissolved in my mouth before I could say them.

"He doesn't want you hurt in any way," she tried to reassure me. "In fact, you'll live in your usual luxurious style and travel frequently. I'll be with you most of the time until the ransom's paid."

I kept shaking my head, almost involuntarily. "I thought he had more money than God," I said. "How could he possibly need funds so desperately he would pick on me like this?"

"The collapse of a dictatorship in Latin America," she explained in general terms. "He had everything invested there, and now the new junta is nationalizing his industries."

I was gradually regaining my composure. "The guy outside the door is a bodyguard then, right?" I conjectured.

"Right," she confirmed.

"How could you do this to me, Laurinda?" I asked her, staring deep into her eyes. "They used you as the bait to get me here, didn't they?"

"I didn't want to do it," she replied in a sad voice. "But Miguel insisted."

"You're in love with him?" I asked.

"Yes," she confessed in a whisper.

It was a great deal to absorb in such a brief time, but I managed somehow. "It won't work," I warned her. "I'm known all over the world."

"Nobody in Trieste seems to have identified you," she pointed out. "Besides, your hair's going to be cut and dyed."

"No," I protested. "At least let me use wigs."

She reached over and stroked my long, golden tresses. I could not really bring myself to be mad at her, so I made no effort to restrain her. "It is too beautiful to cut," she said. "I'll talk Miguel out of that idea."

"What kind of price tag is he putting on my head?" I questioned.

"We all know you're beyond price," she stated, "but just so your lawyers and accountants have a figure to work with, he's asking twenty-five million dollars."

I took that sum in stride since I had no real concept of money   or any real idea of my own financial assets. "And if they refuse to pay it?" I questioned.

She looked out the window and fixed her eyes on some distant spot. "Miguel's desperate," she said ominously, "they'd better pay it   or else."

I lit up a chunk of hash, closed my eyes, and dragged

deeply on my pipe. It had to be a bad dream, I told myself. I was just hallucinating, a bad trip. I took half-a-dozen more tokes and slowly, blissfully crowded out all the evil thoughts from my spinning head. Everything was going to be all right. Nothing could conquer Christina van Bell. With a smile of confidence, I lowered my head onto a sofa pillow and resumed the slumber that had been so distastefully interrupted by an impossible nightmare.

CHAPTER TEN

Disguised once again in a brunet wig, sans makeup, and in a formless, cotton shift, I boarded an eastbound flight with Laurinda Alvarez on one side of me and Jan Dvorak on the other. I needed their support since I had been drugged into semiconsciousness to ensure that I wouldn't attempt to escape.

There was no discussion of our destination. Laurinda skirted the subject by saying that she wasn't sure herself, that further instructions awaited us when we landed. Poor Winnie, I thought. He would be beside himself when he learned of my kidnapping. I asked if I might speak to him by phone to assure him that I was safe and unharmed, but that request was quickly denied.

"Remember, I love you," Laurinda kept repeating. "I won't allow anything to happen to you."

I acknowledged that ruefully. "This is just a little honeymoon jaunt, right?" I responded sarcastically. The downers in my drink soon erased any desire to plot a possible escape. I decided that there had to be other guards among the passengers, so there was little sense in making a scene. They had already convinced the flight attendants that I was ill and en route to a specialist for advanced psychological treatment. There is nothing like being labeled a certified wacko. I was avoided as though I was contaminated.

"Keep me high," I told Laurinda, "and I'll behave like an angel."

"You are an angel," she said.

"Angels can fly wherever they want to," I reminded her. "That eliminates me."

"I don't like this any more than you do," she said once again. "It's just to help out Miguel."

"Poor Miguel," I sighed mockingly. "Why didn't he just ask me for a loan?"

"Would you have really given him one for that amount?" she challenged.

"*I* might have," I replied, "but the guardians of my estate would never have approved it."

"Exactly," she agreed. "Miguel's quite aware of that."

"He'll never get away with this," I said, feeling myself begin to drift.

"He thinks he can," she responded. "He'll move to South America or Central America, where he has political connections."

"I don't care what he does," I said wearily.

"Go to sleep," she suggested. "It'll be a long trip."

I glanced across the aisle to where beefy Jan was sandwiched into a seat next to a chubby, Oriental-looking woman. Stuffed into a space too small for his large frame, he appeared far less menacing than he had back in the hotel. My eyes fluttered as I struggled to focus them, then closed entirely as exhaustion claimed me.

My next remembrance was of coming down from a tremendous but not particularly satisfying high. We were coming down all right   on a steep landing pattern. I tried to shake the haze from inside my head and determine where we might be. It was not a particularly attractive landscape   grayish hills and a muddy kind of light. Gradually I became aware that we were no longer on the same plane that left Trieste. That was strange, I thought. I had no recollection whatsoever of transferring from one aircraft to another. They must have drugged me during the switch, I decided.

That was why I felt so uncommonly sluggish and found it difficult to comprehend and concentrate.

"Christina," I heard Laurinda whisper in my ear, "wake up, we're landing."

I stirred groggily and glanced at her through half-opened eyes. "Where are we?" I asked in a voice thick with sleep.

She smiled enigmatically. "Guess," she said.

The name on a building looming up to the left of us said Kimpo International Airport. Kimpo? It had a very vaguely familiar ring to it. But I was in no condition to search my memory banks very deeply I shook my head.

"I don't know," I admitted

"Somewhere between Japan and China," she said, providing me with a clue.

"We're all the way back in the Orient?" I said with a note of distress. "I just left Singapore a week ago."

"It's not Singapore," she said as the plane's engines cut back to taxi down the runway to the terminal.

"I was hoping for Marbella." I expressed my disappointment.

"That would either be the first or second place they would look for you if you were missing," she said. "We wouldn't want you found before Miguel finds the money."

"This isn't Korea, is it?" I asked with some dread.

She confirmed my guess with a nod. "Seoul," she said. "Ever been here before?"

"I've been everywhere before," I noted with resignation.

"I haven't," she informed me. "I think it'll be interesting."

"It's no Tokyo," I told her. "What on earth made you choose this as a hideout?" My senses and reasoning power were gradually returning to me as the plane came to a halt.

"I didn't," she replied. "Everything that happens is on instructions from Miguel."

"He's a sadist," I snapped.

"You're bitter," she responded. "I really can't say that I blame you."

"Is that hulk a permanent part of the entourage?" I asked, pointing to the morose mass that was Jan Dvorak.

"I'm afraid so," she said, seemingly amused by my disparagement of him.

I rocked my head from side-to-side. "That's the worst part of it all so far," I said. "How about if I promise not to run off and just the two of us hide away together? Can you send this primeval predator back to Prague then?"

Laurinda laughed lightly as if we were off on a holiday together. It hardly seemed a captor captive relationship at all.

"I wish I could say yes," she replied, "but Jan's been with Miguel through thick and thin. I think he trusts him more than he does me."

"Don't let him touch me," I warned, "or I'll scream no matter where we are."

"He won't," she assured me. "Miguel would never allow him to lay a hand on any of his women."

"I don't consider myself *his* woman," I sniffed, "neither now nor before all this happened."

She nodded knowingly. "Your anger will go away in time," she observed. "I think it'll be only a matter of hours before you're free again   once your lawyers get the ransom message."

"They don't know yet?" I reacted in surprise.

"No approach has been made yet," she confirmed. "That'll probably happen tomorrow once Miguel knows we're safely hidden."

"Here I am abducted and nobody even knows it but me," I noted. "It's like getting raped without being touched."

She glanced at me with a puzzled expression. "I'm not sure I follow that," she said.

"Forget it," I responded. "I'm still foggy upstairs."

Jan made it his business always to be directly behind me whenever we weren't seated. Getting off the plane, he practically crawled up my back. "Easy," I cautioned him. "I don't want you avalanching over me. I'd never survive."

"Pardon," he growled, limiting himself as always to the fewest words possible.

For a girl who claimed never to have been in Seoul before, Laurinda conducted herself with remarkable aplomb. English is widely spoken there, so there was no real language barrier for any of us. We all squeezed into a cab together quite a feat, considering Jan's size—and took off for the Lotte Hotel. Thank God for that, I thought, at least I wasn't going to be kept in a dank dungeon somewhere in the forlorn foothills.

"Are you all right?" Laurinda questioned en route.

"Great," I replied sardonically.

"You're not in pain or anything?" she persisted.

"Do I look it?" I asked.

"You look beat," she observed.

"I feel simply marvelous," I lied. My lie was obvious to her, too.

"Let's try to make the best of a bad situation," she suggested. "There's no reason why we can't have some fun."

"Whoopee!" I responded sarcastically.

She looked at me with a pained expression but said nothing. I really wasn't sure how I felt about her now that I was in her custody. She still represented appealing sexuality to me, but I doubted if there could be that special extra spice that genuine affection provided.

"Jan," she said as we pulled up to the hotel, "go ahead of us and make sure we have the top floor rooms I requested. Christina and I will wait in whatever bar or restaurant is closest to the registration desk."

"Uh," he grunted, opening the door and literally rolling out onto the pavement. He was really quite agile for a man of his size, a fact that discouraged any thoughts I might have had of making a run for it. Besides, I doubted that anyone would believe my story. Moreover, I'd been told that one of the conditions of the ransom was that no police authorities be notified.

We went into a restaurant with the odd name of Mug-gunghwa. I was hungry, and remembering the fiery foods of Korea from my last visit, I was eager to set my interior aflame. Everything about me was hot, including my appetite for hotly spiced dishes.

"Order whatever you like," Laurinda said as we studied the menu. "It's all on Miguel."

"I thought he was broke," I responded.

She laughed lightly. "He's not *that* broke," she said.

"I'll have the *bulgoki*," I decided, "with a side order of *kimchi*."

She looked at me in puzzlement. "You'll have to order for me," she said. "I don't know any of these dishes."

I decided not to tell her how hot they really were. Let her find out for herself. "Why don't you get the *kalbi*," I suggested, "and then we can share our entrees?"

"Good idea," she agreed. "How about some wine?"

"Of course," I replied, "although beer is good with the native dishes, too."

"I don't like beer," she said, making a face.

"Okay, wine then," I responded.

When the food came, I urged her to sample the *kimchi* first cabbage pickled in red pepper and garlic and fermented in fish sauce. She lifted a forkful to her mouth as I watched intently. A moment later her eyes looked like pinwheels, her face turned crimson, and she almost choked before pouring wine on the flames.

"I never tasted anything that torrid in my life," she confessed when she was finally able to speak. "Don't tell me you're going to eat that?"

I casually placed a forkful in my mouth, held it to savor the flavor, then swallowed nonchalantly. Even though my throat was burning, I managed to maintain a look of cool appreciation.

"I love it," I said, sipping my wine.

"Now I understand why you're always hot," she said. "Don't tell me these ribs are just as spicy?"

"They're much more subdued," I informed her, "even though *bulgoki* means 'flesh on fire.' "

"If this is the native cuisine," Laurinda declared as she gingerly nibbled on her main course, "I'll self-destruct in a matter of days."

I truly enjoyed it, and for a time I forgot about the circumstances under which I was in Seoul. The Monster my name for Jan   stopped by to report that everything was set and to give the suite keys to Laurinda. Then he took a table across the room and ordered double portions of everything I recommended. There was no negative reaction either as he avidly devoured the scorching dishes, washing the food down with foamy swallows of the native beer.

"Look at him put that away," Laurinda said in amazement. "He must have a cast-iron stomach."

"Then I've got one, too," I noted, patting my abdomen contentedly.

"You're really remarkable," she commented. "No one would believe that someone as beautiful as you could be so down-to-earth."

"I can be haughty," I reminded her.

"Yes," she agreed, "but you'd be acting. That's the difference."

We ordered after-dinner drinks while Jan chose another entree from the menu. "Didn't he eat on the plane?" I asked.

"Everything he could get his teeth into," she reported with a small laugh. "He says that airline cuisine is just toy food."

I felt her eyes upon me as I gazed about the restaurant. No one paid the slightest attention to us, and no one gave the remotest indication of recognizing me. The dark wig and lack of makeup apparently were all too effective a disguise.

"Chris," Laurinda said softly after a lengthy pause, "can you still make love to me?"

My eyes avoided hers. I stared instead into the amber liqueur in my glass. "I can still have sex with you," I replied slowly, "if you understand what I mean."

"I understand," she said, her tone betraying her disappointment.

"Maybe in time . . ." I said with hesitation.

"Being with you under any condition," she responded, "is always better than not being with you."

I reached over and touched her hand, stroking it gently. "I'm trying to see this whole mess with some compassion," I told her. "It's not as though you have a gun to my head or anything like that."

"I wouldn't do that," she said, "not even for him."

I shook my head in agreement. "I know you wouldn't," I assured her.

The return to some semblance of romance between us quickly stirred old passions. In short order my libido was almost as hot as the food I had just consumed.

"Let's go to the room," I said with a sense of urgency. She understood immediately, brightening at the prospect.

"What a marvelous dessert," she responded with undisguised eagerness.

We left the restaurant so abruptly Jan had to abandon half of his second order to fulfill his function as bodyguard. Still we made it to the elevator ahead of him, leaving him frustrated and fuming in the lobby.

The two of us were almost stripped by the time we got the key in the door of our suite. Without even bothering to inspect our accommodations, we fell entangled onto the first available bed. There I lay my face against the nap of her cunt hair and slithered my tongue into the succulent slit, splitting it. As she did the same to me, I then buried my features into the deep, plush, black pile of her pussy. The suck was as sweet as the *kimchi* had been hot, building quickly to a fever pitch. Moaning and groaning, each brought the other to devastating climaxes.

"I brought something along," she revealed as we paused briefly in our wild pursuits.

I watched, panting with passion, as she fumbled through

the garment bags hung in the closet, finally fishing out a long, fat, double dildo. The heads on each end resembled miniature army helmets. She sucked each end in turn, then plunged one into her lush cunt.

"Cock," I said approvingly. "Let's fuck each other."

"Get down on all fours," she directed, doing the same herself.

We lined ourselves up ass-to-ass, reaching underneath our bodies to guide the lovely imitation prick into our waiting holes.

"God, that feels good," I sighed as the cylinder slid deeply into me.

"Fuck it, honey," she urged.

I felt her cheeks bump against mine as we moved in counterrhythm. The contact of our flesh made the thrusts of the dildo even more inspiring. I looked underneath myself and saw the clump of her pussy hanging down like moss from between her shapely legs. The to-and-fro movement made her tits slosh appetizingly beneath her. It didn't matter at the moment whether I was a prisoner or not. All that mattered was condensing this whole scene into the triangle of my crotch, then detonating the biggest orgasm humanly possible.

"Let's get some guys to fuck," I suggested in a reedy voice, utilizing words and mental images to heighten the force of the orgasm.

"Cocksucker," she gasped in response.

"Suck-fuck-cunt-prick," I muttered.

And then it struck, buckling my arms and turning my cunt into a vise around the rigid phallus I shared with her. It must have traveled like a bolt of lightning through the dildo and into her. She screamed in ecstasy as we both collapsed on the floor, our bodies convulsing as one climax tumbled upon another.

It was many minutes before either of us could gather the strength to respond to the insistent knocking at the door.

Jan had heard the screams and moans. He was ready to knock down the door, but Laurinda was able to catch him and assure him that everything was okay.

"I was laughing," she lied, "not screaming. We were telling each other jokes."

"Keep it down," he said through the closed door. "Don't want no cops."

"We will," she promised, allowing him to give her orders just to get rid of him.

I was already playing with the dildo again, sliding one end in and out of me while sucking the end that had been inside Laurinda. She came over and sat on my lap, inserting the head that had been in my mouth into her pussy. When she had impaled herself on it, riding it up and down so that it fucked me as it did her, we faced each other and settled down to sucking tits and deep-throating each other. If there had been any question about the effect our captor/captive relationship had on our sexual relationship, the remainder of the evening served to settle that issue permanently and positively. We simply could not seem to get enough of one another.

The day ended in frustration, though. Laurinda spent several hours trying to contact Miguel but with no results. He had left no word at any of his offices about his destination or whereabouts and, more importantly, no instructions regarding me.

I fell asleep knowing no more of my fate than I had when we left Trieste. A vague sense of insecurity invaded me for one of the few times in my life. I almost never planned ahead, taking one day at a time, but that was when I was in charge of my own movements. Now I had to think about what was going to happen to me. It was not the kind of dilemma Christina van Bell was overly equipped to handle.

CHAPTER ELEVEN

One thing I learned right away about Laurinda   she did not forget what was said in the heat of passion as so many others do. The day after our debut with the dildo, she returned to the hotel from a trip into the heart of the city with two of the tallest, huskiest Koreans I had ever seen. Jan Dvorak, who had been left behind to guard me, was taken aback when he saw them.

"They working for you?" he questioned immediately. He made no attempt to hide his displeasure if that was the case.

"Not in the sense you mean," she replied somewhat impishly. "They're just here to keep Christina and I company for a few hours."

Jan still regarded them with suspicion as he left for his room across the hall. "Call if you need me," he told her.

Laurinda seemed proud of her achievement. She smiled at me provocatively, her tongue protruding devilishly from the corner of her mouth. "You mentioned last night that you'd enjoy a little male companionship," she said, "so I thought I'd go out and get us some *big* male companionship instead."

The two young men smiled engagingly, even though they appeared just a trifle embarrassed up to now. I had no idea if they were just studs that she had chanced upon or working male prostitutes. It really didn't matter, I suppose, but I did sort of rebel at the idea of paying a man to do what I could get any other man to do for nothing.

"You said you were going shopping," I reacted with mild amusement, "you didn't say what for."

She laughed more freely than she had since leaving Trieste. "This is Hwang," she announced, grabbing one by the arm, "and this is Chung. They're professional wrestlers."

I looked at her askance. Was she putting me on? "Hi," I smiled back at them, "I'm Chris." I was allowed to use my first name, but not my last, according to the rules set down by Miguel.

"Let's have some drinks," Laurinda suggested.

"Good," Hwang agreed, suddenly quite at ease after the completion of introductions.

"They both speak excellent English," she pointed out to me.

"We learn from the GIs," Chung explained.

"You might learn all the wrong things that way," I said.

He looked over at me and grinned slyly. "Like you're some hunk of woman?" he asked.

"Something like that," I replied.

"He learned all the four-letter words first," Hwang injected.

"They get you places fast," Chung added to the accusation.

They were quite easy to be with. After the second drink Laurinda was already grabbing at Hwang's cock, teasing it into hidden hardness. "Do the Korean girls like to fuck?" she asked directly.

"Every kind of girl likes to fuck," he replied.

"None more than us," she taunted him.

Chung took that as an invitation to slip his hand into my blouse. He pressed against me, making sure I felt the solidity of his aroused cock.

"Let's get down to business," he said in a voice that honed with lust.

"We'll get down," I responded, "but not if it's a business."

He looked at me cryptically. "What do you mean?" he questioned.

"Laurinda knows," I said. She was already half-naked, ready to suck Hwang's wang.

"They're wrestlers," she repeated. "You don't think I'd . . . ?"

"Forget it," I told her, "there's a lollipop staring you in the face." She was on it in an instant, her cheeks filled like those of a squirrel storing nuts.

Chung had taken out his cock and stood there aiming it at my face. It stood up as though it had a spine of its own, the chablis complexion gradually turning to burgundy as it rose to its full length. I saw that he was wearing a cock ring, engorging it even more.

"Suck like a sonofabitch," he instructed me, pushing my head down on his shaft.

I weighed his balls in the palm of my hand, then let my finger slide into the crevice of his ass. My lips made an airtight seal around his head, holding it in place for the spanking from my tongue. "Mmmmmm," he uttered approvingly.

Laurinda had gotten her man as hard as humanly possible before falling on her back to be fucked. "I like the first load in my southern mouth," she explained to him. "I'll suck off all the others after that if you like." Hwang quite obviously just wanted to get off, orally or vaginally, without any particular preference.

"Your mouth looks like a cunt," Chung picked up the dialogue and applied it to our involvement. "Just like a beautiful pink pussy."

I brought him to a powerful climax, his cum spurting all over me, glazing my face and tits with melted white marble. "Amen!" he gasped, pulling the last pearl from the mouth of his ruddy penis.

"Fuck me, fuck me," Laurinda cried out as she rose and

fell in a frenzy under the steady hammering of Hwang's rock-hard prick. I could tell by the tortured look on her face that she was about to come. His grimace suggested that he, too, was on the verge of a massive orgasm.

"Open that golden hole," Chung said to me as I watched the other two freeze momentarily in the throes of erotic ecstasy. "I'm gonna fuck you till you beg for mercy."

"Do it," I encouraged him, feeding his stiff organ into the silken sheath of my cunt. He buried it deeply, all the way to the titillating little fingers of the cock ring. I closed my eyes to Laurinda and Hwang, now preferring to concentrate on my own succulent seduction.

"Slam it to me," I peppered him with words. "Screw the living fuck out of me."

His hard-headed tool stubbornly sought to strike bottom, pulling in his loose testicles in the effort to drive down as deeply as possible. I clung to his almond skin like a simian to its mother, riding his heaving body with intense dedication.

"Come with me," he urged in labored tones.

"Pop," I encouraged him, tightening the purse of my pussy to strip the head of his cock. It worked just as it almost always did. He came like a blizzard in the snug hollow of my cunt. The warm rain triggered my own orgasmic reflexes, setting me off on a wild, white-water ride of surging climaxes.

"You've got a cunt like a snapping turtle," he told me as he played with himself to keep his erection intact. "Try this mother, Hwang."

"I want to suck it first," Hwang said, crawling over Laurinda to get to me.

"I just came in there," Chung warned him.

Hwang paid no heed, diving head first between my legs, his tongue out front. A moment later his entire face was lost in the swampy delta of my crotch.

We exhausted all the possible combinations for four uninhibited sexual athletes. Then Hwang suggested that we girls deep-throat each other and mutually masturbate while the two of them jacked each other off over our bodies. They formed a kind of bridge over us as we fingered our way to still more orgasms. The view of their cocks and balls suspended over us made an interesting tableau   an erotically inspirational one   and the shower of semen that resulted has us quite literally swimming in cum.

I passed the hashish after that, and when we were all high, we took golden showers together in the bathroom, followed by purifying straight ones. Evening came, scarcely noticed by any of us. The men amused themselves by trying to count our pubic hairs, then when they were stratospheric on cocaine, they provided us with an exhibition of savage sodomy on one another. Somewhere in the proceedings I checked out, not awakening until the scarlet rinse of dawn had begun to remove the gray darkness from the skies. I was hungry beyond description   and not for either of the two Cs, cock or cunt.

"Laurinda." I tried awakening her. She was sprawled out naked across one of the beds. Little puddles of cum had dried on her body like flaking skin. The two men had disappeared, along with a good portion of my hash and coke supply. "Laurie." I tried again. "Wake up, it's morning."

"Ooooohhh," she moaned as though in pain. A second later she was fast asleep again.

I decided to try room service. Instead I got Jan's room, no doubt by some prior arrangement with the front desk. "What is it?" he grumbled.

"I'm starving," I confessed. "Could you order me some food?"

"Where's Miss Alvarez?" he asked.

"She's passed out," I told him. "I tried to wake her, but she doesn't respond."

"She sick?" he inquired with a note of apprehension.

"Hangover, that's all," I assured him.

"What do you want to eat?" he asked.

"Food," I replied without trying to be saucy, "any kind of food. Plus some champagne."

"Breakfast stuff?" he continued his interrogation.

"Breakfast, lunch, dinner," I recited, "I'll eat anything." That was an opening line if I'd ever delivered one. But he was devoid of humor and offered no reaction.

"I'll see what I can get," he said.

"Thank you," I responded.

I had no idea whether he intended to have it sent up or go for it himself. Nor did I care. All I wanted was platters and platters of food to slake my unexpectedly ravenous appetite. Mercifully I didn't have to wait long. I leapt like a kangaroo to answer the knock on my door about fifteen minutes later.

"Who is it?" I asked before opening.

"It's okay," Jan's voice assured me.

I flung the door open. There he stood behind a costumed waiter and a rolling cart pungent with tempting fragrances, bowls of fruit, and steaming covered dishes. "Hallelujah," I cried.

"I didn't know what to get," big Jan said, "so I got some of everything."

"Between the two of us," I replied, pointing at the bedroom where Laurinda lay nude, "we'll polish it off, I'm sure."

"Chow down," he responded in the friendliest manner I'd ever seen from him. I was even surprised that he knew enough to give the waiter a tip. They both went out together, leaving me alone for an orgy of nonsexual oral gratification.

"What smells so good?" I heard Laurinda ask in a tired voice. I looked up to see her standing in the doorway between the rooms, rubbing her eyes.

"I've gone cannibal," I reported, hardly pausing in my gluttony. It was fun to eat without concern for proper table manners. I just dug in like the Arabs do   with my fingers.

"You're not eating that hot stuff for breakfast?" she wondered.

"Nothing could be hotter that what I ate in this very room last night," I kidded.

"What was that suff that sets your mouth on fire?" she asked, moving over to peer tentatively into the clutter of dishes from which I was picking morsels of varied foods.

"You mean *kimchi*?" I inquired. I held up a dish containing the fiery concoction. "Want some?"

Her face pruned. "Ugh!" she reacted. "You must have a grudge against your stomach."

"It's made of the same material as my pussy," I jested. "It can handle anything."

"I believe it," she said, slumping onto a settee near me.

"Have some champagne," I offered. "It's good for what ails you."

"There is nothing good for what ails me except time and rest," she responded. "I'm a wreck."

"Those wrestlers know all the best holds," I reminded her. "I never saw you so passionately involved."

She seemed not to want to recall the previous night. "I've got to get on the ball today," she said more to herself than to me. I continued to indulge myself in the array of dishes spread before me, pausing now and then for a refreshing gulp of wine.

"That sonofabitch Miguel is ducking my calls," she continued her musing aloud. "If I don't hear from him in the next day or so, I'm backing out of this whole mess."

"Maybe he's on the lam," I suggested. "What if they pick him up when he presents the proposition?"

She glanced at me as though I had lost my mind. "You don't think he's going to expose himself, do you?" she scoffed. "This is all being handled by intermediaries on a very high level. It's almost like negotiations between nations."

"Now I'm a territory," I said with mild amusement.

"You're a *cuntry* already," she punned without smiling.

Jan came back to check on the food situation, showing unexpected consideration for my welfare all of a sudden "How was it," he asked after greeting Laurinda. She was still naked, which I'm sure he noticed but probably escaped her.

"You mean how *is* it," I corrected. "I'm not even halfway through it all."

"Good, though?" he persisted.

"Excellent," I replied. That seemed to please him, and he left without any further comments or questions. "What's gotten into him?" I questioned Laurinda. "Being so nice this morning."

She shrugged. "He's moody like everybody else," she answered. "Maybe he wants to get into your panties"

"Him?" I scoffed. "More likely yours. He couldn't keep his eyes off your bare pussy."

She glanced down at herself in mild surprise "Christ," she exclaimed, "I forgot all about being naked"

"Has he ever seen you this way before?" I asked

"He took me by surprise when I was sunbathing once," she reported. "Tried to put the make on me, then Miguel found out."

"He's a jealous bastard," I commented.

She rolled her eyes upward. "You're telling me?" she said "He's got a violent temper."

Again she withdrew and grew reflective as I continued my assault on the feast. "Christina," she said after a lengthy pause, "I've been thinking, I really should let you go I care too much for you to be harming you in this way"

I put down my chopsticks. "You're not harming me" I assured her, "except maybe depriving me of my freedom Otherwise I'd just be jumping all over the globe on my own."

"You're sweet for trying to defend someone else's wrongs," she responded, "but Miguel really shouldn't have done this. There must be other alternatives he could explore to get the money he needs."

"That's his business," I said.

"But it involves you," she reminded me. "Just see how friendly Jan would be if you tried to run away. He's on a mission, and believe me he's very conscientious about it. That change in attitude you just mentioned   that's just to keep himself in condition to cope with the human race. Not that he doesn't like you   I'm sure he'd give a month's pay to just see you naked. But he's the guard and you're the prisoner, and that's the way it'll remain until he gets orders to the contrary."

"I suppose you're right," I responded.

"I know I'm right," she said with conviction.

There was no further discussion of springing me free. Her conscience must have been bothering her, I decided. But after she was finally able to get a call through to the corporate offices in Malaga with word left there from Miguel, she lapsed back into her caretaker role. I had no idea what she had learned, but later in the day she announced quite unexpectedly that we were leaving Seoul immediately for some new, undisclosed destination. The noose was back on my neck and a little tighter than before.

CHAPTER TWELVE

If I had taken an atlas and stabbed a finger at a map of the world, I doubt whether I would have come up with our next destination: Kolonia, Ponape, in the Pacific island group known as Micronesia. For the first time since Trieste, I felt there was absolutely no hope that I might somehow be spotted and rescued.

"How did you ever come up with this godforsaken place?" I asked forlornly as we landed.

"It's really quite beautiful," Laurinda insisted. "Look at the lovely water and the lush vegetation."

"I feel like a pebble in an ocean," I said. "I'm not sure I ever even heard of this place before."

"This is the capital of the Federated States of Micronesia," she lectured.

"Whoopee," I responded with mock enthusiasm.

"We'll be able to do some good swimming here," she said, trying to cheer me up.

"Drowning sounds more appealing to me at the moment," I said despondently.

"It won't be for long, Chris," she assured me. "We can make some side trips to Guam and Saipan later."

"Enchanting," I said with sarcasm. She looked at me obliquely, grimacing in the process.

"You're not making it any easier," she said.

"Sorry," I responded, not sounding in the least bit as though I was.

My bitchy mood continued through the baggage processing and the examination of my forged credentials. They had kept my correct first name in order to avoid any slip-ups in addressing me, but my surname was now Thoreau The customs agent did not question anything, hardly glancing up as he applied the necessary stamps for validation

"You will be staying at the Village Hotel?" he inquired

I looked questioningly at Laurinda. "Yes," she told him, "we have cottage reservations there."

"Taxis are available just outside the building," he said "It's only half-a-mile from the airport."

"Thank you," she replied.

We got there quickly, and I had to admit that it was a charming setting. Our accommodations were individual thatched huts of Ponapean design huddled around a separate dining room and bar, which overlooked a picturesque lagoon. I immediately planned to make good use of the bar and that redeeming feature helped to lift my spirits. For a time I feared I was being taken somewhere so isolated no modern conveniences like a well-stocked bar would be available. That would have amounted to torture as far as I was concerned.

Jan was back to his silent, sulking self. It was good that he would be in a separate hut. The sight of him grimly hovering about could take the luster out of a tropical moon

"Let's go to the bar," I suggested after our clothes had been hung up in the open closets.

Laurinda studied me for a moment. "You really can't wait, can you?" she questioned with amusement.

"I don't have to drink," I told her, "I just like to."

"It is relaxing," she agreed. "But let's let Jan scout the place first."

"Why?" I questioned. "Nobody in the whole world could possibly find us there."

"I have my reasons," she said without elaborating.

I could only shake my head in disbelief. Ponape was as remote and unlikely a place as I'd ever seen. None of my crowd had ever even mentioned it, much less visited it. "Tell him to hurry," I said. "I'm thirsty."

He was back in short order. "Two fat old ladies at the bar," he reported, "that's all."

"Exciting," I said to her. "Nothing like being stuck in the middle of the Pacific Ocean with two fat old ladies."

"I saw some pretty attractive men on our way in from the airport," Laurinda noted.

"Natives," I said. "They can't afford to hang out in hotel bars, I'm sure."

"Let's go investigate," she suggested. There was more of a sense of abandon about her now that we were far from the main traffic lanes of the world. Jan, too, seemed less suspicious, though hardly more personable than he had been before.

In the leisurely setting of the bar with its colorful lagoon vista, I mellowed out to the point where I really did not feel at all intimidated   not at all like a prisoner. I could make myself believe that I was just on another one of my offbeat vacation sorties, experiencing a new little corner of the world. In turn, this restored Laurinda's image to the lovely, sensual state of our first encounter.

"That little hut is going to hum tonight," I warned her playfully.

"It's about time," she replied. "I was beginning to think you no longer cared."

The bartender eyed our hand-holding warily, not certain what to make of it. "You come here on vacation?" he finally summoned the courage to ask.

"Honeymoon," Laurinda teased. The look on his face was priceless, causing us both to burst out laughing. It obviously left him even more confused.

"You two?" he questioned, spreading his middle and index fingers to point at us both. "No," he answered himself, shaking his head in denial.

"Why not?" she challenged him playfully.

"Two beautiful women?" he responded. "No good."

It was diverting and great fun to engage in a kidding session with a stranger for a change. He was a pleasant Micronesian with milk chocolate skin and mischievous dark eyes. It was apparent that he could not decide whether to take us seriously or not. "You two come alone?" he inquired, leaning his elbows on the bar and holding his chin.

"We come together," I said, smiling at the double-entendre.

"No men with you?" he asked, missing my play on words

"Men are no good," Laurinda said with a serious mien

His forehead corrugated, and his eyes crinkled at the corners. "You don't like men?" he said almost incredulously "Why not?"

"Women are more interesting," she declared.

"I think so, too," he agreed.

"But you're a man," I pointed out.

"I don't like other men," he defended himself, "not to make love. No, no."

"Have you ever tried it?" Laurinda asked in an impish whisper.

"Never," he said with macho conviction.

"Then don't knock it," she volleyed with the obvious comeback.

He went down to the other end of the bar, checked the glasses of the two portly women, and then returned. "You know," he said, "I don't believe you."

"That's because you don't want to believe us," I suggested.

"Not two beautiful women," he said with a shake of his head. "Two ugly ones maybe, but not two beauties."

Laurinda and I exchanged sly glances. We were all set to really overwhelm him when Jan Dvorak sauntered in and took a stool next to us. "I checked out some trips we can make in the area tomorrow," he said. "We don't have to stay on this island alone."

The bartender was all grins. "See?" he said triumphantly, "I knew you two were not alone together. You got a big man with you."

Jan stared at him blankly for a moment, then ignored him. "I'm going into town for a couple of hours," he said to Laurinda. "You'll be okay here, won't you?"

"Perfect," she said. He got up and left, having ruined our game with the bartender. Now no matter what we said or did, we could not persuade him that we were anything but one-hundred-percent heterosexual.

I was relaxed for a change, the new sense of limited freedom adding to the pleasure of the drinks. The bartender, apparently greatly relieved that we were in the company of a man   even a man as unlikely a companion as Jan regaled us with information about the island-strewn nation of Micronesia. We learned never to drink with Truks, who inhabited a ring of coral islands to the west of Ponape. "They go crazy with booze," he confided. "Rape women, beat up each other, kill, everything . . ."

"The Ponapes are okay, though?" I questioned.

He grinned slyly. "They become lovers," he related with a wink.

"I believe it," Laurinda led him on, "especially the bartenders."

He glanced up at the ceiling with a sweeping roll of his eyes. It said everything. Rather than continuing into more dangerous territory, he switched the discussion to another part of the nation, Guam.

"You go there to Agana," he suggested. "Everything there is very cheap."

"A duty-free port?" I questioned.

"That's what it's called," he confirmed. "Also go to Talofofo. The beach is all black   black sand."

"I prefer white or pink in beaches," I told him.

"Then go to Tumon Bay," he said.

I looked at Laurinda. "I'm too lazy to go much beyond the hut, aren't you?" I asked her.

"We're not really here for sightseeing," she informed him.

"No?" He seemed surprised.

"We're just stopping over on our way elsewhere," I explained.

"Honolulu?" he guessed.

"Maybe," Laurinda replied. Once again he regarded us with mild skepticism, but he did not question us further. The alcohol was beginning to show on us, and he apparently felt he had ventured far enough into our personal matters. Several others had filtered into the barroom, keeping him busier than he had been earlier, giving us more time to ourselves.

"Are you going to try to reach Miguel?" I inquired.

"He's supposed to contact us," she revealed.

"I wish you'd let me talk to Win Garrett," I said. "Believe me, he wouldn't make any moves that would endanger me. I'll make sure of that."

"I can't make a decision like that, Christina," she replied. "That's up to you-know-who."

I pouted and thought once again about attempting an escape. But Jan and Laurinda held all my credentials, all my money. I would have to throw myself on the mercy of the local authorities, hoping they would believe what would surely sound like a wild story to them. Especially since there was no police report on file anywhere. No, for the time being I would just have to bide my time and make the best of a bizarre situation.

Jan returned a couple of hours later, showing signs of having indulged in a few cocktails himself. Acting even more mysteriously than usual, he took Laurinda aside and whispered something to her. I shrugged it off and ordered us both another drink. When Laurinda returned, she was uncommunicative and preoccupied.

"You act as though you just learned that you've got only twenty-four hours to live," I said.

She looked at me blankly. "What?" she responded.

"I'm the one who's supposed to be down," I said. "Why should you be so forlorn all of a sudden?"

"We can't stay here," she said with a note of regret. "We'll shift to Saipan in the morning."

"Why?" I demanded. "What sense does that make?"

"At times nothing makes sense," she replied cryptically.

We were both plummeted into gloom by the news. Here we had just gotten settled, befriended an amiable bartender, and looked forward to swimming and sunning the next day, and now we were destined to pack up and go on the run again. The short distance to Saipan made the move seem totally ridiculous to me. But I had nothing to say in the matter and apparently neither did Laurinda. As for Jan, he amounted to little more than a portable prison tower.

"I might as well get blitzed," I declared. "Let's get some champagne to celebrate."

"Celebrate?" she responded, tilting her head in puzzlement. "Is that really the word you want?"

"Definitely," I replied. "I want to celebrate the worst itinerary I've ever had to endure. Now I know what it's like to be a gypsy moth, flapping my wings all over the place, landing only long enough to take off again on another dizzy flight."

She nodded slowly, wetting her lips in symbolic distress. "It is a rotten thing to do to you," she said. "You don't deserve this at all."

"Then let's let the inmates take over the asylum," I proposed. "Let's fly over the cuckoo's nest before we go back to the hut." My mock gaiety finally got through to her.

"You're right," she said. "Let's get totally, mortally blitzed. They can take us to Saipan in body bags if necessary."

The champagne was before us in short order. I lifted my glass and touched hers in toast. "To hell with Miguel," I said with gusto.

"Amen," she said.

Hours later we were casualties of our own war the battle to consume every bubble of champagne in the bar's stock. My last words of the day echoed those of the U.S. Marines in World War II: "Saipan, here we come!"

CHAPTER THIRTEEN

Our invasion of Saipan was a foggy achievement from the start. Not only had I been reluctant to go, I couldn't even remember the trip. Had we flown or taken a ship from Ponape? Through eyes murky with only half-realized slumber, I rolled over and squinted at the name embossed on a directory of hotel services to determine where I was. The Saipan Continental. Marvelous, I thought as I rolled over and encountered the body in bed with me. I had to get more sleep, my numbed brain told me. As for Laurinda, she hardly moved at all as I slipped back into something close to unconsciousness.

It must have been hours later when an insistent object as hard and cylindrical as a flashlight rocked me back into a blurry awareness. Eyes still clenched shut, I reached under myself to determine what Laurinda was using to masturbate me. Lo and behold, my probing fingers encountered a handful of hairy flesh enclosing two egg-sized balls!

"What?" I gasped as my eyelids sprang open.

"Relax," a familiar voice rasped. Strong arms prevented me from turning around far enough to see the face of my seducer. But my awakening seemed to inspire him to slam against the cheeks of my buttocks with a new fury, forcing the helmet of his swollen cock to penetrate even more deeply than before.

"Who are you?" I demanded as I clung to the sheets to keep from sliding off the bed. It seemed ridiculous to be demanding identification in the midst of a frenzied fuck, but for some reason my libido was not yet so wanton that it accepted total strangers without invitations.

"Fuck," the faintly familiar voice now honed totally with lust instructed.

Despite my misgivings, the steady impalings all too quickly created a torrid, vaginal friction that I was powerless to hold in limbo. I was hot by now, and when the hands looped around my bosom and sought out the nipples of my tits, I succumbed to an abrupt surge of orgasm. That in turn caused my cunt lips to clutch the head of his prick and literally rip out the pearly pellets of cum waiting to release inside me. He continued to hump right through his climax, determined to maintain the solidity of his cock through another round of orgasms.

"You sonofabitch," I protested, though without much conviction. If I was being raped, I might as well relax and enjoy it. As he grunted and ground away, I threw my body into the rhythm of the fuck with my customary enthusiasm and abandon. It sent him shuddering along the length of my body, his testicles slapping loosely against the loose-hanging lips of my pussy.

"Ohhhhh," he moaned with delight as we galloped together, horseman and mount, through another sequence of spitting cum and surging waves of climax within me.

I wondered vaguely what had happened to Laurinda and Jan as the euphoria gradually faded into the shambles of my monumental hangover. Surely they were aware of a man being in bed with me. Perhaps this was one of her little special treats for me   a surprise seduction that she could watch and enjoy from some private vantage point. That possibility struck me as the most logical and likely of all. It was an assumption that removed any fear or dread from my mind. I was definitely not in the clutches of some mad, violent rapist   even in so remote a locale as the Northern Marianas.

I tried breaking the grip of his hands once again. "Twice is nice." I tried a flippant approach. "But who's the screw?"

"Use your imagination," he suggested, again with a remotely recognizable lilt. It was obvious that whoever it was he was disguising his voice to the best of his ability to prolong the mystery.

"Say something more," I requested.

"Something more," he responded.

I reached behind me and investigated his cock with my fingers. Perhaps there was a clue there. But cocks bore a disturbing resemblance to one another   except in thickness and length   and feeling one without also seeing it made the task of identification more complicated. I gave up, but not before reviving it.

"Cock *al dente*," I noted.

"*Rigido*," he corrected.

I knew in an instant who it was. "Miguel!" I blurted out in an odd mixture of surprise, anger, and frustrated happiness.

"I must have you again," he declared, "then we will talk."

"You bastard." I feigned resistance. "I should bite your cock off for what you've done."

"Suck it instead," he responded, pinning me to the bed with his knees and feeding his prick to my mouth.

"I'll decapitate it," I threatened.

"Suck it," he repeated. His hands brought the gleaming corona to my lips. It slipped in like a snake finding its habitat.

The shock of it all and the welter of emotions over this bizarre reunion spurred me on to inspired oral athletics. I ate him like a starved cannibal at a feast   licking, chewing, salivating, swallowing, and gurgling the way a baby teethes upon a pacifier   until he erupted from the depths of his balls, shooting molten cum over my face and down my throat, milking every last pearl onto my gaping features. I made no attempt to wipe it away immediately, preferring to let it rest upon my skin like an exclusive facial. Despite the silken lacquer, I still found it difficult to believe that he was here. The brazen kidnapper I could not bring myself to regard as my abductor, despite all the evidence.

"You're as delectable as ever," he said with his customary charm. "It's been a long time without the pleasure of your company."

"Whose fault is that?" I countered, forcing myself not to succumb totally to his wiles.

"Things happen, Christina," he replied. "Circumstances sometimes force us into odd resolutions."

"There was nothing odd about your resolutions just now," I responded with a touch of sarcasm.

He smiled. "It gives a nice patina to your face," he said.

I had great difficulty formulating a consistent attitude toward him in view of all that had happened. There were times such as now when it seemed that nothing really substantial had taken place between us. Yet at other moments I felt that he had used and betrayed me, and then I despised him. Whatever the emotional mixture, it was a volatile one and made lovemaking with him intense and disruptively satisfying.

"Why did you decide to come here of all places?" I questioned.

"That's obvious, isn't it?" he replied. "Remoteness. Anonymity. Beautiful, lonely beaches on which to make love to a beautiful woman."

"Do you actually think you can just pick up where we left off?" I asked in amazement. "Don't you think I feel trapped, a prisoner on the run?"

"I don't want you to feel that way," he said blithely. "That's why I came here to be with you."

I shook my head in disbelief. "Miguel," I said, "I think your financial problems have made you lose your mind."

He cocked his head and looked off into the distance. "It's

only temporary," he said. "I consider what I'm after from your trustees just a loan."

"Then why didn't you just apply for it?" I questioned. "This foolish scheme of yours is liable to land you in prison and leave you penniless besides."

"Obviously I don't agree," he said. "You're the only one who knows I'm directly involved. The negotiations are all through professionals who haven't the vaguest idea for whom they're working."

"That's movie scenario stuff," I snapped. "You treat twenty-five-million dollars as though it were pocket money."

"Isn't it, Christina?"

I paused and thought it over. "I guess in a way you're right," I reluctantly agreed.

"We're both members of the MINO club," he said.

"Explain that."

"Money Is No Object," he replied crisply.

"I wish you had come to me and discussed your problem on a businesslike basis," I told him. "I could have worked something out."

He shook his head. "Nobody must know my situation," he said slowly. "Your lawyers would never willingly agree to advance me the capital on my terms despite the fact they'd get it all back very quickly."

"I stay out of business affairs," I responded, "but it seems to me that this is a terribly drastic way to go about financing your recovery."

He patted my thigh with his open-palmed hand. "That's not your concern," he said softly.

Laurinda interrupted us from the adjoining suite. "I hope I'm not breaking up anything personal," she said in mock apology.

"Oh, no," I replied. "I always sit around with a naked captor, wearing the milk of his manhood in place of skin lotion."

She laughed. "I'll bet you were surprised," she said.

"It's the only known cure for a hangover," I told her. Incidentally, why do you look so fresh?"

"Fresh?" she retorted. "I feel like one of those dead fish on the beach."

"You two both outdid yourselves on the other island," Miguel observed. "I couldn't communicate with either one of you last night."

"You established an effective pipeline this morning," I noted.

Laurinda looked at me slyly, strangely showing no jealousy over my relationship with the man of her dreams. She had not always seemed so generous.

"How long do you intend to stay with us?" she asked Miguel.

"A few days at most," he replied. "But then again, maybe longer."

"That's what I call a definitely indefinite response," I said.

"It all depends upon outside factors," he explained without elaborating.

I got up and looked out of the windows at the ribbons of white sand curling through the lacy surf. "It's much prettier than I would have expected a famous battleground to look," I noted.

"Some bitter fighting took place here and over there on Tinian during World War II," he said "You'd never think it to look at its peacefulness today"

"The same applies to you," I said He glanced at me questioningly.

"You never forgive," he said, "or forget."

"I forgive," I replied tartly, "but I don't forget"

Laurinda interrupted again. "Let's have some breakfast Christina-style," she suggested.

"What is Christina-style?" Miguel asked He seemed to welcome the opportunity to change the conversation.

"Anything at all," she told him, "as long as it's served with champagne."

We decided on a buffet of cold, native fish and local fruits with champagne, of course. "Have it sent up," Miguel instructed.

"By the way," I injected, "where's your mobile mountain?"

Miguel frowned. "I don't appreciate your metaphor," he said.

"Jan's out there in the surf playing whale-on-the-beach," Laurinda jibed.

Miguel shook his head. "You two have no respect for a man doing his job," he complained.

"I have no respect for the job he's doing." I rearranged his words.

"It's only temporary, my dear Christina," he replied. "You have my word on that."

I threw him a skeptical glance. "I don't know why I don't hate you," I said while Laurinda was in the next room, calling down our order.

"Because you love me," he responded confidently.

I thumbed my nose and stuck my tongue out at him.

"Don't tempt me again," he warned.

"Excuse me while I rinse off." I excused myself. He grabbed for my cunt as I got up, but I drew in my stomach automatically, eluding his grasp. "Your timing is off, señor," I goaded him.

"That butterfly will be caught again," he predicted. I had no reason to doubt him, even under the less-than-ideal circumstances.

After a leisurely breakfast, the three of us went to an isolated stretch of beach to sauté in the warm sun and dip ourselves in the azure waters. With my eyes closed, I could actually make myself believe that I was on a holiday somewhere with old friends—the Riviera or Costa del Sol perhaps. Only the occasional bursts of Japanese patter with its prolonged vowels and little whiplashes of staccato whines interfered with that illusion.

Miguel persuaded Laurinda and I to strip away our minute bikinis and indulge in subdued sixty-nine with only he and the sun as witnesses. The hardness of his cock as he watched, propped next to us on one elbow so that his body acted as a shield against potentially prying eyes, was like a barometer indicating the effects our activity had on his ever-resilient libido.

"How beautifully your bodies blend," he observed with a lusty edge to his voice.

I peered out from the damp and dense foliage of Laurinda's crotch to see him stroking himself gently but firmly. One in the hand was worth two in the bush, I thought to myself, except when you're talking about jerking off as opposed to fucking or sucking.

"Ooooh," I groaned from deep within. Laurinda had a reptilian tongue flicking at my most sensitive pussy meat like a lizard capturing delicate tidbits.

Miguel could not restrain himself from becoming a full participant as we slithered and writhed in the warm sand. Crouching above our heaving bodies, he entered the silken sheath of Laurinda's cunt as I continued to lick at the tensed finger of her clit atop the entrance. His balls jostled against my chin as we collaborated in the simultaneous fucking and sucking of her succulent love hole. It quickly proved to be too much for all of us, setting us off in all different directions as climax after climax tore us asunder. Or so it seemed. All I knew was that each time I had an orgasm, I felt that I'd been shattered to pieces only to be magically restored like the characters in animated cartoons ready to be destroyed once again by the same sweet, satanic force.

"Into the sea together!" Miguel trumpeted. His cock was still dripping and at half-mast as we scampered hand-in-hand into the turquoise tranquility of the vast Pacific.

It turned into an idyllic day. I was free of concern for the first time since the whole nightmare began. None of us spoke of reality. Miguel had smuggled in some pristine cocaine, and we sat snorting it under the graceful palms, letting its magic erase all worries for the time being. We fucked as well—the slow, leisurely interweaving of bodies that brought on absolutely ecstatic climaxes. By sundown I was positively euphoric, the most willing captive in history. Of course the feeling couldn't last. The next morning Miguel was gone   and, worse, we were moving again. This time our destination was Manila.

I wanted to cry. And I did.

CHAPTER FOURTEEN

Even with a lei of sweet-smelling sampaguita around my neck, I felt anything but fragrant and flowery. The hopscotching travel patterns I'd been undergoing since Trieste were beginning to show on my features as well as my disposition.

"I don't understand why we have to move so often," I complained bitterly to Laurinda on the flight from Saipan. Omnipresent across the aisle from us, Jan Dvorak had become the oaf he was originally, a sort of big bad, brooding Buddha stuffed into an undersized airline seat. I was tempted to spit on him on more than one occasion — not for any particular offense other than being present in my life.

"Miguel wants it that way," she replied as if that explained everything.

"He took off without even a goodbye." I added another lament.

She smiled tolerantly. "Didn't that day on the beach say it all?" she responded.

"Maybe for you," I said, "but not for me. He knows I could just start screaming in one of the airports and get him in more trouble than he's ever been in his life."

"You wouldn't do that," she reacted blithely.

"Never bet on Christina's reaction to anything," I warned.

"I'm an instinctive person, and sometimes I don't even know myself how I'm going to respond to pressures."

She took my hands in hers in a gesture of asssurance. "Miguel told you it would only be for a short time," she said with concern. "Bear with it like I do. We both love you."

It was idiotic, but in my continuing quandary it made some sort of oblique sense. I stayed passive for the rest of the flight and entered the terminal in a glazed zombie state. As I got off the plane, some flashing-eyed, dazzling-smiled young girl hooped me with a lei and welcomed me to Manila. I fleetingly thought of myself as a stray cow being roped with a lasso.

"How long will we be here?" I finally managed to ask. I hadn't said a word in so long I wondered whether I still had the capacity to speak.

"What, darling?" Laurinda bent over to ask.

"Will we be here long enough to sleep late tomorrow?" I inquired with deliberate sarcasm.

"Definitely," she said. Her eyes ricocheted off Jan, obviously warning him that I was showing signs of stress. He moved in closer, virtually smothering me with his bulk.

"Get this elephant off my back," I snapped at her, pushing him back at the same time.

"What's the matter?" she asked in an anxious tone. "I thought we'd agreed on the plane to make the best of things for a little while longer."

"I don't want him touching me," I said emphatically.

"Jan," she said, directing her attention to him, "back off a bit, please?"

He gave her a dirty look but did as he was told. Laurinda put her arm around me and stroked my short, black hair. I felt like ripping off the wig and letting my golden tresses spill over my shoulders to declare to everyone present that Christina van Bell was alive and well and living on the lam. But I did not. The friendliness about me was all of the welcoming tourist variety. I could not depend upon strangers to provide me with a possible escape, especially since my real passport was somewhere in the locked vaults of Miguel Clemente far away in Malaga.

"Let's go into the bar and have a drink," Laurinda suggested. "It'll help calm you down."

I was weeping quietly by the time we took a small table for just the two of us. "It's beginning to get to me," I confessed to her. "I'm really beginning to feel trapped despite all the movement."

"Poor dear," she responded with genuine sympathy. "I'll let Miguel know that."

"I think it was yesterday   the tranquility and companionship of it all   that reminded me of how much I miss my freedom," I continued to ramble. "I miss all my friends on the Riviera, in Paris and London and New York. I was never meant to be a fugitive like this."

"It won't always be this way," she repeated once again. "It's a very temporary state of affairs."

"It's been weeks," I reminded her.

We stayed in the bar until I was sufficiently tranquilized to make the trip into the city. The hotel that had been selected for our stay was the Manila Mandarin in the suburb of Paseo de Roxas. Its subdued greens and the blond wood were restful to my eyes after the burning of tears. But over-all Manila, with its air of martial law subtly suffocating the environment, was not my kind of city. The once and future Christina van Bell would hardly make more than an airport stopover in such a controlled climate.

In the course of the next few days, I must have slept fifty to sixty hours. I had little desire to go out, preferring to dine on a mixture of Chinese, Japanese, and Filipino cuisine in our top-floor suite. Laurinda kept encouraging me to accompany her on a shopping tour, and finally, bored beyond belief by my self-imposed confinement, I agreed.

"Good," she greeted my decision, "you're much too young and beautiful to lock yourself in like this."

"The other places I wanted to stay longer," I said, "and we left too soon. Here, where I'm ready to shove off at a moment's notice, we linger and linger."

"I haven't heard from Miguel," she explained.

I looked at her a trifle incredulously. "He's either paying you a fortune," I declared, "or he's got you totally brainwashed."

"Neither," she insisted. "I do it out of love and concern for his welfare."

"He'll never need welfare," I punned lamely. She ignored my comment.

"I've been to the markets," she said. "They're fun."

"Hilarious," I said disparagingly.

"You've turned so bitter, Chris," she noted. "You're not yourself at all lately."

"I haven't been leading my old, carefree life at all lately either," I pointed out.

I picked out a very revealing outfit to wear on our junket. Laurinda quickly vetoed it. "Miguel insists on nothing that will attract undue attention to either of us," she announced. "Pick out something fashionable but not ostentatious."

"Who could possibly recognize me here?" I protested.

"It's a fairly cosmopolitan city," she disagreed. "There's always that chance."

I pouted "I don't think I want to go after all," I said.

She reacted by embracing me warmly "Please?" she requested. "For my sake?"

My holdout was brief I really did want to get out for a while. "Get out my nun's habit," I jested "and my chastity belt."

"Thank God you haven't lost your marvelous sense of humor," she reacted with a pleased smile.

"I thought you were going to say my marvelous sense of chastity," I responded

The brief bit of word play brightened us both. We sauntered through the lobby of the Mandarin, laughing, and continued behaving merrily at the Pistang Filipino, a flea market glutted with handmade bags, embroideries, and shells. All kinds of bamboo furniture were available as well.

"Let's set up housekeeping," I suggested as a joke. "We've been here five days already."

Laurinda laughed, then bought me a basket and a bottle of wine to put in it. We decided to take a stroll, nipping from our wine as we walked. It brought smiles from the friendly Manilans as we ambled along President Roxas Boulevard, through a place called Rizal Park, then Circle Intramuros, and finally Fort Santiago. From there we took a cab to the San Andres fruit market, bought some champagne to wash down the native fruits we purchased, and finally returned to the hotel exhausted but far less tense than when the journey had begun. To cap the day, there was a message at the desk for Laurinda to call Miguel in Bogotá, Colombia.

"I hope this means we're leaving." Laurinda voiced my sentiments as she closed the door separating our bedrooms to make the call.

It did. We were on our way to far more sophisticated and therefore to me far more acceptable Tokyo. For some intuitive reason, I had a feeling that this move signaled that the end of this butterflying was near. Rightly or wrongly, I was buoyed considerably by that possibility.

I caught my breath when I heard Laurinda tell Jan that our destination in Tokyo was the Okura Hotel. As a blonde to say nothing of as a free spirit I had stayed there any number of times. Would anyone there recognize me in my pale and subdued brunet trappings? I had reason to hope that someone would perhaps some member of the formidable Japanese paparazzi. They were unusually good at detecting celebrities in various forms of disguise, a necessary skill for their professional survival. At least here there was an opportunity for me, unlike in Manila.

The dream was short lived, however. No rooms were available on such short notice at the always crowded Okura. We wound up instead at the Ibis on the Ginza, a pretty place but somewhat less of a celebrity hangout than the Okura. I was disappointed but not devoid of hope. If I could persuade Laurinda to make the rounds of fashionable restaurants, nightclubs, and discos, I might still be spotted by the roving paparazzi. It was distressing to realize that none of them had the vaguest idea that I was in any form of trouble other than the usual trouble of my own making. Miguel's representatives had struck a hard bargain, one which Winston Garrett apparently respected because of the danger to my life.

Immediately after checking in, I had *sashimi* and *sushi* at one of the cute restaurants within the hotel. With ample *saki*, of course.

"It's good to see you looking so exuberant for a change," Laurinda noted from across the table.

"I like Tokyo," I confessed. Then slyly I added, "Do you suppose we could go dancing later? The discos in Roppongi are really fun late at night."

"You wouldn't try to whisper anything to one of your partners, would you?" she questioned coyly.

I responded with my best Who?-Me?-Never! expression. "Laurie," I said with conviction, "I'd never do that to you and you know it."

"I don't think you would," she replied, "but I do have to be careful for Miguel's sake."

"Then take Jan along," I proposed boldly. I was basing my main hopes on being recognized, not enlisting some baffled Japanese man or woman into a plot to escape.

"Oh, certainly," she said. "We couldn't go out wandering around this huge city safely without him."

"But you will go?" I persisted.

She smiled and nodded agreement. "I want you to be happy," she said.

We returned to our rooms and melted into one another, the *saki* seeming to liquefy us as we collapsed into a fluid pool of arms and legs, lips and breasts. But as always the chief allure was at the joining of the thighs   the delta of mossy softness and warm pungency.

"Love me," she sighed.

At that moment there was something small and tender about her, delicate as violets, sweet as lilacs. It provided that fleeting moment of contrast before those same features were overtaken by lust, turning my aesthetic appreciation into savage desire. I slid over her smooth, almond curves until I was face-to-face with the dolphinish smile of her pulsating pussy. It seemed to wink at me slyly, this chameleon cunt that changed not only its color but the geometry of its contours each time I approached it.

"How suckable you are," I pronounced before my plunge into the depths.

Her hands drew my buttocks down, masking her face with the fevered flesh of my own aroused vagina. "Smother me with pussy," she moaned as she lost herself in the intricacy of my molten maze.

We lay together, immersed in one another for what seemed like hours in one sense but like minutes in another. The joy was in the sharing of one orgasm after another alternately smooth and gently mesmerizing, then dramatically convulsive as though it were the last, euphoric destruction of all that was mortal on the precipice of eternity. I clung to her, and she clung to me, two on a raft in a swirling sea of passion, extracting all we could from each other, yet sharing the entirety of it all both willingly and completely. It was exhausting and uplifting. It was total communication, yet neither of us spoke for long moments after we finally released one another in our reluctant return to reality.

"That was *soooo* good!" she gushed finally Her hands pulled at her crotch as though reassuring it that it had all really happened.

"I never thought I'd stop coming," I sighed with contentment. "It was like one never-ending orgasm."

"Wouldn't it be wonderful to lead your whole life that way?" she asked.

"Uh-uh," I disagreed. "You wouldn't know the difference that way."

"I figure that's what heaven must be like," she continued. "Just coming and coming and coming."

"But first you have to go in order to come," I laughed lightly. We sprawled out on the bed, peering at the ceiling, reluctant to let go of the experience.

"Speaking of coming and going," she responded, "we'd better stop coming if we're going to be going."

"Vertical dancing will never replace the horizontal kind," I said, "but it'll renew us so we can go back to the other later."

"Is that a promise?" she asked.

"I've never made a more definite one in my life," I said.

With that in mind we dressed hurriedly, ready to explore the darker reaches of Tokyo. I hadn't been so optimistic and so sexually satisfied   in weeks and weeks.

CHAPTER FIFTEEN

Across the crowded floor of the Blue Shell disco, someone shouted, "Christina!" I looked up startled, breaking the intense concentration I'd devoted to my dancing.

Laurinda froze in her own gyration a few feet away. But she recovered quickly, summoning Jan from out of the kaleidoscopic shadows. Before I could respond to the call, I was whisked out into the pewter-gray night. "Quick," she instructed my unwanted bodyguard, "get her back to the hotel. I'll deal with whoever that is inside."

He looked at her skeptically. "You sure?" he questioned.

"Positive," she assured him.

The door to the disco had already swung open, several camera-necklaced members of the local paparazzi literally tripping over one another in pursuit of us. Laurinda stepped forward to challenge their assault as we sped off. I turned to see them gesturing angrily, even threateningly at her. Then we rounded a corner, and the scene was erased.

"What're you doing?" I quizzed Jan back at the hotel. He was pulling everything out of our closets with no concern for their condition, simply piling them in a heap atop one of the beds.

"We're getting out of here," he informed me with authority.

"We just got here, for God's sake," I complained.

He ignored my statement. "She'll meet us at the airport," he declared. "Come on, help me stuff this crap into the suitcases."

St. Laurent, Givenchy, Halston—some crap! It was no use arguing with a man of his limited finesse and even more limited awareness. I salvaged what I could of the outfits he had not already wrinkled to ruin. "Let me handle the dresses," I said, "you stick to the hard goods like shoes and belts."

The phone rang, and he pounced upon it. It was Laurinda. She had managed to convince the photographers that I was not Christina van Bell but rather someone else often mistaken for her. To aid in convincing them, she had allowed herself to be photographed sans bra and described herself as a "mysterious new starlet on the Tokyo nightlife scene." I had to admire her ingenuity and unselfishness under stress conditions.

It was really all too much. The period of elation had been so brief that it was almost negligible. This time I didn't even ask where we were headed. What did it matter? It wouldn't last. I swallowed a pair of tranquilizers and drifted off into a state of semicomprehension aware of what was going on about me but indifferent to it. I rode to the airport at Narita without saying a word, which seemed to suit Jan just fine. He always treated routine conversation as though he was being subjected to a third-degree interrogation anyhow.

Laurinda was in an agitated state when we arrived. She cursed at Jan for taking so long and regarded me coldly, as though everything was my fault. "I couldn't reach Miguel," she told Jan. "This is an emergency move I'm making on my own."

He took that news with a look of apprehension. "Try him again here at the airport," he urged her.

"There's no time," she told him. "I told you, I'm taking full responsibility."

He continued to be hesitant. "Señor Clemente said all orders were to come from him," he reiterated stubbornly.

Laurinda became furious. "You stupid ass," she snapped, "I'm in charge now, and you do as I tell you or I'll have you replaced."

A reluctant Dvorak slouched toward the check-in counters, shaking his head as he moved. We followed behind, Laurinda's teeth clenched and jaw set in obvious determination. I had never seen her usually soft features in such a hard pattern. It diluted her attractiveness considerably as far as I was concerned.

"You go between us," she instructed me, following our set pattern. This kept me sandwiched between them in case there was any problem boarding or checking through customs. The short, bespectacled man at the counter glanced up at me with fleeting curiosity as we handed him our documentation. Any hope I might have had that he recognized me in my disguise disintegrated quickly.

"You sisters?" he inquired with a smirk.

"No," Laurinda said with a forced smile. "Just friends."

"Pretty," he noted succinctly, then waved us through. The lunk ahead of us cleared customs without comment.

I had read the electronic destination board over our counter so I knew now that we were en route to Honolulu. Under other circumstances that might have made me rather happy, but now I was incapable of any reaction at all. Laurinda was tense and moody, no doubt troubled by having to accept responsibility for shifting our position without Miguel's knowledge or blessing. Surely we could have remained somewhere in Tokyo a city that size afforded thousands of hiding places but I was just as glad to be going to a beach resort If a move had to be made. Sun and surf were a balm to troubled nerves and I had developed an extremely active set of them in recent weeks.

Laurinda had hastily booked a four-bedroom suite at the venerable, pink Royal Hawaiian on Waikiki Beach. That meant Jan would be figuratively on top of us for the first time. Up to now he had always had separate quarters, which suited both of us better. But she was more than usually apprehensive about the flight from Tokyo right into the midst of an international resort. I wondered about that decision myself, but naturally I didn't express it. The more people around, the more chance I had of perhaps making my plight known.

Laurinda's nervousness translated into hypersexual arousal. "I feel like a wild sex orgy," she confided to me. "The whole works from dogs to de Sade."

"Tell me about it," I encouraged her. "Only rub my lamp and make the genie happy while you do it."

Her hand quickly went to my crotch, separating the lips like the petals of a rose with her adroit fingers. She found my clit immediately and flicked it delicately but firmly as she pushed her body against mine. "I'll charge it all to Miguel," she said in breathy tones, "a pair of hung studs, some delicious Polynesian girls, a pussy-fucking dog. . ."

"Mmmmmm," I purred, lifting my furry mound in response to her touch.

"We'll suck and fuck for a few days," she continued, exciting herself along with me as she projected the scene, "wipe out everything else except coming and coming and coming. . ."

My ass lifted from the bed, and my cunt seemed to go liquid like a spring breaking forth in a mountain meadow. I moaned with pleasure as my juices surrounded her finger. My orgasm was audibly succulent, inspiring her to dive face first into the seething swamp of my pussy to savor the frothy warmth of my special juices.

"Eat me, honey," I encouraged her, "and then I'll eat you raw." It was no idle promise. Only in sexual activity could I now become the Christina of yore, and I longed to fulfill myself again and again. Laurinda had the appetite of a born cunnilinguist. "You must have licked your way out of the womb," I complimented her as she brought me to one climax after another. Finally, when she was unable to free herself from the magnetism of my cunt, we compromised by settling into a torrid sixty-nine with both our faces lost in the hairy triangles of the other's glorious vaginal geometry.

"You weren't kidding about the orgy, were you?" I questioned her when we were finally sated with sucking.

"I don't kid about holy ceremonies," she responded.

"I want to do it," I told her.

"So do I," she confessed. "I want to get lost in a sea of cum."

"I know someone who can arrange it all," I said.

She shook her head. "That wouldn't be wise," she noted "Anybody who's ever been involved with you would not fail to recognize you. You're as special in bed as you are to look at."

"They wouldn't remember me," I argued. "Everybody was smashed on coke and 'ludes at the time. Cocks were going off like geysers all over the place, and there hasn't been that much sucking in a litter of Hawaiian pigs since."

"Good recommendation, baby," she said as she lit up some hash. "But let me set it up with my own people. I'm not exactly a stranger to the scene either."

"I'm sure of that," I agreed without trying to be snide. "I do like the idea, though. Just thinking about it is relaxing."

"You deserve it," she told me. "I've really been rough on you the last few days."

"Blame it on Miguel," I said.

"When he hears that we're here in Honolulu," she responded, "ten to one he'll fly here. He loves it."

"So did I," I noted, "in my free days."

Laurinda's hardness had softened in the process of working out her frustrations through oral involvement. "It hurts me to hear you put it that way," she sighed.

"I'm a truthful person," I replied. "I call them the way I see them."

"Sex is the only escape," she suggested.

"Take me to your libido," I said with a hint of a smile, my first in at least twenty-four hours.

Jan found himself a plump native girl with skin the color of dark rum and a merry laugh. It was a discovery that turned his disposition into something almost human. Since Laurinda and I were occupied with the arrangements for an all-out orgy, we both welcomed his preoccupation with the Polynesian gal. Miguel had not objected to the transfer from Tokyo at all in view of the circumstances an attitude that relieved the bodyguard's tension over Laurinda's decision. He now seems to regard her with the respect of an employee dealing with a superior. When she suggested that he enjoy a bit of romance himself, he welcomed it as a reward for a job well-done and went at it with more vigor and virility than I had thought he was capable of exhibiting.

"You should see them fuck," Laurinda confided to me after making some stealthy observations through a crack in the door. "It's like two barrels trying to get together And she laughs while he's trying to make the connection."

"Laughing and fucking don't mix," I noted as I had many times in the past.

"Nothing could stop him," she stated. "He's so hard up if he went to a *luau*, he'd try to fuck the roast pig before he ate it."

"Don't knock it," I kidded her, "if you haven't tried it "

"Speaking of food. . ." she said with sudden concentration.

"We can't live on pussy alone," I agreed.

"How about some *laulau*?" she suggested, licking her lips.

"Is that on the orgy menu?" I teased.

"Forget the orgy for a minute," she said, smacking her lips audibly now. "Think of suckling pork and fish cooked in Hawaiian spinach and wrapped in leaves till the taste gets so divine you come when it crosses your lips. "

"Come to me, porkie," I jibed, moving my mouth like a fish.

"How does that sound?" she persisted.

"Yummy," I replied. "Get it up here before I take a bite out of your suckling thigh."

"Anything else you want?" she asked as she picked up the phone.

"Marinated salmon," I responded, "and a bucket of booze."

"I'm starving all of a sudden," she reported after placing the order.

"Lick on these for an appetizer," I suggested, offering her my tits on the platter of my upturned palms. She reached for a bottle of cherry liqueur and poured some on each nipple before surrounding them with her lips. I did the same to her moments later, and we continued to repeat the process until the food finally arrived.

"As spectacular as this looks and smells," she said when the waiter had left the steaming cart and closed the door behind him, "nothing could equal your scrumptious tits, darling."

"Sometimes you say the nicest things," I responded. "Especially since this food looks like heaven itself."

"You're so beautiful," she paused to say, "but I'm so hungry I'm going to close my eyes and just stuff my mouth."

"Amen," I agreed.

For the next hour our oral sex was confined to lusty mastication accompanied by as many oohs and ahhhs as any other oral orgy. At the end, like true gluttons, we fell back and postponed any further involvements for rapturous rest. To the sound of Jan Dvorak's headboard pounding against the wall as he indulged in his own Polynesian dish, Laurinda and I slipped into slumber, the all-consuming orgy left on the planning board for another day.

CHAPTER SIXTEEN

Like the pink stucco of the hotel's facade, her pussy stared into my sleepy face, yawning sensuously. She had thrown the room open to the sun, letting its morning goldness gild everything it touched. Instinctively I uncurled my tongue and let it slither into the pale red crevice before it.

"Good morning, love," she trilled in a sultry voice. "I tried waking you with my tongue, but you were deeply involved making love to Morpheus."

I woke up fast, playing my mouth organ and bearing witness to her lovely labia. That faintly aromatic pungency of prime pussy stirred my senses into a fresh confrontation with the new day. "Mmmmmm," I groaned appreciatively.

"Today is the day," she announced as she rode my face, making a saddle of my features. I knew immediately what she meant, and it inspired me to an accelerated tempo. "Boys, girls, bow-wows everything," she elaborated. My tongue felt as though it was tearing away from my mouth as I strove to reach her ultimate depth.

"Suck me, you sonofabitch," she gasped. A moment later her body crumpled over my head as she was racked with overlapping climaxes.

I was fully awake by now. And fully aroused. "I want cock," I demanded almost savagely.

"You'll get it," she promised. "Later."

"Now," I insisted. "Fuck me any way you can." I lay on my back, my legs spread into a fleshy V, my feet pointing toward the ceiling.

"I'll eat you," she proposed.

"I said *fuck*," I rasped, my voice thick with sudden lust.

Laurinda moved about with a kind of quick desperation, searching for some phallic object to satisfy my desire for malelike penetration. She resorted at first to probing my pubes with the handle of a hairbrush. But that failed to satisfy my quivering quoin of fevered flesh.

"Cock," I reiterated, writhing as though in anguish.

"Jan," she uttered breathlessly, testing my reaction.

"Cock," I said again. She took that as an affirmative and dashed into an adjoining room of the suite. A stoic but slightly startled Jan Dvorak followed her back into the room.

"Fuck her," she told him in a commanding tone. It was one order to which he had no audible reaction only a visible one. His pants were tensed by the pole that had risen against the fabric like a pitched tent.

"At last," he said with an air of triumph. Laurinda helped him pull his clothes off until he was stripped to his socks. A thin ribbon of advance cum dripped from the end of his fat penis as he fell to his knees to enter me.

I clenched my eyes shut, seeking only the friction of flesh against flesh. "Fuck me, you big bastard," I groaned.

"Give it to her," Laurinda exhorted him. She accentuated her words with several sharp slaps to his undulating rump, something like a jockey encouraging a racehorse to pick up speed.

"Good ass," he grunted as he pumped in and out of my wet well.

"Too good for you," I heard Laurinda say. It only provoked him into more furious fucking.

"Deeper," I urged as his head grazed the walls of my cunt in a futile quest for the bottom.

"Move it," he retorted, picking up the cheeks of my

derrière like two melons in his huge hands. I felt spindled on the stiff angle of his wide prick as he brought me up and down against his thrusts.

"I didn't realize you were that good," Laurinda observed as she watched in fascination. I reached over and squeezed her hand in gratitude. I would have taken on a horse if that was all that was available. Somehow I had never really considered Jan any kind of sex partner until now. Yet he was proving himself more capable than either Laurinda or I could have imagined.

"I'm coming," I announced dramatically. My body was already shuddering on the brink of explosion as the words escaped from my lips. The declaration had a detonating effect on the oversized cache of human dynamite pounding at my entrance. No sooner had I heralded my imminent orgasms than he lost control of his weapon. It reared back howitzer-style, then scattered soft, alabaster bullets all over my silken sheath and into the woolly mound of hair surrounding it. Laurinda was still milking stringy strands of cum from my cunt when I came out of my almost convulsive battery of climaxes. I was limp from the mental and physical exhaustion of it, but the savage tension I had felt earlier was at least temporarily relieved.

"Leave me alone." I dismissed him when he attempted to continue his invasion.

"I'll handle it from here," Laurinda declared, pulling at his sweaty body.

"What am I?" he demanded with a hint of anger. "A fuckin' stud or somethin'?"

"You had your taste," she told him coldly. "Consider yourself lucky to have been around in an emergency."

Jan crawled off me reluctantly, scratching his head in disbelief. "It don't make sense," he declared to no one in particular.

"It's a disease," Laurinda said, "called acute horniness. We all have attacks of it once in a while."

"I feel used," he lamented as he struggled back into his

pants. I was surprised to see that he had enough insight to have such a reaction.

"Lucky," she corrected him, "not used. You've just had one of the most beautiful and desirable women in the world "

He looked me over with a mild air of disdain. "Yeah," he commented, sounding unconvinced.

"Go back to your Polynesian pig," she said derisively How chilly and cutting she could be when she chose to be

"She sounds like fun." I attempted to dilute her remark

"She likes to fuck," he said.

"That's eighty-five percent of it," I noted.

"Just remember who you are and why you're here," Laurinda reminded him. "I don't want hanky-panky to lead to hocus-pocus. If Christina vanishes, you might as well jump into one of those Hawaiian volcanoes."

"I never lose my head over women," he said.

"That's what Louis XVI said, too," she responded It went over his head like a gaggle of geese.

"Never," he reiterated.

Laurinda watched him as he moved toward the door "Don't bother us for the next twenty-four hours," she warned. "Christina and I will be entertaining some local friends."

"Another one of your orgies?" he inquired boldly

"Just don't bother us unless I call for you," she emphasized.

He looked at her skeptically. "Does Señor Clemente know?" he inquired snidely. There was a vein of threat in his tone.

"You do as you're told," she snapped with irritation

"*Si, señorita*," he said with more arrogance than I'd ever heard from him before. She turned away from him haughtily as he disappeared into the next room.

"I guess it was a mistake," I said apologetically

"It was an emergency," she responded, in a tone that said the matter was closed.

"I'll try to keep better control of myself in the future," I said   a highly unlikely prospect.

Laurinda and I sunned ourselves behind a protective canvas shield to thwart prying eyes. I had been simmering even more passionately than usual ever since our arrival in Honolulu.

"Are you sure you didn't inject me with some powerful aphrodisiac aboard the plane while I was sleeping?" I teased her.

"Darling," she said in her throatiest voice, "you're hotter than the equatorial sun without a drop of anything."

"I don't know what's wrong with me lately," I confided. "All I can think about is sex."

"That puts you in the same condition as a few billion others on earth," she commented.

"I mean hot, urgent fuck-and-suck sex," I said.

"Is there any other kind?" she inquired flippantly.

"You seem cool," I noted, removing my sunglasses to survey her supple body.

"That's only by contrast," she responded. "Next to you a forest fire would look like candlelight."

"Is everything set for later?" I asked.

"Our little soiree?" she responded.

"Must you be so formal?" I retorted.

"What do you want me to call it?" she inquired.

"Our big, fucking orgy," I said, savoring the words.

"You are turned on," she observed.

"Heavy *pupus*," I laughed.

"What is that supposed to mean?" she wondered.

"It sounds raunchy," I explained, "but in local lingo. All it means is lots of hors d'ouevres."

"You'll have plenty of those," she assured me. "I've got a pair of guys coming with balls as big and hairy as coconuts."

"Full of coconut milk?" I jibed.

"Full of good, native cum," she said.

"What about girls? Did you get what I wanted?" I asked.

"A young one without pubic hair, you said," she recalled.

"Right."

"I got two of those and two more with the blackest bushes this side of the lava pits," she said.

"Keep talking," I encouraged her. "I can get myself off on the descriptions alone."

"Why don't you finger yourself?" she suggested.

"What do you think I'm doing down there?" I responded. "Curling my hair?"

"Oh, yes," she said, "I wasn't really paying attention before."

I groaned low and long as the wave of a climax surfed through me, followed immediately by another.

"The Lord helps those who help themselves," she commented. "But don't use up all your firepower before sundown."

"I've got enough of that to take on the American army," I boasted.

I managed to fall asleep for an hour or so despite the heat of the sun. There were always refreshing breezes to dilute its potency, and I really needed the rest. It also quieted my libido slightly, though hardly enough to keep the promises of the evening from crowding my senses.

Jan steered clear of us all day, preferring to keep his eye on me from the terrace of our suite. At times it felt as though his binoculars were laser beams cutting into my psyche. I had no desire to cohabit with him again, and in a sense I was annoyed with myself for having had to resort to his services even once. He was just not Christina van Bell material, no matter how I analyzed him. Oh well, it was only a brief encounter in a sea of copulations, I consoled myself.

"Let's go in and have cocktails," Laurinda suggested a little past mid-afternoon.

"Cock and tail," I jested, "my favorite combination."

"You're impossible," she laughed. "I hope you get stuffed with both tonight."

"I'll do my best," I promised.

We decided to welcome our guests in the most attractive outfits we owned — our naked bodies. In spiked heels our calves tightened and curved sensuously, just the right pedestals for the crowning glory of our cunts. I poured chartreuse into my crack, and Laurinda drank from it happily. Then she poured for me in her own vulva.

"Here's to a great party." I toasted her before licking the sweet liqueur from her equally sweet pussy.

By the time the first of them arrived, we were both in marvelously randy moods, ready for anything and everything.

"Welcome," Laurinda shouted as she flung open the door and revealed herself in all her natural glory.

The two men — both tall and muscular with tawny skin and lustrous, onyx black hair — immediately took out their cocks and rubbed them against her. "Which one's Dick, and which one's Peter?" she laughed gaily.

"I'm Kiko," one said, "and this is Kuhio."

"Hi," she greeted them, kissing the heads of their organs in turn. "I'm Laurinda, and that gorgeous hunk of woman over there is Christina."

The women in the small assemblage hung back until the male introductions were completed. They were dressed in mid-thigh length, kimono-style wraps, which I soon discovered constituted their entire clothing for the night. They were nakedly nubile underneath, the two youngest of the quartet deliciously pink and hairless in contrast to the hirsute abundance at the crotches of the other two.

"The hell with names," I proclaimed in my high state, "let's get with it."

One of the men responded immediately by ripping off his robe, leaving him clad only in leather sandals. His cock stood out from him like a flagpole, a pair of fist-sized balls swinging pendulously below it. He mounted me with a vengeance, grabbing and sucking my tits as he entered me

"You," I called out to one of the younger girls, "come sit on my face."

She swung her legs over my head with a graceful swoop, her petite pussy hovering above my profile momentarily before settling over my nose and mouth. How marvelously fresh and pink it looked, glistening with delectable newness. I drew in her nectar hungrily, my appetite whetted even more by the force being applied and withdrawn alternately inside my cunt.

"Good fuck," Kuhio related to the girl straddling my face. His positioning put him face-to-face with the girl as the three of us formed a feverish triangle. One of the others knelt beside us and fed her tits to the two of them while I fingered her juicy clit. I was in some sort of heavenly limbo, feeling, fucking, and sucking all at once   oblivious again to the fact that I was really a captive. How could anyone complain about this kind of captivity, I asked myself Squeals of delight, groans of passion, and the thud of bodies making ripe contact punctuated the atmosphere I couldn't see Laurinda with all the mahogany flesh surrounding me, but I could hear her shriek with pleasure now and then as her body was rent with orgasms.

Kuhio pulled out of me to come all over the young girl, splashing her with his glut of rich, whitish cum that trickled down her sleek body onto my gyrating torso. The warm ooze of it invaded my pores, stirring another batch of climaxes inside my lust-crazed body. I wanted to come endlessly, perpetually, eternally   my cunt forever filled with tongues and cocks and everything that moved and licked and spat out the hot hail of overloaded pricks. The girl astride me, whose name I didn't know, baptized me unexpectedly with the warm, pale chablis of her snapping-turtle pussy. I welcomed its sweet rinse as my tongue continued to tap its faucet throughout the springlike shower. Not to be outdone by so young a collaborator, Kuhio opened the bung of his barrel and released a glittering stream of golden liquid so concentrated and intense it literally drilled into my skin before pooling beneath me.

"Let's shower together," I suggested after all our resources had been temporarily drained. We crowded into the stall gleefully, playing with each other like so many toys until once again we fitted our bodies together for another exercise in sucking and fucking the stand-up variety this time.

They had brought a large, shepherdlike dog a beautiful animal even if you ignored his almost human sexual prowess and left him tied in the corridor. In the midst of our most heated involvement, the dog had begun barking plaintively, ending each bark with a desperate whine. I was sure he understood what was going on and was eager to join in the festivities.

"You like dog-fucking?" Kuhio questioned me with a big grin.

"I'm a total liberal when it comes to the fine art of fornication," I responded.

"Good," he said, "I'll get Mahalo."

I laughed. "You call the dog 'Thank You'?"

"He is very good," the little girl with the big brown eyes confirmed.

"You like him, huh?" I asked, rubbing her roselike vagina. She nodded with conviction and leaned forward to suckle my nipples. I could mother her indefinitely, I thought to myself, then smiled at the realization that that would make her a motherfucker.

Mahalo came charging in like a wild animal, quickly sniffing every bit of genitalia his eager snout encountered. I spread my legs wide to welcome him, but Kuhio pulled him off me.

"Turn around," he said, "and get down on all-fours. That's his favorite position."

"You want me to be a bitch?" I jibed.

"Exactly," he agreed.

The dog's long, slender penis looked raw and sensitive as it gleamed from beneath him. He mounted me with familiarity, wrapping his front legs around my waist, his paws touching my tits. The smooth firmness of his cock slid snakelike into the nest of my cunt. I felt the warmth of his fur against my body as he began humping me at a furious pace.

"He's horny, isn't he?" I observed through the strands of my hair surrounding my face.

"He loves beautiful women," Kuhio said.

"Does he do it with dogs, too?" I asked, swallowing hard as his length uncoiled inside me. He was touching tender areas no human cock could reach and I loved it.

"He's too spoiled for that," the girl replied. She stood next to me, letting Mahalo lick the syrup of her cunt as he drove rapidly in and out of mine.

"He's woman-crazy," Kuhio laughed. "He only likes two-legged bitches."

"Aughhh," I groaned as the first of multiple orgasms racked my body. The girl petted my back as though I were some sort of special creature.

"He likes you," she said. "I can tell."

It was a unique experience not my first time with a four-legged animal but undeniably my best within recent memory. Mahalo certainly inspired "thank yous" for his sexual artistry. Even his loose-tongued panting was sensual and stimulating. I came more times than I could count, especially after Kiko confronted me with his upright organ while the dog was still pumping away. I sucked him while my four-legged lover licked the girl and fucked me. Laurinda was so busy pretzeling herself around the other members of the party I wasn't sure she even knew about Mahalo's presence. But she did. As soon as I broke away from the dog, she grabbed him by his testicles and directed him into herself.

"Who needs men?" she gasped as he found her tender

track. Her eyes were glazed from cocaine, her nipples scarlet from having been so ardently sucked. I lay back in a trance to watch her, but almost immediately one of the lovely women who'd been with her slid her face between my legs.

"Help yourself," I invited her. What a surprise followed! She seemed to have a tongue a foot long, able to reach everywhere the dog had with his serpentine cock. "Oooooooohhh," I reacted, my body corrugating from the sudden rush of pleasure.

The other prepubescent girl offered her pinkness to me as an hors d'ouevre while I was being eaten with such fervor by her older companion. I accepted her lovely pussy, which seemingly winked at me while still looking like a fragile, crushed carnation. The combination of the pair made a roller coaster of my body, the orgasms causing my skin to ripple up and down with breathtaking effect. I couldn't believe the range of the woman's tongue as it slithered about my cunt and along the crack of my ass. Later I learned her secret   she had undergone a frenulotomy just to become the superstar of island cunnilinguists. She had a surgical incision made in the tissues holding the tongue to the floor of the mouth. The operation had increased her cunt-lapping range by almost four inches to say nothing of her improved fellatio powers. Why not? I thought to myself. Women underwent all kinds of plastic surgery to improve their appearance, including silicone injections for bigger busts. So why not a little knife work to become a queen of the oral sexualists?

"I want to take her home with me," Laurinda said later during a recess in our orgiastic pursuits. Everyone was so high now it was impossible to maintain any type of activity through to climax. So we all flopped about, snorting coke, slurping champagne, and puffing on hashish, hardly aware that we were diminishing our appreciation of the amorous even more. That was the way it was when things got out of hand.

"That's the best tongue I've ever had," I agreed. "It's like an eel the way it slides around inside."

Lilo, the tongue woman, stacked us atop one another for a final double suck of our combined anal and vaginal tracks as Mahalo feverishly fucked her at the same time. He was the only creature in the suite who wasn't high, which gave him a decided advantage over the rest of us. But who cared? Together Laurinda and I achieved overlapping orgasms so intense that I felt our bodies had melted together. Clinging to her tits, the remarkable tongue of Lilo slathering away at us, I drifted into a fiery, kaleidoscopic unconsciousness. When I finally awakened, there was only Laurinda and I, naked and splattered with cum, entwined amidst the litter of the ravaged hotel suite. It had been some night. Some night indeed.

CHAPTER SEVENTEEN

After the delightful debacle with the Polynesian boys and girls, I was not surprised to learn that we were moving on once again. The hotel management could hardly be expected to tolerate the wanton destruction our prolonged orgy had visited upon our suite. I hid as much of myself as possible behind oversized sunglasses and a turbanlike snood as we made our escape through a rear exit.

"Miguel's coming," I overheard Laurinda reveal to Jan. He looked wounded both physically and mentally with this abrupt departure. Obviously the plump lady with the big pineapples had gotten under his tough skin and lacerated a little corner of his heart. For the first time since I'd been forced into his company, I felt a small tinge of sympathy for him. He was human after all, despite his sloth-like appearance and manner.

"Too bad we can't take the tongue lady with us," I lamented.

"Lilo?" Laurinda responded "If I tell Miguel about her, he'll send for her."

"Miguel's coming?" I pretended to be surprised.

She glanced at me coyly. "You're not supposed to know," she said.

"I don't know anything," I replied with a toss of my head.

155

"He's meeting us at Kailua-Kona," she elaborated. "We'll take an island jet there."

"You mean this was all planned before last night?" I questioned.

She smiled enigmatically. "What do you think?" she asked.

I shrugged. "Beats me," I confessed.

"Do you know how much in damages we had to pay for that little circus we staged?" she queried. "Fifteen-hundred dollars."

I was surprised. "Nothing was broken that I could see," I said. "But then I didn't exactly take inventory."

"Your friend Mahalo destroyed a tapestry, among other things," she revealed.

"The dog?" I reacted. "The only thing I saw him do aside from the obvious   was take a leak on Kuhio's leg."

"He did?" Laurinda laughed. "I missed that."

"That's about all you missed," I teased her.

"You didn't exactly shortchange yourself either," she accused me playfully.

"It was a great session," I agreed. "I could take one of those about every three days."

"You'd be dead in a month," she predicted.

"With an ear-to-ear smile on my face," I said.

Jan was sullen en route to the airport and slept during the short flight to the big island of Hawaii. The resort of Mauna Kea sent a station wagon for us, and we all lapsed into our separate contemplations as it sped along the black lava beaches of Kealakekua Bay to the hotel.

"Is he here already?" I whispered to Laurinda as we pulled into the posh resort grounds. The air was perfumed with native flowers, adding sweetness to my lightheadedness.

"No," she said. "Tomorrow."

Either I had been totally brainwashed or I was simply more adaptable than I had imagined myself to be, but I no longer thought very much about being kidnapped and held for ransom. We were moving from place to place with such frequency that I felt somewhat like the Christina of bygone days.

"Go suck a macadamia nut," I declared out of the blue. Laurinda looked at me as though I had flipped.

"What're you on that I don't know about?" she questioned.

"I'm high on ohelo berries," I jibed.

She continued to scrutinize me as we got out of the station wagon. "Were you sniffing on the plane?" she asked.

"I was breathing," I replied airily. "Are you planning to ration my oxygen intake?"

"You seem, uh, just a little wacko today," she said.

"That's my normal state," I responded in a breezy fashion. "You just don't know the real me."

She seemed dubious, but she did not quiz me further. Checking in took over her thoughts as we casually sauntered into the lobby. But later, after we were settled into our suite minus Jan, thank God she resumed her interrogation.

"You're sure you didn't light up or snort anything on our way here?" she asked again.

"What difference does it make whether I did or didn't?" I replied.

"Because if you did, I'm concerned about my failure to catch you doing it, that's all," she stated crisply.

"Ever the guardian angel," I taunted her, stroking her panther-black hair in a condescending manner.

"Don't do that unless you mean it," she warned. "I don't like being toyed with."

"Whatever makes you think I'm toying with you?" I cooed. I enjoyed playing bitch every now and then—and this was one of those times.

"You're fooling with me," she accused, pushing my hands away.

"No, darling," I assured her with a sultry reedıness to my tone, "it's just that you're the only one I mıssed at our little party last night. Let's see. I had Lilo, Kiko, Kuhıo, Mahalo, the two little sweethearts with the pınk centers every man, woman, child, and animal there except my own magical Laurinda."

She leaned back, mollified momentarily. "You're right," she sighed, "we mıssed each other in all the madness."

I knelt before her and gently parted her legs. There at the apex was her pussy, suddenly tense and expectant, its lips puckered and pursed, wet with fresh anxıety. My bitchiness turned to passion at the sight of it

"Make love to me," she begged, making a fleshy oval frame with her thumbs and ındex fingers. It accented the plump ripeness of her lovely cunt

I slid my tongue along the ınsıde of her thıgh, leaving a silvery saliva trail to her entrance. Once there I cupped my hands around the peach halves of her buttocks and pulled them gently but firmly apart. Like a sleek fish entering an underwater grotto, I slid my funneled lips and cheeks into its inviting darkness. Breathing like a scuba diver and sucking like a dolphin, I nourished myself on the rich harvest of her crotch.

"Eat me, honey," she admonished me. "Suck me dry."

I drew in the sweet juices as I would those of a succulent pineapple, savoring each drop as it oozed down my open throat. The tip of my tongue danced on the tiny stage of her clitoris, tapping a frenzied jungle rhythm as primitive as it was timeless. Inevitably she rose and fell in carnal counterpoint to my tempo, her body buckling under the savage intensity of my attack.

"Chrissssst, Chris!" she screamed as the fragile structure of the preliminary climaxes towered within her and then abruptly collapsed, shattering the delicate fibers of her libido and rushing a turbulent torrent to the harbor of her cunt My face was flooded with the silky abundance of her orgasm—a silvery balm that warmed not only my features but my entire inner body as well. I came in sympathetic response to her mighty upheaval, reluctant to break contact with the tender flesh that constituted her most precious treasure.

We fucked after that, nipple-to-nipple and tit-to-tit, a pulsating vibrator shared between our two pussies. I rode atop her, imagining my cunt lips transformed into a healthy cock. That fantasy combined with the steady vibrato of the vibrator to provide us both with enormously enriching orgasms. It was so vividly real and overpowering that I swore cum had spat from me and drenched her with its pearly goodness.

"Come to me," Laurinda requested hoarsely, like me ever unwilling to break contact after climaxing. She pulled at me, indicating that she wanted to suck my tits with me remaining atop her. I inched downward until I could feed one of my breasts to her gaping mouth. Silently her lips drew in one nipple and then the other, siphoning them with single-minded dedication. I wanted to give her milk almost as much as I had wanted to give her head earlier.

"Milk me," I told her, swallowing hard. She sucked like an unweaned baby as I resumed humping her with the vibrator. If there was to be no milk, I was determined that there would be more cum.

"Baby, baby, baby," I cried as my nipples swelled with the fervor of her suction. I was coming in ripples now, one climax after another, my body addicted to orgasms, yearning for the next fix before the last had even worn off. I had the fever   the fuck fever I called it   and the only antidote was sex and more sex, any kind, any place, with anyone at all.

It was an auspicious moment for Miguel to arrive   ahead of his schedule but right on time for mine. "Don't even talk," I greeted him in the moist and musky throes of nymphomania, "just fuck."

"Stick your prick anywhere you want," Laurinda gasped, surprised by his premature arrival but too lost in lust to care. "We're going to suck and fuck all day now."

If he was taken aback by the uninhibited welcome, he quickly recovered and fell into it. We both attacked his cock the moment it was free, collaborating on a frenzied blow job that included sucking his entire sack of nuts along with the full length of his proud prick.

"*Sensacional*," he kept repeating in his Spanish accent, "*sensacional*."

He spurted forth thick bolts of milky cum that streaked the air like white lightning. Laurinda and I rubbed the love lotion into each other's tits and then set about reviving his cock for another assault. This time I mounted the organ while she straddled his face, facing me. We deep-throated one another and fondled each other's tits while Miguel sucked and fucked us both simultaneously. It was a glorious reunion, topped off with some super cocaine that Miguel had smuggled in for us. For a kidnapper he was really something else. I could almost like him as much as I had before my captivity.

Almost but not quite.

CHAPTER EIGHTEEN

Three whole days at Kailua-Kona.

Three whole days of nothing but eating, drinking, snorting, fucking, and sucking.

Not once was the ransom discussed. Not once did Miguel make me feel that I was anything but free to come and go as I pleased. It was a lovely illusion, one I enjoyed enormously, so I did nothing to test its reality. I simply relaxed and let go, Christina-style, knowing it had to end.

It did just when it seemed that it might not. Miguel had gone to Honolulu on business on the morning of the fourth day. When he returned that evening, our stay at Mauna Kea was over. We were moving on to Mexico this time. There was one significant difference about this trip, however. Miguel was coming with us.

"Did you look up Lilo in Honolulu?" Laurinda questioned him as we boarded the interisland jet for the international airport on Oahu.

"I looked her up all right," he confirmed, "and she licked me up and down."

"Isn't she sensational?" she asked, knowing there was only one possible answer.

"*Fantástico*," he confirmed with a smile of remembrance.

"A human anteater," I suggested.

Miguel looked at me with amusement in his eyes. "Aunts, uncles, nieces, nephews," he recited, "I think she'll eat anyone."

"The tongue lady," Laurinda mused. "She's worth a trip to Hawaii every now and then just to get thoroughly reamed."

Anyone overhearing our lighthearted conversation, even with its sexual content, would have assumed we were just a trio of friends on a holiday. Except for the hulking presence of Jan Dvorak, there was nothing to indicate that this was a ransom-inspired relationship and abduction. That pleased Miguel enormously now that he joined our hopscotching little group for the first time in the air.

"What's new from London?" I finally asked after we had transferred to an overseas jet bound for Acapulco. That was not to be our ultimate destination, however. Miguel was opposed to any more resorts with their hordes of international travelers, so he had arranged for us to stay in a quieter place northwest of Acapulco called Zihuatanejo. I had heard of it but had never been there.

"We're making progress," he said somewhat cryptically.

"How much longer do you think it'll take?" I persisted.

He shrugged. "Maybe a week," he replied, "maybe a month but no longer. I have only four more weeks to resolve my own matters."

"Have you talked to Winston Garrett?" I inquired, trying my best not to be pushy. Miguel had a Latin temper, and I had no desire to see it in action just now.

"I am not involved, I told you," he snapped irritably. "My name is not known to anyone in the negotiations."

"I forgot that," I confessed.

His hand cupped over mine in a gesture of reassurance. "You will have it all back within a month after it's delivered," he promised. "It's really just a short-term loan."

I nodded, unconvinced but unwilling to pursue the matter further. "You're a man of your word," I told him. "Let's drop the subject until something new develops."

"Precisely my feeling," he replied.

There was only one other person   a swarthy, mustached man of Latin extraction   in the first-class section with our party of four. He was buried in a Spanish newspaper from which he didn't emerge even once during the first hour of our long hop across the Pacific. After a while it hardly seemed that he was there at all, especially when he did not react to my lighting up some strongly aromatic hashish. The smoke clouded the small compartment and turned on everybody in the group. Or so it seemed to me, now floating both figuratively and literally above the clouds.

"Everything all right?" the flight attendant inquired, pretending not to notice my violation.

"Any more champagne?" I asked flippantly.

"For beautiful ladies there is always champagne," he responded.

Miguel shook his head. "You're a chronic flirt," he noted.

"I try to stay in practice," I replied, "even in captivity."

He frowned at my snideness and pointed a warning finger in the direction of the man behind the newspaper. I took a long drag on the hash and waved my hands in a pooh-poohing gesture toward the stranger.

"No problem," I said airily.

Another bottle of champagne arrived, and I sipped from it grandly, enjoying the bubbly high it gave me with the hashish. Miguel held himself in check, drinking minimally and refusing all drugs of any kind. One of us had to stay clear-headed, he said, and he appointed himself to that task. Dvorak sat propped like a jumbo mannequin in the corner of the compartment, snoring like a walrus as the plane droned over endless blue water. The presence of Miguel relieved him of some of the round-the-clock pressure he had endured as my guard, and obviously he was taking full advantage of it.

"How big he is to look so much like a child when he's sleeping," Miguel observed.

"He's love-sick," Laurinda said.

"Who? Dvorak?" Miguel reacted with surprise.

"He fell for a little fat Hawaiian woman," she revealed. "All three hundred pounds of him."

"No!" Miguel could not hide his amusement.

"I'm telling you, Miguel," she assured him. "Isn't that right, Christina?"

I nodded in confirmation. "We watched them fuck." I embellished the verification.

Miguel laughed aloud. "Does he know it?" he inquired, his eyes at their merriest.

"We are very subtle voyeurs," Laurinda declared with mock solemnity.

"Then you have been enjoying your little hops, skips, and jumps?" he asked. He looked to me for a response.

"We can make the best of a bad situation," I said. It was obviously not the answer he wanted or expected.

"I've tried to provide you with the best accommodations possible under the circumstances," he told me in a slightly wounded tone.

"It beats a cell all to hell," I responded.

Laurinda moved in to smooth any ruffled feathers. "Christina and I have developed a really beautiful one-on-one relationship," she told him.

"Which one on which?" he parried, still showing signs of being hurt because I did not fully appreciate his treatment of me. It was ridiculous even to consider being grateful to a man holding you captive, regardless of the conditions of your confinement. But he stubbornly refused to see things that way. A true and unrepentant chauvinist, I thought to myself.

Laurinda ignored his question. "When this is all over," she said with conviction, "I hope we'll all still be friends intimate friends."

"What do you say to that, Christina?" Miguel inquired.

"I never predict my reactions to anything," I replied. Now Laurinda appeared hurt.

"You could just go away and forget us?" she asked in a

low voice, "forget about me and all we've meant to each other?"

I sucked deeply on the end of a joint, then stuck the final shreds in the ashtray within the seat divider. "I am Christina," I declared with the dramatic eloquence of a stoned woman, "playgirl of the Western world, beholden to no one, beloved by all. . . "

"She's higher than this jet," Miguel noted. "Let her come down off it before she makes any more silly statements."

"Let's hear some music," I demanded, "let's have a goddamned stratosphere party. . ."

"Whoa, girl," Miguel interceded, grabbing my wrists. "Calm down before the people in the coach section take notice."

"Fuck them all," I laughed. "Hey, that's a good idea."

Laurinda moved over and held me down along with Miguel. "Take it easy, Chris," she urged. "Don't get everybody aboard excited."

The man with the newspaper abruptly lowered it, then crumpled it aside. He began to rise as though heading for the lavatory but stopped suddenly in the aisle and reached inside his jacket. Even in my heady state, I was astonished to see his hand emerge, clutching a silver pistol.

"Nobody move," he rasped menacingly. Our group seemed frozen in time like in a snapshot, all eyes on the man with the mustache and the gleaming revolver. "Carlos!" he shouted back to the long, rear cabin, "make them all strip!"

We became aware in that instant that he had a confederate aboard, although we could not see him from where we sat like statues. My high dissolved like fog in the sunshine as reality crushed in upon us. We were being skyjacked to where we would find out later. The man with the gun reached behind him and flung open the metal door to the cockpit.

"*El Capitán*," he shouted over his shoulder at the startled flight officers, "I am commandeering this aircraft in the name of our beloved Fidel Castro and the people's revolution of Cuba. You will proceed not to Acapulco but to Jose Marti Airport in Havana. *Comprende?*"

"I'm not sure about the fuel," the captain responded in a remarkably calm voice.

"It is sufficient," the skyjacker assured him "That has been checked out in advance."

I could see the pilot shrug as his eyes skimmed over the elaborate gauges on the control panel. He was already speaking in low, staccato phrases over the radio to air controllers monitoring flights in the area. This was not a usual skyjacking route, which accounted for the general surprise of both the passengers and crew. Actually I was rather enjoying it, even entertaining the notion of going in with the skyjackers in order to effect my own escape. That possibility must have dawned on Miguel as well. He stared at me oddly during the takeover a strange, haunted look that altered his features.

"My name is Ricardo," the gunman announced as he positioned himself in the oblong passage between the first-class section and the cockpit. "This will be a pleasant flight so long as no one attempts to be foolishly heroic. As you see, my partner Carlos has taken the clothes and belongings from those in the next section. It is now my pleasure to request that you people the crew as well also remove all your clothing, jewelry, etcetera. This is not robbery, merely a precaution. It will all be returned to you once we are safely in Havana."

"Hey," I said with feigned exuberance, "this could turn into quite a ball with everybody naked."

Ricardo flashed a lecherous grin in my direction. "You are one beautiful señorita," he said with a wave of his gun.

Everyone stripped slowly and reluctantly, peering in disbelief at the scene to the rear. Most of the passengers there sat huddled behind their seats, embarrassed by their nakedness and hiding as much as possible through careful posturing.

"Can you help me with my zipper, Ricardo?" I flirted

shamelessly with the skyjacker. He seemed tempted momentarily, but then remembered the seriousness of his mission.

"That man with you," he gestured, "he is a Latin, no? He knows all about ladies' zippers I am sure."

Miguel nervously tugged at the silver tract that led to the crack of my derrière. When the zipper was all the way down, I stepped from my dress totally nude.

"You wear nothing beneath?" the skyjacker asked, salivating slightly.

"Never," I quipped. "A girl never knows when she might be skyjacked and have to undress in a hurry."

He smiled thinly. "You have the body of a goddess," he said, "and the mouth of a bitch."

I stuck my tongue out daringly and made a fellatiolike gesture. "Bitches are the best," I stated with a flash of my eyes. I was sure I could play on his libido to my own benefit as well as for the other passengers aboard. It was a long way to Havana, and there was no reason to have to endure it under extreme pressure if it could be avoided.

"Be careful, Chris," Laurinda whispered. "You're toying with a madman."

"All men are mad," I flipped, still high enough to be relatively immune to danger. "How come you and your partner don't strip like the rest of us?" I challenged him.

He laughed thickly at my impudence. "For you I would bare myself any time," he declared.

"Let's see," I proposed, moving toward him with my fingers spreading my cunt.

"Hold it," he warned, the smile dropping from his face. "No one moves about the cabin without permission." To underline his warning, he pointed the gun directly at my crotch.

"You wouldn't shoot a poor little harmless pussy, would you?" I asked plaintively.

"Don't move." He repeated his command. "We'll deal with that later." He glanced into the cockpit, and for the first time I noticed the hard glint in his eyes. "Hurry it up in there," he said sharply. "Get those shorts off, captain. Your balls get no special privileges when I'm in charge." It was said without humor.

Jan was still stunned by what had happened while he was dozing. At first he refused to remove his clothes, thinking it was some sort of joke, but a few pokes of Ricardo's gun in his ribs convinced him otherwise. He sat now in moody silence, sulking with his hands cupped over his genitalia, his large chest sagging into a pair of unattractive but ample tits. He was hardly the image of a ruthlessly efficient bodyguard, but then few of the people aboard looked any better with their clothes off than with them on. Laurinda and I were among the exceptions, I contemplated.

"Did you ever see so many naked people without one man wearing a hard-on?" I asked Laurinda.

"This isn't exactly conducive to sex," she said.

"Oh, I don't know," I disagreed. "I could get hot in a hurry if I wanted to."

"You could get hot on an iceberg with Bluebeard," she said with a tinge of disdain.

"Why waste nakedness?" I retorted. "We could start a new club called The Skyjackoffs."

"Are you ever serious?" she asked. "Doesn't it bother you that we're being held prisoner by two potential lunatics?"

"I was already in that condition before the skyjacking," I responded snidely.

"I won't even honor that with a comment," she snapped.

"Go fuck yourself," I whispered in her ear. "I'm going to get high and fuck and do anything I want on this trip   and watch how I get Ricardo to let me do it."

"You'll get us all killed," she warned.

"That can't happen," I replied, "because first I have to get into the *Guinness Book of Records* as the only woman in history kidnapped, skyjacked, and fucked at forty-thousand feet."

Miguel could not hear our dialogue, despite his straining

to decipher it. He was quite paralyzed by the situation, his eyes seldom leaving the gun in Ricardo's steady brown hand. I looked at him and winked, unnerving him even further.

"Hey, Ricardo." I approached our captor again. "How about letting Carlos watch over our playmates while you and I get it on together."

He glanced at me with a kind of wry amusement. I could tell that he was intrigued not just by my body but also by my provocative daring. "My gun shoots bullets, too," he jibed, poking his crotch with the barrel of his pistol.

"Soft ones," I responded, "warm and juicy."

Despite all the tension, his trousers began to bulge as I gyrated and fingered myself before him. If he was like most of the criminals I had met or read about, then this climate of fear and apprehension did something erotically stimulating to his psyche. In other words, he thrived on the excitement of his illicit power. By playing up to it, I was turning him on tremendously, perhaps almost uncontrollably. I inched my way toward him, pushing out my mound of Venus like an ID badge while jiggling my tits in the palms of my hands.

"Let's fuck, Ricardo," I gushed through liquid lips.

"Hey," he protested lamely.

"Come on," I teased him, "the plane's going where you want. What harm can a little fucking do?"

"Carlos!" he shouted down the long aisle. We both turned to see his confederate waving his gun in the air as a young girl and what appeared to be her mother were energetically sucking him off. Instead of being angry, Ricardo laughed at the spectacle. "Some Communist," he scoffed. "He likes fellatio more than Fidel."

I was impressed with his use of language. Skyjacker or not, he was not just some illiterate, scatter-brained zealot. He apparently knew what he was doing but did not let his mission smother his senses.

"Let me take it out for you," I proposed, reaching for his

fly. Instantly the gun was against my forehead, cold and demanding of respect.

"Easy," he warned. "No tricks."

"I just want you to have what Carlos is having," I assured him.

"Too many people watching," he hesitated. "Hey, everybody turn your heads. Look away."

Heads swiveled obediently as I slowly pulled down the tab of his zipper and freed the lonely soldier inside. He sprang to attention in my face, his crimson helmet gleaming. "Good boy." I petted it, hardening it to the point of bursting.

"You like to suck," Ricardo suggested.

"Love it," I agreed, confirming my predilection with a succulent kiss that surrounded the entire head.

Ricardo pointed his revolver into the pilot's cabin. "No funny business in there," he warned the naked crew.

"We're on compass to Havana," the captain assured him.

Ricardo grunted approval, then turned his attention back to my efforts. I had both of his balls in my mouth the way a squirrel stores nuts in his cheeks. With both hands I stroked the taut skin of his cock against the solid inner core of his swollen organ. The head strained against the pressure, its mouth gasping for air like a drowning man trying to stay above water.

"Son'bitch," he moaned, "that hurts good."

It did not take long before molten cum boiled over the rim of his prick, lacquering my face and dripping in elasticized loops on to the carpeted floor. Ricardo's knees buckled momentarily from the shock of a climax so copious it seemed impossible that there could be a drop of semen left anywhere within him. I wiped him off with one of the headrest covers, returned his cock to its hiding place, and pulled up the zipper, like an efficient professional.

"There we go," I announced with a pat to his crotch.

"I think we will keep you in Cuba," he said without smiling.

"Why not?" I retorted boldly. I could see Miguel wincing at that, though he still did not dare to turn around

"We have some fun now," Ricardo said to me under his breath

"Now?" I reacted with feigned indignation, "I thought what I just did for you was fun."

"Different kind of fun," he assured me. "Watch."

He strode over to Miguel and tapped on his bare back with the butt of his revolver. I could literally see his flesh creep. "Hey, you," Ricardo addressed him, "I want you to take that big man there and blow him."

Miguel turned and looked up in anguish "Me?" he asked. "I'm not that way."

Ricardo's eyes narrowed, and he glared at him "You be that way now or you'll be no way at all," he threatened.

Jan appeared just as distressed at the prospect as Miguel. But he kept his lips pursed and simply waited, uncertain how to react.

"That's a terrible thing to make a man do," Laurinda objected. Ricardo scowled at her.

"I'm gonna do something special for you, too," he said, biting his lips.

"You started this, Chris," she accused me.

"Me?" I responded. "Look back there in the other cabin. Everybody's doing everything to everyone! How can you blame me?"

"Shut up," Ricardo ordered.

Miguel looked grimly at Jan, apparently unable to let his eyes fall to his crotch. I really felt sorry for him, but I knew there was nothing I could do to stop Ricardo. This was his way of humiliating an aristocrat and enhancing his own sense of power and worth.

"I won't do it," Miguel finally managed to utter. The gun barrel immediately went into his mouth.

"Then it will be *this* on which you perform," Ricardo announced in a no-nonsense tone, "your first, last, and greatest blow job."

"No," Laurinda cried. "He'll do what you want."

It was obvious Ricardo was enjoying this entire drama immensely, particularly the distress of Miguel. He sat there dry-lipped and trembling, a look of terrible apprehension clouding his eyes.

"I give you sixty seconds to begin," Ricardo said. To emphasize the time, he held the gun to the side of Miguel's head and counted. "One, two, three, four . . ."

At the count of sixteen, Miguel pitched forward and fell upon the limp prick and balls of Jan. His eyes were clenched shut as he took the flesh between his lips, sucking in his cheeks as he sought to make it rise.

"Hee-hee-hee," Ricardo squealed gleefully. He was alone not only in his giggling, but also in his delight with the scene.

"Ugh." Laurinda dared to express herself.

"Some cocksucker, huh?" our skyjacker commented as he watched intently.

Jan grimaced as his cock rose seemingly against his will. I could appreciate his discomfort at having his boss playing a forced oral tune on him. It was one of the few times in my life that I was witness to the performance of a sex act that did not have any erotic effect on me. Laurinda kept her gaze askance, refusing to look directly at the two men despite Ricardo's insistence.

"Swallow it," he insisted when Jan finally came. It was a weak amount, scarcely more than a few drops and a good indication of how uninspired they had been.

Miguel contorted his face as he forced the cum down his throat. "Ugh," he choked out.

"Now that wasn't bad at all, was it?" Ricardo taunted him. "Maybe you'd like some more before we land."

The look of horror on Miguel's face could not be faked. He gave no other response. One ordeal was over, and he could only hope and pray there would not be another. I slipped him a couple of uppers, and his eyes expressed his gratitude. He was normally not a pill taker, but this had been too much to endure undiluted. They went down his throat with a wash of champagne to dissolve the memory of the ejaculation that preceded them.

Carlos ventured into our section for a brief look around, making sure the passengers in coach were aware that he had his eyes and his gun aimed in their direction at all times.

"Hey, Ricardo," he said to his colleague in crime, "that one there. I like her." He pointed directly at me.

"You got taste," Ricardo responded. "You want to fuck her?"

"First-class or tourist?" he laughed.

"Take her back there with you for a while," Ricardo said. "I haven't even looked over the stewardesses yet."

They were remarkably nonchalant, considering what they were up to. It seemed at times that they had all but forgotten the nature of their mission. But that was all an illusion. The moment anyone, passenger or crew member, made any sort of suspicious move, the guns went to the heads of the offenders to remind them who was in charge.

"Come here with me," Carlos said, gesturing with his gun. He pointed to the empty row of seats against the first-class bulkhead.

"What do you have in mind?" I asked coyly.

"Get down on the seats on all fours," he instructed.

"Doggie-style?" I toyed with him.

"Dogs know how to fuck right," he said.

"You like bitches?" I asked as I assumed the requested position.

"I like girls who fuck like bitches," he replied.

"That's my style," I said.

He probed my cunt with his gun barrel before slipping his cock into the handful of damp flesh separating my legs and the cheeks of my derrière.

"Good ass," he noted as his prick responded to the sweet suction of my pussy.

I glanced up to see Laurinda in the same position up ahead with Ricardo slamming back and forth into her.

Somewhere about that time the combined effect of everything the booze, the hash, the pills, and the excitement caught up to me and did me in. The next thing I remember we were descending and I was wet all over with the sticky residue of cum. I learned later that when I passed out on him, Carlos angrily made all the men on board masturbate on my unconscious body. The cruelest part of it all was that I hadn't even been awake to enjoy it.

CHAPTER NINETEEN

We were not in Cuba.

Fuel problems had forced us down on some remote Pacific isles off the coast of Mexico called Revillagigedo. The skyjackers, Ricardo and Carlos, were tense and suspicious during the hour-long ordeal, forcing everyone to keep their hands over their heads and keeping their guns against the heads of the pilot and copilot the entire time. No one came aboard, and only the fuel truck driver and one assistant even approached the aircraft.

"There's not enough time to get the federal police here," the captain assured Ricardo. "We didn't radio for clearance until the last possible minute."

"I trust no one," he was told.

The transaction went smoothly and almost silently. It seemed that everyone on the plane was holding his breath, anticipating some unexpected disaster. Then when the jet engines began to whine once again, there was an almost audible, collective sigh of relief from all concerned.

"*Adios*, motherfuckers," Ricardo sneered as he waved his gun in farewell.

"It went well," the captain said, visibly relieved.

"You wouldn't be speaking now if it hadn't," Ricardo informed him. The look on his face confirmed that he wasn't jesting.

"Acapulco is just south of here," the captain announced wistfully as we flew over the mainland below.

"Havana, Havana," the skyjacker reminded him.

The captain nodded. "I'll start making radio contact as soon as we cross Mexico," he told him.

"*Viva Fidel*," Ricardo chanted.

"*Viva Fidel*," Carlos recited after him.

"I hope you're going to let us put our clothes back on before the landing," I heard the captain say.

"The men, maybe," he was told. "The pretty ladies look better without them."

He returned to the first-class cabin, swaggering, and deliberately waving his cock from one thigh to the other. "The one who is called Laurinda," he announced. "I promised you special attention before all of these interruptions."

Laurinda was high, having snorted some coke while the skyjackers were concentrating on the refueling. She stood up and sauntered brazenly over to him. "What's your problem, mustache?" she challenged him.

"You have the problem," he countered, "not I."

Something about her posturing and her impudence made her more voluptuous than ever. She radiated sensuality as she tossed her head defiantly. It obviously had its effect on him, too, because his cock was pointing up at her face with its own special arrogance and chauvinism.

"Sit down," he ordered her, "right there in front of me."

"Why?" she responded flippantly.

"Sit down," he repeated, pushing down on her shoulder this time. She sank slowly into the nearest seat as we all watched the action peripherally.

"You want me to suck it?" she asked matter-of-factly as he crouched over her, his arms braced against the headrest.

Abruptly a torrent of amber shot from the mouth of his prick, splashing over her like warm cider from a nozzle. She threw up her hands instinctively to thwart the hard stream.

"Piss on you," he growled, smirking with pleasure at her frantic efforts to duck the shower of urine.

"You bastard," she gasped, only to have her mouth fill up with the juice of his bladder, overflowing onto her chin. In no time at all she was drenched from head to toe, after which he pulled himself off onto her tits, adding an ample batch of cum to the wine of his cock.

"You're baptized now," he announced after the last pearl had been milked from the helmet of his prick.

"You're a real sonofabitch, Ricardo," she reacted. "I hope your balls fall off."

He laughed in a weirdly high-pitched tone, like the cackle of some jungle vulture. It was plain to see that he enjoyed dominating people, women in particular, and degrading them through sexual humiliation. If I had softened toward him since the moment of the takeover, I had now renewed contempt for him and his accomplice. I decided to fake sleep for the remainder of the flight in the slim hope that that would keep him from bothering me. Apparently I was not alone in seeking refuge from the bizarre proceedings through slumber. At least half the passengers were cuddled into their seats in fetal positions, their eyes closed.

"How much longer to Havana?" Laurinda asked in a hoarse whisper.

"I'm no good at geography," I confessed, "but if we're over Mexico, we must be getting fairly close."

"I hope so," she sighed. "These assholes are getting more and more revolting."

"Play dead," I advised, slouching low in my seat so as to be mostly out of the range of Ricardo's vision.

"I don't have to play it," she responded. "I am dead physically, mentally, spiritually."

"You'll survive," I assured her. "Miguel is the one who surprises me. He doesn't take stress very well, does he?"

"He's always had things go his way," she confided. "Why do you think he resorted to something as drastic as holding you for ransom?"

"Even that he's done in a real pussyfooted way," I whispered. She looked at me strangely and did not respond.

For the moment I'd forgotten that she was in love with the man   good, bad, or indifferent.

Ricardo lurched overhead. "What's all the psssst-psssst-pssssting about?" he inquired gruffly.

"Woman talk," I replied.

"Stop it," he rasped. "In fact, nobody talk anymore until we land. Understand?" He ricocheted his eyes off each person in the cabin, then strode forward to pass the word to Carlos. "Only the flight crew can talk from here on," he declared. "We're approaching Jose Marti Airport, isn't that right Captain?"

"Roger," the captain responded through the open door to the cockpit.

"Do we have clearance?" he asked, obviously seeking repetition of what he already knew.

"We've got emergency landing clearance, yes," was the response.

"Good," he said. "Now everybody shut up and let the captain do what has to be done."

Like shooting you between the eyes, I thought to myself. Silently I wriggled toward a cabin window to watch our landing. Would we be detained in Cuba or allowed to move about freely? I had no idea what the procedure was with respect to hijacked aircraft, especially in a Communist country such as Cuba.

It was odd how prolonged nakedness made one more or less oblivious to the nudity of others. My pussy almost seemed like a fur pelt donned to keep me warm, and since I seldom wore a bra, my tits moved about in their usual state. It was only the sight of the men with their dangling prongs and hairy testicles that seemed slightly out of kilter when I stopped to observe them.

"Fasten your seatbelts, please," the captain's voice hummed over the intercom. "For safety's sake that should include everyone."

Ricardo's eyes flashed as he braced himself in the passageway between the front cabin and the cockpit. "I will stand," he declared resolutely.

The captain shrugged. "Suit yourself," he replied. "You'll be the first to go if anything goes wrong."

Ricardo cocked the trigger of his revolver and pushed aside the safety catch, then held the barrel to the back of the captain's head. "Nothing will go wrong," he said in an even, intense voice.

The plane obeyed the staccato chatter from the flight tower and landed smoothly and gracefully on the white-striped runway. I swallowed hard at the first bite of the wheels to the asphalt, moved by the realization that another chapter in my recently hectic life was ending with a new one about to begin. It seemed at times that it was all a nightmare, a trance from which I would suddenly awaken with no recollection of what had transpired. But then reality in some guise or another would slap me in the face.

"Clothes on!" Ricardo commanded as we taxied to a hangar separated from what appeared to be the main terminal. There were olive-drab jeeps filled with rifle-bearing soldiers over the entire area, somber-faced young men peering grimly at the windows of our plane as they followed its progress.

The jet was like a can of sardines suddenly restored to life as everyone squirmed and wriggled to get back into their clothes. Ricardo and Carlos could no longer maintain the edict of silence and made only a perfunctory effort to enforce it.

"Shut up!" they shouted at the chattering, revitalized passengers. But it was to no avail. They were nervous and apprehensive themselves, too much so to worry any longer about controlling their human cargo. Now that the deed had been done and they were back in Cuba in temporary possession of a multimillion-dollar aircraft, they seemed uncertain about their mission and perhaps also about their fate.

"The field commander wants to board the plane," the captain relayed to Ricardo. He in turn peered out through the front window of the plane at the approaching limousine with flags flying from either side of its hood.

"Open it then," Ricardo instructed. He sounded much more tentative than the positive manner he had projected earlier.

"They may put us all in prison." Miguel made a hoarse prediction.

"For what?" I questioned. "Being the victims of a pair of lunatics?"

"Cuba doesn't observe international laws," he replied. "They make their own rules to suit the situation."

"Then Ricardo and Carlos could be in trouble, too," Laurinda said.

"It's very possible," Miguel agreed. "I think Castro's developing a new policy toward skyjackings."

"We'll know soon," I noted. "Here comes the big man up the ladder."

The big man was actually rather short in stature, but the power he wielded was obviously large. Surrounded by a retinue of machine-gun-toting soldiers in green fatigues, he appeared cold and efficient as he greeted first the captain and then the two men responsible for diverting the aircraft to Cuba. There was a brief, low-voiced discussion in Spanish, followed by the departure of Ricardo and Carlos in the company of two armed soldiers. They did not even turn back or utter a word of farewell as they were escorted off the plane.

"Everyone will bring his passport and other credentials," the captain announced calmly, "for processing in the terminal. The commandant assures me that no harm will come to any of you and that after the customs check, we will be permitted to resume our flight to Acapulco aboard this plane . . ."

Applause and cheers greeted his declaration, bringing a thin smile to the lips of the field commander. We trooped down the steps behind him, sharing a mood of subdued festivity. It had been an ordeal, but now there was real hope that it was almost over.

Our captain drew up alongside me as we walked behind a group of soldiers to the processing area. "The commander tells me we just set a record for the longest skyjacking ever   at least to Cuba," he said. "That makes us all a part of history."

"I feel like ancient history myself," I laughed. "That was some trip."

"I saw you," he reported with a grin, "and you certainly didn't look ancient in any way, shape, or form."

"You peeked?" I teased him.

"No," he corrected me, "I gaped."

The check was routine, swift, and impersonal. We then learned that the plans of Ricardo and Carlos had backfired. They were already in custody and would face trial for illegally commandeering an international aircraft. Later the captain made an official statement condemning them for sexual abuse and lewd conduct as well. "The authorities assured me that they'll get ten to twenty years for this," he informed us when we were once again airborne. This statement brought another surge of cheering and applause. Moments later the plane became a magic carpet of camaraderie and celebration with even the flight crew joining in the party. Thank God the captain and his navigators remained sober or we would never have made it to Acapulco. But we did   and each of us joined hands to kiss the sweet earth of Mexico after disembarking. But then I realized that I alone was still not free.

CHAPTER TWENTY

Something about the experience of being skyjacked had soured Miguel, making him fretful and uncommunicative. Laurinda and I tried to get him out of his irritable mood by making repeated sexual overtures to him, toying with his genitals, and going through exaggerated posturings of our pubes in front of him. But he continued to be sullen and more or less oblivious to our gestures, behaving relatively impotently on our first day in Zihuatanejo.

"Where do you find these out-of-the-way places," I questioned him sardonically on the beach, "in the Yellow Pages of the Albuquerque phone book?"

"This is a developing resort area," he replied in a miffed voice, "deliberately kept subdued so it isn't overrun with the picnic crowds."

"It's pretty," I conceded, "but I feel like I'm at the edge of civilization somehow."

"You're spoiled rotten," he responded. "You'd complain about a suite in Buckingham Palace."

"Definitely," I retorted, "it's cold and drafty and have you ever tried skinny-dipping in the Thames?"

He stared at me with something between a scowl and a frown, then resumed reading what looked like a financial report in a leather portfolio.

"What's that?" I goaded him, "the first draft of your memoirs?"

"Why don't you run off and play sixty-nine with Laurinda?" he sneered.

"Not until you tell me why you're so bitter," I said.

He laid the report in his lap and looked directly into my eyes. "Your goddamn lawyers are making things unnecessarily difficult if you must know," he told me.

"Good for them," I responded. "They know I'm a survivor, no matter what tortures I might be subjected to."

"That's a laugh," he snapped. "I've kept you in luxury the entire time."

"Luxury is not leaping from place to place like a frog," I pointed out. "It entails some degree of stability and serenity as far as I'm concerned."

"That's not possible just now," he said. "You have to understand that."

"I don't *have* to understand anything," I replied. "If you think I couldn't have escaped from Laurinda and that ape you have guarding me a dozen times in the past few weeks, you're underestimating Christina van Bell."

"Why didn't you then?" he countered.

"To save your ass," I said. "You could do life in prison for what you're doing to me."

"I'm not doing anything to you," he responded with an air of hostility. "You're not being held, and you can't claim that you are."

I stood up and brushed the sand from my bikini. "In that case," I announced, "I think I'll spend the afternoon in Acapulco."

"Why not?" he reacted. "I'll have a chauffeur drive you and Laurinda there if you like."

"Alone," I specified.

He arched his eyebrows. "Okay," he agreed hesitantly.

"What's the catch?" I challenged.

"No catch," he replied. "Jan will drive you there."

"I knew there had to be a catch," I said, snapping my fingers to accentuate the discovery.

"You don't really expect me to allow you to go there all alone, do you?" he asked.

"If I'm free to come and go as I please as you just claimed," I replied, "then the answer is yes."

"You're too much of a realist to expect that," he said.

"Too much a captive is more like it," I responded.

He shook his head in quiet exasperation. "Truthfully, Christina," he said, "I didn't expect this whole thing to drag on so long. It's put me in one hell of a bind."

"I used to feel sorry for you, Miguel," I told him, "but I think I've gone beyond that."

Laurinda came back from her swim in the warm waters of the bay and stood next to us, blotting herself with a towel.

"Christina would like to go to Acapulco for some reason or other," Miguel told her. "Would you care to join her?"

"I don't really want to go," I protested. "I was just testing Miguel."

"I'll go if you like," she replied, "but not today. We just got here yesterday."

"You're right," I agreed. "I don't even want to move more than a few feet from the hotel for the next few days."

Miguel made a face and returned to his documents, the matter closed as far as he was concerned. I caught Laurinda's eye and stuck my tongue out at him while wiggling my hands from my ears. She laughed aloud, but he did not look up.

"Let's go to the patio for cocktails," I suggested, "and leave old sourpuss to his adding and subtracting."

She glanced at him for his approval, but he ignored us both on purpose. "Sounds like a good idea," she said tentatively. "I'll get my robe."

"You can go like that," I assured her. "It's very informal."

She smiled. "I should've known you'd checked it out already," she said.

We skipped off together, leaving Miguel to his business concerns. Not far away Jan basted in the sun like a beached whale, his gimlet eyes ever aware of everything about him. After the hysteria of recent days, this was an extraordinarily peaceful setting studded with coconut palms and papaya trees, the waters turquoise and tranquil. My intermittent desire to escape took a holiday once again, relaxing me more than I had been in over a week.

"He's a grouch," I complained to Laurinda as we sat down at a rattan table with a huge yellow umbrella over it.

"Things aren't going well, I gather," she responded.

"That doesn't mean he should take it out on us," I reminded her.

"True," she agreed, "but then again this is all new to him to be under this sort of pressure."

"I'm not exactly accustomed to being a captive either," I said.

"I wish you wouldn't use that term," she replied with a wince.

"Should I call myself your guest then?" I suggested in jest.

"That would sound a lot better," she said.

We both ordered rum punches and leaned back nonchalantly to study the other guests at the hotel. It was called the Posada Caracol, which meant "Inn of the Snail." I liked its Spanish, white stucco design, the wide arches, and the way it sat on the edge of a cliff overlooking the beach. I made a mental note to keep it in mind for a hideaway at some future date when I was once again in charge of my own itinerary.

"The flight captain liked you," Laurinda observed casually.

"What makes you say that?" I asked.

"He asked me for your name and address," she revealed.

"Of course you gave it to him," I jested.

"I'm sorry, Chris," she apologized. "I would have liked to, but you know the circumstances."

"Oh well," I sighed, "when you've fucked one flight captain, you've fucked them all."

"That's one piece of cynicism I won't buy," she laughed, "not from you or anyone else."

"I liked him," I recalled. "Nice cock, too."

"Wasn't that wild, seeing everybody on the plane naked?" she remembered.

"How many times have you sat on a plane and mentally undressed people?" I questioned. "I've done it lots of times with certain individuals. But this is the first time it actually happened en masse."

"Crazy, wasn't it?"

"It almost seems like it never really happened to tell the truth," I noted.

She grew wistful. "I wonder if that's how you'll feel about me after this is all over," she pondered aloud.

"You're unforgettable," I assured her.

"I feel the same way about you, Chris," she responded. "I only wish I could see you in those golden tresses again. You were made to be a blonde, not a brunet."

"Do you suppose Miguel would let me take down my own hair while we're here?" I inquired hopefully.

"I doubt it, honey," she said honestly. "You're too well known that way to take a chance."

"Here?" I reacted in self-defense, "I can't even remember the name of the place."

"Zihuatanejo," she said.

"Don't even bother spelling it," I responded. "If ever there was a spot where nobody had heard of Christina van Bell, this is very likely it."

"It's not as remote as you think," she said. "We're only a hundred-and-twenty-five miles from Acapulco."

"It could just as easily be a thousand miles," I insisted.

Laurinda shrugged. "Try that argument on Miguel," she said, "but don't get too optimistic."

"The way he's acting," I said, "I wouldn't even ask him the time of day."

"If anybody can get anything out of him," she said, "it's you."

I gave her a look of amused skepticism. "That's why I'm his captive," I said.

"There's that nasty word again," she objected.

"Guest," I said quickly. We both laughed and ordered another drink.

Miguel eventually joined us after taking his business

papers to his room first. He seemed considerably more amiable than he had been earlier. "The two schemers," he greeted us, "adding chemicals to their constitutions."

"What happened?" I responded. "Somebody inject you with cocaine or something?"

"Why?" he asked.

"You were lower than the legs of a lizard before," I pointed out, "now you're almost human again."

"I was inspired by a pair of Mexican teen-agers in bikinis," he reported. "My mood went up almost as fast as my Tinker-Toy."

"We were beginning to wonder if you'd gone impotent," I said offhandedly, "weren't we, Laurie?"

She seemed reluctant to make such an indictment, even in jest. "Miguel's been working too hard," she said in his defense.

"Too soft," I corrected. "Didn't you notice during that entire flight from Hawaii with everybody letting it all hang out that Miguel didn't raise his bridge higher than his balls once?"

"Christina!" she cried in feigned embarrassment.

Miguel allowed the head of his penis to peek out from under his trunks. It glistened in scarlet splendor, like a small shiny apple against his thigh. "Kiss it and see what happens," he challenged me.

I looked around, saw no one watching, and took a fast suck of it. Immediately his bulge swelled, and the head fought to free itself from the elastic leg band. "Take it all out," I dared him.

Laurinda looked aghast. "Not here," she pleaded. "Let's go to the room before we get thrown out of the hotel."

"I can't go like this," Miguel said, leaning back to display the full-scale erection harbored in his scant bikini trunks.

"I'll pull it off," I volunteered, digging my hand under his bathing suit and clutching the cluster of cock and balls.

"At least cover up with a towel," Laurinda insisted. She flung a large beach wrap over my pumping hand and his naked genitalia, looking furtively about the open-air lounge for prying eyes. No one seemed to be looking, but I made fast work of it just the same. Miguel spouted like a whale, his cum splattering over my hand and against the towel, a few drops falling to the stone terrace. I wiped him off along with my hand, then artfully returned his equipment to its hiding place.

"Now where were we?" I jibed as I resumed sipping my drink.

"We were on our way back to the room to indulge in a little rubbing of the flesh," he said matter-of-factly.

"Your flesh has already been rubbed," I retorted.

"That was only a preliminary massage," he said.

"Has the swelling gone down yet?" Laurinda inquired.

"It's in the limber, rubbery stage," I reported, feeling his crotch.

"The south shall rise again," he proclaimed, "so let's get out of here before the shooting starts."

We made it to his room just in time. Our combined attention to his crotch had brought another full-blown hard-on to blossom en route. Laurinda gave it immediate oral attention while I smothered his face with the full flesh of my meaty cunt. Before an hour had passed, there were no more doubts about Miguel's virility or potency. He came four times in the process of being acrobatically fucked and sucked by two of the horniest women ever to invade Zihuatanejo   or anywhere else on earth for that matter.

CHAPTER TWENTY-ONE

Miguel decided that the three of us should make a day trip to Acapulco together There was not that much to do in Zihuatanejo after several days of sipping, sunning, and sinning, therefore he was more restless than even I The negotiations seemed stymied by Winston Garrett's insistence on hearing directly from me before considering any ransom offer at all. For all I knew, Winnie might have been thinking I was involved in some crazy international game thought up by some of my jaded millionaire friends. He knew me well enough not to rule out that possibility.

"Let's have fun for a change," Miguel declared en route. It earned him questioning looks from both of us.

"We always manage to have some measure of fun," I informed him. "It's you who usually puts the damper on things."

"That's what I mean," he said. "I want to let myself go and forget about this whole mess for a day."

"How about letting me go natural then?" I proposed.

"You mean naked?" he countered.

"I mean blonde," I replied. "I'm sick of being a brunet."

He thought it over briefly. "I wish I could say yes, " he said, "but it's too dangerous   especially in Acapulco. Anybody could be around at this time of the year."

"I'll deny I'm Christina van Bell," I said.

He smiled tolerantly. "Some things just can't be denied," he told me, "and that hair combined with that face and figure add up to only one person on earth."

"If I'm supposed to be flattered, I'm not," I pouted. "The only time I see myself the way I really am is in my own bedroom."

"That's your main source of life anyhow," he teased me.

"I can do it anywhere," I volleyed back.

"You won't get any arguments from me on that," he laughed.

In lieu of Jan our driver was a man only about a third his size a small, slender Mexican with skin the color and luster of polished mahogany. He understood little English, taking his orders from Miguel in Spanish. Miguel in turn conversed with us in English to keep him out of the conversation.

"He can get us some very attractive young people, he says," Miguel reported primarily to me since Laurinda could understand the Spanish as well as he.

"Teen-agers?" I inquired.

"Fifteen, sixteen in that general age," he confided after another exchange with the driver.

I jutted my lower lip out and nodded affirmation. "I could use some fresh material," I said. "How about you, Laurinda?"

"Foolish question," she laughed.

"What do you say?" Miguel asked, his eyes glinting at the prospect.

"*Si, si, si, si,*" I voted.

"Laurinda?" He turned to her.

"Miguel, you know better than to ask me that," she said coyly.

He immediately launched into more detailed negotiations with the man at the wheel. The boys were rock divers, I learned, the girls recruited for their beauty from inland farms. They worked the resort circuit in season, offering their bodies for hire for any purpose whatsoever.

"They do everything but set themselves on fire," he reported with obvious anticipation.

"I'm already on fire myself," I confessed.

"I want a boy and a girl for myself," Laurinda declared, lighting up one of the marijuana joints Miguel had supplied us. I did the same, leaning back to close my eyes and envision the lays that lay before us. Miguel really was uncoiling a bit. It made it much easier to look over my situation regarding him—at least temporarily.

"Anybody in need of practice?" Miguel asked, taking his hard cock out of his slacks. It bobbed about like a loose Leaning Tower of Pisa until Laurinda fell upon it like the prize apple in the Garden of Eden. The driver giggled at the scene in his rearview mirror, unfazed by the unorthodox proceedings in his taxi. He had already told Miguel that he was three things rolled into one—promoter, pimp, and chauffeur to the rich and famous. It was apparent that he enjoyed his work.

Fellatio aside, we arrived more or less intact at a small seaside cluster of cabins, unmarked except for an arrow pointing to what I assumed was the office. The grounds were quite heavily wooded, and if anyone was around, they were certainly hidden by the foliage. I did hear laughter and shouts of glee coming from the direction of the sea, so it was obvious we were not being stranded at a deserted campsite.

Miguel went inside the main cabin with the driver while Laurinda and I got out of the car and stretched.

"How do you feel?" she asked me.

"With my hands," I replied, utilizing one of the oldest clichés in my repertoire.

"I never would have expected such a tired line coming from you," she sighed.

I laughed lightly. "I'm numb from the ride," I explained.

"And high from the pot," she added.

"A little," I admitted.

"Want to share another one?" she offered.

"Sure."

She lit a stick, sucked in its sweet smoke, and handed it to me. "Let's turn the kids on when we get them," she suggested.

"Great idea," I agreed. I inhaled a deep drag, reveling in the smoke curling through my system like a prolonged orgasm. "Good stuff," I noted as I handed it back to her.

"Acapulco Gold," she said before pursing her lips for another heady drag.

We were floating when Miguel returned. But he was so enthralled with the arrangements he'd just made, he paid little or no attention to our euphoric state. "I got three boys and three girls," he reported. "We can use the beach or any of the cabins here."

"Where are they?" I asked, looking about for some sign of them.

"I told you, they're divers," he reminded me. "They have to go get them off the cliffs."

"The girls, too?" Laurinda wondered.

"No," he replied, "they're down on the beach."

"Swimming?" I teased.

"Among other things," he said. "This place is pretty well-known to the jet set so they're busy most of the time."

"Let's go down there and join them," Laurinda proposed.

"Don't you want to wait for the boys?" Miguel asked.

I looked at him with feigned surprise. "Girls fuck, too, don't they?" I inquired.

"Let's go," he responded, grabbing us both by our wrists and pulling us toward the beach.

Our three girls—Margarita, Theresa, and Rosita—were lying naked on a huge, Indian-pattern blanket at the water's edge. They were uniformly tanned to a rich, walnut shade, and all three were adorned with lustrous, ebony hair. The six lovely cheeks of their asses looked as appealing as half-a-dozen gourmet-roasted Cornish game hens basting in the sun. The three of us licked our chops in gustatory anticipation almost in unison.

"Girls," Miguel addressed them, "your newest friends are here—Miguel, Christina, and Laurinda."

They looked up in mild surprise, all dazzling smiles and flashing dark eyes. They immediately revealed six scrumptious tits with starry nipples glistening in the sunlight. "Hello," one of them said in a girlishly cute voice. "I am Rosita, and these are Margarita and Theresa."

"Dolls," Laurinda appraised them with a smile, "a trio of living dolls."

"Usually we don't get such good-looking people," Margarita confessed. "Making love to you will be easy."

"A pleasure in fact," Theresa said.

"That goes both ways," I told them. They were sizing us up very openly and directly, prompting me to suggest that we strip down immediately.

"You're undressing us with your eyes," I accused them merrily.

"Would you like some marijuana?" Laurinda asked before discarding the purse containing the pot. The girls giggled in eagerness.

"*Si, si, si*," they chorused.

"Are there no boys coming?" Rosita wondered as she lit up.

"They're on their way," Miguel told her. "The girls here just couldn't wait to get on with it."

"Oooh," Theresa said, "I like that honey hair." She pointed to my pussy.

"Why is it black on top and gold down there?" Margarita asked.

I glanced at Miguel before answering. He was already half-stoned on three drags of pot. "Blond is my natural color," I replied.

They all started talking at once. "Then why don't you keep it?" Rosita's voice emerged from the chatter. "In Mexico everybody has black hair. Blond is so much better."

I laughed. "I don't know if it's better," I said, "but it is lighter."

"Is that a wig then?" Theresa questioned. I nodded affirmation. "Take it off, Christina, please?"

"Yes, do," the other two urged. "We have so few blondes."

"It's up to Miguel," I responded.

"Why?" Margarita asked. "He is only a man, and besides it is your hair and not his."

"Hear that, señor?" I challenged him, emboldened by the grass I was puffing.

"It wouldn't hurt way out here, would it?" Laurinda joined in on my side.

"Take it off," Miguel shrugged, "and let's start fucking for crissake."

The girls eagerly joined in unpinning the brunet wig and then unraveling the tightly compressed curls of my real hair. There were multiple ooohs and ahhhs as my golden tresses cascaded over my shoulders.

"So beautiful," Rosita said breathlessly.

"A goddess," Margarita sighed.

"You should never, never hide such golden treasure," Theresa said with awe in her voice.

In the process of releasing my hair, I was surrounded by succulent, fresh pussy. The bristly curls of their cunts brushed against my bare flesh and sent tremors of desire coursing through me. And there was something distinctly erotic about having the hands of pretty young maidens raking through my locks, stroking them in admiration.

"Kiss me, darlings," I encouraged them, and they did, heatedly and wetly, all over my body. Theresa, who had been the first to express her appreciation of my golden cunt, found her way into its interior first.

"You're not commandeering all three of them," Miguel protested. "If they're going to continue kissing you, baby, I'm going to fuck them while they're doing it."

He had no difficulty finding a smooth and willing ass to enter as the six of us gathered as close as bees around a hive, licking, kissing, fucking, and sucking. In the midst of it all, the boys descended upon us with whoops and hollers of joy, adding their stiff pricks to the proceedings without interrupting any of the fervid activity.

I was caught in what literally seemed to be a blizzard of cum from the talented young cocks of the diving boys. They were cliff divers, but they were also muff divers, and among the nine of us there was so much tongue-thrashing and anal-slathering we created our own pool of warm saliva on the beach.

It took a combined total of perhaps fifty or so orgasms before any sort of order returned to our patch of sand. The boys Pedro, Juan, and Jesus were just as spellbound by my blondness as the girls, guaranteeing me the most attention of anyone. I think that annoyed Miguel, but it galled Laurinda. Her beautiful cunt suffered from the competition of the three younger and just as black pussies, causing her to resort to licking assholes to command the attention of the boys. Even at that, they probed away at me at every opportunity until finally Laurinda herself took over my cunt with a full-faced invasion that kept any cocks from entering.

We dipped into the warm sea at intervals to rinse the cum and perspiration from our bodies, refreshing us as well in the process. The afternoon eased into evening before anyone thought of food other than of the cock and cunt variety.

"I ordered a feast for all of us," Miguel announced. "We'll have a picnic right here on the beach."

"We've had a circus already," I quipped.

He looked at me oddly. "I never realized what a totally horny creature you are," he said with what I interpreted to be just a hint of disdain.

"Maybe you don't really know me at all," I retorted.

Laurinda caught the sparks flying between us and seemed pleased. "Now, now," she said, "jealousy's not permitted at orgies. That's the number one rule."

"I'm not jealous," I snapped, "I'm just myself now that my hair's down where it belongs and in the color God intended it to be."

"After chow you'll put it back up the way it was before," Miguel ordered. "It's too late to get back to Zihuatanejo tonight—we'll have to stay in Acapulco."

"Shit," I said. He turned away and offered his cock to the waiting mouth of Margarita.

"Don't get him mad and spoil everything," Laurinda counseled me.

"Fuck him," I hissed. Just the feel of my hair on my shoulders and the realization that I was once again Christina van Bell restored some of my natural spitfire quality. I was in a dangerous mood, capable for the first time in weeks of entertaining thoughts of escape. Who needed Miguel Clemente to arrange my sexual dalliances? I needed no one for that nor for anything else for that matter. The pot, the pussy, and the prick had recharged me and rearranged my thinking as well. Something had to break and soon.

Pedro fucked me during dinner in casual Roman-style, entering me from the rear as I lay stretched out and propped on my elbow, eating from a tray of enchilladas, tacos, refritos, and assorted other native delicacies. "You should come watch me dive from the cliffs," he said as he pushed against the curve of my buttocks. "I am the only naked diver who always plunges from the rocks sporting a first-class hard-on"

"I'll bet it smarts when it hits the water," I laughed.

"It goes in first," he reported, "like an arrow."

"It couldn't go in any better than it's going in right now," I said.

"You like the way Pedro fucks?" he asked.

"Love it," I replied.

"*Gracias*," he said, punctuating his thanks with a quick flurry of milky cum pellets that fed my lower mouth while I continued to stuff the upper one.

We left the kids reluctantly, promising to return another day. I knew it was an empty promise, for on this continuing run for anonymity, Miguel would never retrace any of our route. Besides, he had allowed me to be seen as myself for the first time since Trieste, and that made it doubly important that we not be seen by the same people again. I had taken advantage of his being high, and after he thought about it en route to Acapulco, his resentment became apparent

"No more blond stuff," he said out of the blue

"Are you talking to me?" I asked.

"Are there any other blondes in this car?" he countered.

"Don't you snap at me, you sonofabitch," I warned him.

I could see that he was tempted to slap me, but he restrained himself. Everyone had been getting edgy lately, and the long afternoon of sexual abandon only heightened our awareness of how frayed our nerves really were. There was always a sort of desperate quality to overindulgence, as though surfeiting oneself in endless fucking and sucking would somehow pacify the flesh and spirit. But instead it only stirred hunger for more and more.

"Let's cool it tonight," Laurinda injected, putting her hand on Miguel's shoulder as a calming gesture. "Just have a few drinks maybe and go to bed."

"Why go there then?" I questioned. "I thought we were going to make the rounds."

"You made the rounds already," Miguel said. "Daisy chains and circle jerks."

"I didn't notice you putting your cock to sleep anytime today," I fired back. "Since when did kidnappers become moralists?"

"Keep it up and I'll have your tongue removed," he threatened, wagging his index finger for emphasis.

"I'll remember that when the judge asks me if my life was ever threatened during captivity," I responded.

"You bitch," he sneered, "I told you I am not in anyway involved in holding you either for ransom or anything else."

"Off comes the wig then," I taunted him, pulling at my hairpiece.

"Leave that on," he said through clenched teeth.

I noticed that the driver never looked around anymore. In fact he had said absolutely nothing since our afternoon at the seashore. Miguel must have bribed him to play the three monkeys—hear no, see no, speak no evil.

"This is getting a little out of hand, Miguel," Laurinda said to him. "I don't know how much longer we can keep it up."

"That's not for you to decide," he snapped at her. "I'm the one who's in charge."

"Why don't you beat your chest like the gorillas do?" I needled him.

"Go smoke yourself wacky," he suggested. "I've heard enough of your snide remarks for one day."

An afternoon of uninhibited carnality had deteriorated into an evening of bitter verbal exchanges. I no longer had any real interest in going out. In fact I didn't even want to sleep with Laurinda according to the usual arrangement.

"I want a room of my own at the hotel," I informed him as we neared the city.

"That's impossible," he retorted. "Jan's not with us, so you'll have to stay with Laurinda."

"I don't want to," I said. She looked over at me in surprise. "What have *I* done?" she asked.

"You're the aide and accomplice of a man I despise," I announced dramatically.

They looked at each other, frowned, and shook their heads slowly. "Don't start making things difficult, Christina," he said in a hushed but positive voice.

"That's exactly what I intend to do," I ranted. "I've been playing ball too long because I felt sorry for you. But now I'm beginning to feel sorry for the three real victims of this sordid mess me, myself, and I."

"You're stoned," he snapped in a disparaging tone.

"Driver," I shouted over the intercom, "stop this car and let me out. I'm being kidnapped."

Miguel pounced upon me and locked my head in a vise-like grip. The sleeve of his jacket acted as a gag in my mouth, preventing me from talking further. I kicked at him and bit into the fabric as hard as I could. He held on briefly, then relaxed his grip. "Don't you ever say anything like that again to anyone," he rasped, his breath coming in heavy gulps.

"Don't you ever manhandle me like that again either," I warned him. "Nobody touches me against my wishes, and it's against my wish for you to touch me again. Ever!"

"I don't want to believe all this," Laurinda said with a hard edge to her voice.

"We won't even go back to Zihuatanejo," Miguel announced. "I'll have Jan bring the stuff to Acapulco, and we'll get out of Mexico first thing in the morning."

"I don't think we should even wait until then," she said. "Christina's behaving dangerously, Miguel."

"Christina is behaving like Christina," I injected. "She's through playing patsy, through being shipped around like a prize heifer, through being treated like a dumb animal."

"Ignore her," Miguel said. "We can't get a flight out at this hour. It'll have to be morning."

"I wish Jan was here," Laurinda responded. "What if she tries to escape?"

"She wouldn't do that," Miguel said. They talked about me as though I was on another continent instead of sitting right next to them. In a sense that was how I felt disconnected, removed, no longer a part of either of them.

I lapsed into a sullen silence, my anger dissipated but my unhappiness intact. Earlier the combination of drugs and sex had distracted me from my plight as they usually did but with the breakdown of our already shaky relationships I now felt suddenly and sadly alone. I would have cried except that I would not give them that satisfaction. Besides, they would mistake it for weakness on my part just when I felt stronger and more determined than I had in weeks.

It was already mid-evening by the time we got to the

hotel. The lobby was practically deserted as the two of them hustled me to a waiting elevator. "I'm not an invalid," I protested as they took me by the arms to escort me.

"Don't get any funny ideas," Miguel warned.

"I'm also not a comedienne," I said in a tone of resignation.

I didn't get my wish regarding a separate room, but I did get twin beds, which helped. "You don't want to be with me," Laurinda commented, "so I don't want to be with you either."

"Good," I retorted, "let's keep it that way."

"You'll get over this," she predicted. "We've all been under too much strain."

"You call it a strain," I parried, "I call it captivity."

"Miguel doesn't want you to use that word," she reminded me.

"As I said so eloquently before," I replied, "fuck Miguel and what he wants."

"Get some sleep," she sighed, "you need it."

"There's only one thing I need," I shot back, "and it's spelled f-r-e-e-d-o-m."

She rolled over in her bed, putting her back to me. "If you want to crawl in with me later," she purred, "you're welcome."

"Save it for Miguel," I said.

There was no further exchange after that. What was the sense of volleying words when they accomplished nothing? I lay awake for a long time, mulling over my possible alternatives. When none of them brought anything more than a yawn, I let myself succumb to sleep. Maybe my mind would be sharper in the morning. I could only hope so.

CHAPTER TWENTY-TWO

Unlike the night before, the lobby was jammed with newly arrived conventioneers in the morning. They all wore ID tags and stood around greeting one another like long lost friends. I thought of how ridiculous they looked peering first at the name tags and then pretending to remember each other. It was just something to amuse myself while Miguel checked us out at the desk.

"Are you talking today?" Laurinda inquired. "Or do we play cat's-got-your-tongue all day?"

I awarded her a disdainful scowl. "The less said, the better," I replied.

"Have it your way," she shrugged. "I'm talked out anyhow."

"What's holding us up?" I asked.

"We're waiting for Jan to get here," she explained.

"He had all night," I said coolly.

"He also has to sleep," she pointed out.

"I thought zombies never slept," I remarked acidly.

"It's going to be one of those days, huh?" she reacted.

I nodded with conviction. "Every day from now on," I said.

She looked away in frustration. "I knew it couldn't keep going so smoothly," she lamented. "I kept telling Miguel to speed things up."

"He doesn't take orders very well," I noted, "particularly from women."

"I hope this is the last leg," she said. "I haven't been home in ages."

We went into the coffee shop for a breakfast of papaya, pineapple and cantaloupe with hotcakes but no champagne then returned to the lobby. Miguel was pacing about nervously, stepping outside now and then to survey the road for a sign of Jan Dvorak. I sat back in one of the soft lounges, trying to lose myself in the billowy cushions. Abruptly a familiar-looking man approached me.

"Christina?" he asked tentatively. Laurinda's hair almost stood up on end at the sound of my name coming from a stranger.

I hesitated, staring at his name tag. Dr. Dirk Boland! "Dirk!" I reacted excitedly, jumping to my feet.

"I · · · I wasn't sure," he stammered, "it seems like so long ago . . ."

"Oh, I'm so glad to see you," I gushed. "You'll never know how glad." He seemed overwhelmed by my enthusiasm.

"Your hair that's what threw me," he said, "but as a born pathologist I always probe beneath the surface of things. I was studying you from across the lobby, and then lo and behold, I got the confirming clue . . ."

Laurinda looked around frantically for Miguel, uncertain whether to risk leaving me to search for him. In the meantime she just stood there, looking distraught while our conversation continued.

"What was it?" I asked buoyantly.

"That bastard who did me in in Bristol," he said "That was him talking to you, wasn't it?"

"Yes," I replied without hesitation.

"Christina, we have to go," Laurinda insisted, taking matters into her own hands.

"No," I said evenly and firmly, "I'm not going with you."

Dirk looked on quizzically. "I'm afraid I don't understand," he said.

"They've kidnapped me," I blurted out. "They're holding me for ransom."

"That's a lie," Laurinda screeched.

Dirk's eyes spun about trying to size up the situation. Just then Miguel reappeared at the hotel entrance, and she bolted for him. "Are you serious, Christina?" Dirk asked in a breathless voice.

"It's the truth," I said, almost choking on my own words. The rush of excitement inside me all but clogged my vocal cords. "Look at them take off."

Sure enough, Miguel had seized Laurinda's arm and pulled her into a waiting taxi. The sight of Dirk Boland obviously caused him to panic. I collapsed onto the lounge and began sobbing uncontrollably while Dirk petted me like a wounded child.

"It's all rather baffling to me," he said softly, "but don't worry. I won't let anything happen to you."

"Oh, Dirk, I'm so grateful to you, so happy you're here," I muttered. "I just can't believe it, that's all . . . you here in Acapulco of all places . . . it's just too wonderful, too marvelous . . ."

"We're holding an international pathology forum here," he explained. "There are doctors from all over the world attending."

"God bless all pathologists," I laughed through my tears.

"You weren't harmed by them, were you?" he asked.

"Only mentally," I replied.

"Just relax now," he prescribed. "We can go into details later."

"Do you think they'll come back?" I inquired apprehensively.

"It certainly didn't look like it, the way they took off," he noted.

"I've got to call Winnie Garrett," I said, "that's more important than anything."

"Whoever that is," he said with a sympathetic smile.

"My lawyer in London," I explained. "He's handling the negotiations with those bums."

"They really did kidnap you?" he asked a trifle incredulously.

"Not in the bound-and-gagged sense," I elaborated, "but I *was* being held against my will."

"It's almost unbelievable," he said. "An international figure like you just pulled right out of the mainstream and nobody notices?"

"It was kept a secret," I responded. "Otherwise they never could have gotten away with it so long."

"Interpol must have known," he said.

"I'll find out when I talk to Winnie," I told him. "I'm still shaking from it all."

"Come," he suggested, "I'll get you a sedative."

"I'd rather just go the bar and have a drink," I replied.

"Okay, let's do that then," he agreed.

No sooner had we seated ourselves than the hulking silhouette of Jan Dvorak looked in the lounge doorway. He spotted me immediately, but the sight of Dirk made him wary. "That was my guard," I informed Dirk.

"A real behemoth," he observed.

"I should turn him in," I said, "but right now it's too complicated."

"They'll get him if he's involved," he predicted. "But you'd better talk to your lawyer before you start pressing charges in foreign countries."

"Good advice, doctor," I said, clinking my glass against his.

Dvorak moved away slowly, no doubt puzzled by it all. I saw him go to the desk. There he would learn that his bosses had flown the coop without him. What happened to him now was no concern of mine. The drink reached inside me like the soft caress of a lover. I could hardly believe it was true. I was free of them at last. Or was I?

I had no clothes except the ones I was wearing. But that would be resolved with a single call to Win Garrett.

Acapulco offered an array of smart boutiques and couturiers, so I had no reason to fret over a temporary inconvenience. Besides, after what he had done for me, I intended to be naked and available for Dirk Boland much of the time I would be with him.

Even before calling Winnie Garrett from Dirk's room, I had to let my hair down—hopefully for the final time. Dirk, with his surgically skilled hands, helped me remove the bobby pins and combs that held it tightly against my skull. When it had spilled down over my shoulders once again, he offered to brush it to its full glory.

"I love doing it," he confessed. "Sometimes I think I'm really a frustrated coiffeur."

"You have a nice touch," I complimented him. I felt as radiant as the sun now that I was truly Christina van Bell again.

"It's as soft and smooth as silk," he said, "the most beautiful hair I've ever seen."

"Even prettier than this?" I surprised him, spreading my legs and exposing the curly lamb's wool of my cunt.

He wet his lips with his tongue, his eyes intent on my furry triangle. "Oh, Chris," he sighed, "don't show me that unless you're serious."

"I'm always serious about my pussy," I purred.

He fell to his knees as though he had seen a vision, deftly parting my thighs to make room for his face. "A fleur-de-lis of sacred flesh," he declared before worshipping it with his tongue.

I was in such an elevated state, so keyed up over the sudden change in my life, he brought me to orgasm in record time. Then while I was still reveling in the aftermath of the triple climax, he shed his clothes and plunged the rounded arrowhead of his cock into the quivering mound of my cunt. His prick was truly a monument to his manhood, hard and slick as marble. He, too, was mightily aroused and quickly heated himself to the point where part of him seemed to melt, spurting from the tip of him like liquid marble. I reached down and pulled off the final drops, letting them form a small puddle on the flatness of my abdomen.

"That was a good, ripe load." I smiled at him.

"Christina," he said solemnly, "you'll never know just how many times I jacked off in memory of you—in tribute to you, really."

"I'm honored," I responded.

"If all the oceans of the world were filled with fresh cum, it still wouldn't be sufficient to do justice to you," he declared.

"That's sweet of you, Dirk," I replied.

"Let me stay in you just a little while longer," he requested. "I feel almost spiritual having relations with a goddess like you."

I laughed lightly. "What a way to find religion," I said. "A born-again cocksman."

"It would be very easy to fall in love with you," he told me.

"Do," I said, "but forget about marriage. I love being loved, but not being possessed."

"I know that," he replied with just a trace of sadness. That note ended the eroticism for the moment as far as I was concerned.

"Not to interrupt a lovely connection," I remarked while pushing myself up on my hands and bracing myself against the bed, "but I have some serious business to attend to—if you remember."

He pulled out of me and fondled himself fleetingly. "Of course," he said apologetically, "I'm really taking advantage of you. I'm sorry."

"Please, Dirk," I scolded him, "that's uncalled for. I loved the reunion as much as you did. But I do have to call Win, and the sooner the better."

"I know you do," he said, handing me the telephone. "Be my guest, and talk as long as you like."

"Thanks," I responded. "I'll see that you're reimbursed."

"Nonsense," he said. "Just to have you with me, I would pay for all the calls made in the world since Alexander Graham Bell."

"You're sweet," I told him, throwing him a kiss.

Before I could pick up the receiver, the phone unexpectedly rang. "Should I pick it up?" I asked him.

"Certainly," he replied. "I'm not expecting anyone, and I'm not hiding from anyone."

I put the dildolike receiver to my ear. "Hel-lo," I cooed into it, exaggerating the syllables for the fun of it. But any sense of play I had disappeared the moment I heard the voice on the other end. It was Miguel, threatening me with all sorts of dire consequences if I didn't report immediately to Jan Dvorak's car waiting half-a-block down the avenue from the hotel.

"Never!" I screamed into the sievelike mouthpiece. "You'd better run for your life because the police are already after you!" With that I slammed the telephone back into its cradle as Dirk stood by helplessly.

"You don't have to explain who that was," he assured me quietly.

"Imagine the gall of that sonofabitch," I fumed, "daring to track me to your room and threatening me when he's the one who's in trouble."

"It's obviously a desperate move," Dirk reasoned. "Looking at it from his standpoint, I guess it was worth a try."

"He says that big lunk of a bodyguard is waiting for me downstairs," I revealed. "They must be at the airport, hoping I'd join them. It's sheer idiocy to think I'd ever go back with them after the last couple of months on the run."

"People think irrationally when they're under severe stress," he said. "Just calm yourself down and let them be the ones to self-destruct."

"You don't think I should go down there and tell that fat-head where to go?" I asked agitatedly.

Dirk smiled patiently. "Of course not," he said. "He's liable to throw a net over you and drag you away."

"Fat chance," I bristled. "I'd kick him right where he lives."

"You're a tigress when you're aroused," he chuckled. "No wonder you're such a super fuck."

"That sounds funny coming from you, doctor," I teased him. It did seem to calm me down slightly. It always amused me when people who chose their words carefully unexpectedly resorted to slang and obscenities.

He offered me another tranquilizer, but I opted for hashish instead. "Nature's own sedative," I explained as I drew in the sweet smoke.

"I think you should call this fellow Garrett as soon as possible," he suggested. "Especially with those people still lurking around somewhere."

"Good idea," I agreed. "That call threw me off the track."

I gave the hotel operator Winnie's name and the firm's address. I didn't know the telephone number by heart, and my little blue book was with my wardrobe. She informed me she would call back when the party was reached.

"Dvorak's got my things in the car," I told Dirk. "Do you suppose we could send somebody from the hotel for them while he's still waiting?"

"You don't think he would just relinquish them, do you?" he questioned.

"What good are they to anybody else?" I replied. "Naturally it would involve a bribe, too."

"I say let them go, Christina," he advised. "You don't need them really—not as long as I'm here. It would be too risky even to make the slightest overture to desperate people like them."

I frowned briefly. "The trouble with doctors is they're too damned logical," I complained.

He smiled. "Wait for the call," he said, "and enjoy your smoke."

The room was cloudy with my exhalings by the time the phone rang. I seized it immediately, eager to spill out my story to Winnie. But as luck would have it, he was away in the country and couldn't be reached until the following morning. "Tell them it's Christina van Bell calling," I notified the operator in London, "and tell them it's urgent."

"That message will be conveyed to Mr. Garrett," I was told with typical British aplomb and reserve.

"I'm dead until tomorrow," I said to Dirk.

He slipped next to me on the bed and ran his hands over my naked body. "Yours is one body this pathologist doesn't want professionally," he said with soft sensuality honing his voice. "Let's see if we can perform some form of resuscitation to keep it alive."

His mouth surrounded the lips of my cunt and succeeded admirably in restoring me to life. So much so, in fact, that we hardly slept, too busy pumping life into one another throughout most of the night.

CHAPTER TWENTY-THREE

Winston Garrett was beside himself with joy when he finally reached me. I could have sworn the old gentleman was actually crying during the early part of our long conversation, but he naturally denied that, attributing his sniffles to a lingering head cold. He said he had never been through such a torturous ordeal in his long and distinguished legal career   desperate to protect and free me, yet sworn not to notify the police, fearing for my safety.

"Death no longer frightens me," he told me. "I've died a thousand times since the day I was informed of the ransom demand."

"Your voice sounds positively angelic," I said. "Just hearing it makes me feel warm and safe and protected."

"You're not out of danger, my dear," he warned. "These are reckless and thoroughly desperate people we've been dealing with."

He still did not know the identity of the man behind it all. And for some reason I was reluctant to tell him, despite all that had happened to me. I decided as I spoke that I was really an incurable romantic, disturbed by the idea of figuratively decapitating a once precious lover. But it had to be done, like it or not.

"You do know who's behind it all, don't you, Winston?" I finally forced myself to say.

"Not absolutely, no," he admitted. "I have some ideas, but nothing substantial to back them up."

"I hope you're sitting down," I said, "because this is liable to knock you off your feet."

"I am sitting," he said, "if that makes you feel any better, my dear."

"The mastermind of it all is . . ." I paused for dramatic effect, "Miguel Clemente."

There was silence for a moment, then a raspy clearing of his throat. "Christina," he said slowly and deliberately, "I'm not surprised."

More than enough money was transferred to an Acapulco bank in my name the following day. Winston insisted that a bodyguard be hired for me even if we remained there only another twenty-four hours. So now I not only had my own suite near Dirk but also a handsome Mexican gunman at my side.

"The bodyguard I can see," Dirk kidded me, "but the handsome part is just overkill."

"All the men in my life are handsome," I retaliated, "including my sandy-haired pathologist."

"Dishwater blond, my mother called it," he said with a grin.

"Wheat-colored," I suggested.

At any rate Luis Puente was polite and unobtrusive as befitted a hired guard. His presence freed Dirk for some of the meetings he had come to Acapulco for in the first place I felt guilty for having kept him away from too many already.

"I should have been a gynecologist," he lamented good-naturedly. "The topic of discussion at their conventions is much more interesting."

"It's never too late to learn," I responded. "And I've got a specimen you can practice on."

"The offer is gratefully appreciated," he said, "and will be acted upon at a later hour."

"At your convenience, doctor," I quipped.

I took advantage of an afternoon meeting he wanted to attend to go shopping for the nucleus of a new wardrobe. Luis, with his shoulder holster adding an extra bulge to his broad chest, rode in the cabs with me and walked only a half-a-step behind me as I foraged about among the posh boutiques and sports shoppes. How marvelous it felt to be on my own   even with a mahogany shadow following.

"Christina van Bell," I heard salesgirls whisper as I moved about examining the latest resort styles. My own name, my own identity again. I vowed never to take it for granted in the future   not after what I'd been through.

Luis had a sly way of appraising my figure, skipping his eyes over me whenever he thought I wasn't looking. But I was equally sly and coy in catching men in the act. After the third or fourth ricochet of glances, I drew up provocatively close to him and asked, "What do you find most interesting about me, Luis?"

He was momentarily taken aback by my unexpected confrontation. But with true Latin poise, he quickly recovered his equilibrium. "Everything, Señorita van Bell," he said with a beguiling smile, "everything you have and are."

"There must be some special attributes you find more intriguing than others," I persisted.

"*Si*," he agreed, "but it would not be proper for me to say."

"With me," I told him, "propriety goes out the window when I so desire."

"But I am in your employ," he hesitated.

"Tell me," I taunted him, pressing against him now.

"Your body," he said softly.

"Which part?" I continued to press him.

"All of it," he said.

"Come in here with me," I said in a sultry, low voice. I was in an elegant salon with several plushly furnished dressing rooms provided for its patrons. I opened the door to the nearest one and directed Luis inside. He looked apprehensively over his shoulder as I quietly locked the door behind us.

"Now," I said, unzipping the gown I had been trying on and letting it fall about my ankles, "point to what you like best and then sample it, courtesy of the management."

He looked stunned by my sudden nakedness and availability. I knew it was like a fantasy coming true for him and that made it more enjoyable for me as well. "*Bello*," he whistled long and low. I understood "beautiful" in practically every language on earth.

"Take me," I urged him, spreading my cunt with my fingers. At the sight of that action, he moved swiftly to get out of his pants and into my beckoning pussy.

"You want me to stand up to you?" he asked, his cock denting my stomach.

"Let me get up on this bureau," I said. It was really just a counter with a mirror behind it. I lifted myself onto it and grabbed my legs by my ankles. "Fuck me," I said, offering him the whole triangle of my vaginal apparatus.

"*Magia*," he gasped. Then he entered the magic with his wand.

I looked over my shoulder to watch it in the mirror. There was no sleight of hand involved in my clutch and squeeze of his hairy balls.

"*Zorra*," he said. Then translating it, he uttered, "Bitch."

"Bastard," I shot back at him. "Fucking bastard."

He responded with a vigorous assault on my cantilevered cunt. It was the kind of savage attack I expected from a man of his low breeding and position. He harbored a vague contempt for successful, aristocratic people like myself, and I was exploiting that disdain for a special kind of resolution. It worked beautifully. I almost fell off the bureau from the force of my response to his temporary arrogance. His cock lofted over the rim of my cunt and shot looping arcs of cum onto my bare belly. It was a personal Mardi Gras, the confetti coming in liquid pearls of semen that lacquered my assets with a lotion no store could supply.

"Lick it off me," I ordered him.

He looked at me in disbelief, his chauvinism rampant. "Me?" he questioned.

"Lick it," I repeated.

"Myself," he queried with an incredulous look, "me eat myself?"

"Lick," I said again.

He backed away and stood like a sentry at the gate to his macho country. "No," he said firmly, "I won't."

I stared at him with the fiercest look I could muster. "Lick it," I insisted. The bewildered look on his face was too much for me. I burst out laughing at his dilemma. "You proved yourself," I said. "You're all man."

"What is this?" he asked in confusion.

"Nothing," I assured him. "Give me your cock and let me suck it."

In utter confusion he fed his prick into my open mouth. I had toyed with his masculinity, and I felt guilty about it. I was taking advantage of his unsophisticated nature, and the only way I could make instant retribution was to bestow upon him the best blow job he had probably had in weeks and months—if not in all his life.

By the time we returned to the hotel, Luis Puente was my friend for life. There was no sense explaining it to Dirk Boland. He would never understand.

"You're later than you said you would be," he greeted me when we returned.

"I got carried away," I explained. "Remember, I've been a prisoner so long I don't know how to behave when I'm free."

"Buy anything?" he asked.

"A few things," I replied. "I only want enough clothes to get me to Paris."

"You don't need clothes to get you anywhere," he remarked. The shift of his features and the tilt of his eyes told me he suspected me of more than casual shopping. I chose to ignore the implication. He had been my savior, but he was not my god.

"Can we leave tomorrow?" I asked.

"You can leave anytime you want," he replied.

"Is that what you want?" I countered.

"Christina, you're so beyond me I can't even hope to focus on you."

"You're mad because I went with Luis?" I asked.

He shrugged, but there was exasperation in his face. "No single man can ever hope to contain you," he philosophized. "I'm just happy to have you for a little while."

I felt guilty for some strange reason. He was so kind and good and patient I wanted to fuck it all out of him to justify my own selfish desires.

"Come here," I purred, opening myself to him.

"It's not necessary, Chris," he hesitated.

"Come here," I repeated.

He stood staring at me, obviously trying to resist. I fingered my cunt and ran my tongue over my lips. Slowly, but with rising desire, he came to me.

"Baby," I said as I ran my fingers through his sandy hair, "let's be happy."

The fever rose in both of us in the following moments. Whatever had briefly stood between us was gone. There was a chemistry between us now that could not be denied, and we succumbed to its catalytic force with little or no resistance.

"You're bad for me," he said, "and I'm bad for you."

"Let's be bad together then," I whispered, sucking on the lobe of his ear.

He entered me with surgical finesse, practicing proctology instead of pathology for a change. "Your asshole is almost as smooth as your cunt," he said in quick puffs of exertion.

"Your cock is almost as smooth as your tongue," I returned the compliment.

I was on all fours, taking it up my ass dog fashion. His slender, skilled hands cupped the curves of my cheeks, steadying the fulcrum for his seesaw attack on my third most popular hole after my cunt and mouth. As he rocked to and fro, his balls slapped against the loose outside petals of my pussy. It was a stimulating syncopation, progressive in the effect it had on my taut and expectant libido.

"Your posterior should be preserved for posterity," Dirk commented with mock professionalism. I think he got his kicks from mixing intelligent lingo with provocative profanities.

"Fuck it," I responded with double-edged connotation.

There were only gasps and grunts after that as Dirk drove us both to the brink of orgasm. I felt him tense and hesitate when the moment was at hand, the realization of its arrival flooding me with climaxes a split-second before I felt the hot, pearly rain from his cock in and around my twitching hole.

"That felt good, doctor," I purred contentedly.

"The operation was a success," he responded, reaching under me for a handful of wet pussy. "The patient will live to love again."

His prediction came true sooner than anticipated with the spirited recovery of his prick. I took it in the missionary position this time, enjoying the pounding of his whole body against mine. In all we fucked and sucked for three hours before deciding that we needed some nutrients.

"I prescribe champagne and chateaubriand for two," he said with pseudoseriousness, "to be taken orally as soon as possible."

"It would be nice to have some meat that I can bite and swallow," I agreed.

We showered together, almost winding up in another sexual embrace. But other appetites prevailed this time, and we managed to survive the intimacy of the shower stall without indulging in another impromptu fuck.

Dinner was a delight, and for the first time in months I felt like my old self in public, complete with pesty paparazzi snapping photos and pestering me for the name of my escort and an explanation of where I'd disappeared for the past few months. I brushed aside their questions, refusing them anything more than a smile and my plunging décolletage for their lenses. Those were Win Garrett's strict instructions, pending a full report to Interpol. Still, the mere presence of the quasi-journalists with their impertinent cameras cheered me greatly, and the food seemed even better than it was.

Dirk noticed the change in me. "This is your life, Christina," he said benignly. "Nobody in the world has the right to deprive you of it."

"I do love it," I admitted. "I can't wait to get back to Europe and the Riviera."

"It won't be long," he assured me. "I really have only two more days of meetings. The rest are just routine conferences I didn't plan to attend in the first place."

Luis Puente was waiting for us as we emerged from the restaurant more than two hours later. The two men looked at each other guardedly but without hostility.

"Are we being followed?" I questioned Luis gaily.

"Only by the Nikon brigade," he reported with a half-smile.

The remainder of the evening was as dreamy and sparkling as the velvet Acapulco sky. I was high on life again and that was higher than the best cocaine on earth could get me.

CHAPTER TWENTY-FOUR

Interpol wanted to question me in Madrid. They had taken Miguel Clemente and Laurinda Alvarez into custody in Spain on charges filed by Winston Garrett on my behalf. It was a sobering revelation as Dirk and I flew over the Atlantic—enough to all but dispel the pleasant memory of the last few happy days.

"What was that you gave Luis at the airport?" Dirk inquired in the first hour we were aloft.

"Just a little memento," I replied.

"It looked like a gold medallion from what I could see," he said.

"A very personal one," I noted.

"You can tell me," he responded. "I'm beyond jealousy at this stage."

I looked at him and smiled mischievously. "It was a gold capsule on a chain," I elaborated. "Inside it has a fresh cutting of my pussy hair."

He laughed. "He'll probably have a mustache made of it," he jibed, "so that he can lick it whenever he wants."

I joined him in laughter, eager to distract myself from the unpleasantness ahead. "I don't relish being interrogated," I told him.

"Remember, they showed you no mercy," he reminded me. "They deserve to be punished."

"I know," I replied slowly and thoughtfully, "but Miguel is one of my set—a cultivated man, a wealthy man until recently. Any sort of imprisonment is going to have a devastating effect on him."

"There's an old street saying that is most appropriate to that," he noted. "It goes something like this: If you can't do the time, don't do the crime."

"You're right, of course," I agreed, "but still . . ."

"Christina, despite all the surface cynicism and glittering jadedness you try to project, you're really just a sweet, cuddly little softie underneath it all," he diagnosed.

"I can't help it," I admitted. "Miguel and I had some good times together over the years."

"What about the woman?" he inquired.

"What about her?" I tossed the question back to him.

"How do you feel about her?" he asked with obvious interest.

"I used to feel quite close to her," I said. "Now I'm not so sure."

"She was in on it all the way, wasn't she?" he persisted.

"You sound like you're the investigator," I told him.

"I am a coroner, remember?" he reminded me.

"But these two aren't dead, at least not yet."

"Would you consider either of them suicidal?" he wondered.

"Him, yes—but not her," I decided.

"Weak male, strong female, eh?"

"I didn't mean it that way, Dirk," I responded sharply. "I'm merely making a character judgment based on observation. Miguel's whole world has collapsed, but Laurinda was only his employee—and part-time lover."

"Interesting," he mused.

"Are you staying with me in Madrid?" I changed the subject.

"I don't think so," he replied with a touch of sadness. "I do have to get back to Bristol."

"I wish you could be with me," I reacted. "It's going to be an ordeal for me, and you're such a tower of strength."

He reached over and took both my hands in his. "I wish I could, too," he said with conviction. "I will get back there if it drags on to any degree."

"Winston will be there, at least," I told myself aloud.

"He sounds like quite a man," Dirk noted. "I'm impressed by him without ever having met him."

"I'd be lost without his wise counsel," I said. "He's like a father to me as well as my top legal advisor."

"That's a good, solid relationship," Dirk responded. "I envy you."

We both sipped cognac and drifted off into private thoughts for a time. It was amazing how utterly horny I could be at some times and how almost asexual I could be at others. Thankfully I didn't get into the latter condition very often.

Floating through the clouds always mesmerized me, especially with the aid of my little powdered and capsulated friends. Dreamily I recalled the sweet innocence of Laurinda at our first meeting on the Costa del Sol. How fragile and vulnerable she had seemed to me then, and how different she appeared to me now. I was still physically attracted to her—that I could not deny even to myself—but now that her loyalty was more to Miguel than to me. Whatever had transpired between us was momentary and fleeting, like the clouds outside the plane windows. As for Miguel, his first love was for Miguel, then for others. I could not tolerate taking second place to anyone in the affections of another. The more I thought of it, the more determined I was to reclaim my title as the number one playgirl of the world; empress of hedonism, queen of erotica, princess of pleasure. Miguel and Laurinda had swept me off my multiple thrones, diminished my luster through disguise, and subtly brainwashed me into believing I might be less than I really was. It would never happen again, I vowed once more.

We landed in the early evening at Barajas Airport. The timing was perfect since nothing much happens in Madrid before ten P.M. In fact the restaurants don't even open their doors until nine.

"Will Garrett be meeting us?" Dirk inquired as we waited for the customs inspection.

"Either he or someone from his office will be here," I said. "Remember, I'm traveling under a forged passport. Win assured me he'd have everything straightened out at the arrivals counter."

"What is your other name in case I ever lose track of you?" he asked.

"Nicole Stevens," I replied.

"Hey," he said, "that's not bad."

"I prefer Christina van Bell the blonde," I responded, "to Nicole the brunet."

"You know something?" he smiled. "So do I."

I was surprised to find a trim, efficient, but nonetheless stunning young woman attorney awaiting us. "Christina?" she approached me tentatively. I smiled and nodded. "Hello, I'm Margo Wells from the Garrett office."

"Hi, Margo," I returned the greeting. "This is Dr. Dirk Boland, a good friend of mine."

"Of course, doctor," she said cordially, "we all appreciate how much you've done for Christina in this terrible time."

"She's done equally as much for me, I assure you," he replied graciously, "if not more."

"Come follow me into the office of the chief of customs," she motioned to us. "Everything is in order, but there are a few documents Christina will have to sign."

"Committing me to prison for life," I kidded.

Margo did not smile at my jest. "A little warning, Christina," she related in a low voice, "they take themselves seriously around here. I would suggest that you not be flippant about any official matters."

"That's good advice," Dirk agreed. "They've had a lot of

terrorist activity in these parts, and nobody in uniform makes light of things."

I shrugged. "I'm used to following orders lately," I said.

Everything went reasonably smoothly for a change—no small achievement in any Latin country. I was frisked by a customs matron who luckily did not discover the small cache of cocaine I had in my cunt. That would have definitely led to complications, but I took the risk anyhow. I couldn't bear the thought of being without any white lady if I had to undergo prolonged questioning by the international police.

"Winston is coming in tomorrow," Margo answered my question before I could utter it. "He'll meet us at the hotel, and then we'll go to headquarters together."

"Where are you staying?" Dirk inquired.

Margo looked surprised by the question. "The Ritz, of course," she replied without being haughty.

Dirk smiled. "Of course," he said.

"Will you be staying with us?" Margo asked him.

"I'm afraid not," he replied. "But I'd like to take you both to dinner before I return to the airport for my flight to Bristol tonight."

"Not even one last night together?" I asked him plaintively.

"Don't tempt me," he chuckled. "The morgue's already overflowing with bodies awaiting autopsies."

"One more night won't matter that much, will it?" I persisted.

"At the risk of a bad pun," he responded, "the question of my staying in Madrid overnight is a dead issue. I simply have to get back to be in my laboratory in the morning."

"Boo," I pouted.

"The doctor's a professional man, Christina." Margo came to his defense. "He has to do what he has to do."

"Necrophiliac," I taunted him.

"Anyone who's been with someone as alive as you could

never be rightfully accused of that," he said with a quirky smile.

Margo's eyes pingponged between the two of us. Her green eyes twinkled beneath the rusty highlights of her neatly coiffed hair. Winnie still had very good taste in selecting the junior members of his staff.

"Does necrophilia really go on frequently?" she asked him with no fear of appearing naive.

"I don't know the frequency rate," Dirk said, "but it certainly does go on."

"Among pathologists, too?" she questioned.

"They've been known to climb on a corpse now and then," he related with apparent amusement, "but I think the main offenders come primarily from the ranks of morgue and mortuary employees. It's not the kind of employment that attracts your average, adjusted heterosexual with normal carnal appetites."

"Screwing dead people is creepy," I commented, making a face in the process.

"I've heard many a married man complain that his wife's a dead lay," Margo laughed.

"What an invigorating discussion," I said. "Let's get off the subject before I lose my appetite for dinner."

"You're right," Margo agreed. "No more cadaverous conversation until after dinner."

"Until after Christina is tucked away out of earshot," I appended her statement.

We dined at Zalacain with no further mention of anything even remotely related to necrophilia or even pathology. I adored the strawberry soup almost as much as the truly exquisite champagne. It was a breezy, informal meal with lots of laughs and little or no serious conversation. Margo was a fun person once her professional barriers were down. As the evening wore on, I felt myself becoming more and more attracted to her, envisioning the fiery bush that surely nestled at the meeting place of her thighs. The anticipation of possibly making it with her eased the pain of saying goodbye to Dirk. He had to excuse himself before dessert due to the time.

"I'll just make it to the airport in time if I leave this very second," he said.

I stood up and embraced him fully. Our lips met in a long, liquid kiss that was perhaps a bit out of place in such an elegant restaurant, but I didn't care. This man had literally saved my life and restored my freedom. I would be forever indebted to him.

"You will come back as soon as you can?" I said to him, my eyes misting.

"Of course," he said, turning away quickly to hide his own eyes. "Margo, it was a pleasure meeting you. If I ever need legal representation in London—or anywhere else—I'll certainly call on you."

"Goodbye, Dirk," she responded. "We're all so very, very grateful to you for what you've done for our Christina."

He nodded and left quickly, visibly moved. "He's such a sweet man," I said, dabbing my eyes with my napkin.

Margo smiled sympathetically. "Sweets for the sweet," she said.

The sadness of parting later dissolved into the joy of meeting. Margo was one of those deceptively calm, cool, and collected people who behind closed doors become uninhibited hellions. Before I could even suggest any form of carnal collusion between the two of us, she was all over me with wet kisses and wandering hands. We fell into the natural position for mutual cunnilingus as though we had rehearsed the act repeatedly for this premiere performance.

"I love to suck pussy," she confessed in the brief wrestling match before beginning. "Cock is great, but cunt is superb."

"You said it for both of us," I agreed. Then my tongue tangled eagerly with the sweet scarlet croissant of her cunt. What a pussy it was, moist and ripe with just enough musky pungency to make me savage in pursuit of it.

"Mmmmm," she hummed from my depths, sucking like a drowning person going for her last breath.

I rammed my face into her flaming ruby hole and drank in the warm nectar as my tongue fenced with the hardened tip of her clit. She writhed and squirmed, lifting her ass off the floor to absorb every minute calibration of my tongue. My fingers ran up the split of her buttocks and dug deeply into the moist river bed. The more I ravaged her, the more I came. It was like fireworks exploding inside me—stars, rockets, and comets that set my entire insides burning.

We did not relent in cannibalizing each other for hours, not until sheer exhaustion overwhelmed us and sent us into each other's arms and then into the arms of Morpheus. It seemed like only moments later when the phone rang to announce the arrival of Winston Garrett, but the sky's bloody rinse confirmed the unbelievable. It really was morning, hours and hours since our combined collapse.

CHAPTER TWENTY-FIVE

Behind dark glasses, I sat with Margo Wells and Winston Garrett, breakfasting on the outdoor terrace of the Ritz. It had taken a long, long shower and a quick exchange of cunnilingus to get us into any kind of shape at all for these important meetings. Winston, as always, observed everything but kept any critical thoughts to himself. The old fox had probably sent Margo on this mission deliberately   he was no stranger to his client's special needs and appetites.

"Christina," he said, "you look remarkably fit for one who's been through such an ordeal."

"Winnie," I responded, "you'd tell me that even if I looked cadaverous."

Margo laughed lightly at that, no doubt recalling the night before with Dirk. "She already has her own pathologist," she pointed out. "How many people can say that?"

"I dare say, not a great many living creatures," Win fell into the preliminary lightheartedness. He was a well-rounded man and not just physically, able to enjoy a joke at the appropriate times.

"I may be needing him professionally soon if this hangover doesn't subside," I said with a tap to my inwardly swollen head.

"I understand you two had quite a night of it," Winnie injected, peering paternally over the rims of his glasses.

"It was kind of a hello and goodbye party," I explained. "Hello to Margo, goodbye to Dirk."

Winnie nodded, smiling to himself. "Well," he said, "it was a good way to forget about all you've been through, poor dear. Our prayers were with you during that long period of uncertainty."

"What's going to happen to them?" I asked with concern.

"That's up to the courts to decide," he answered noncommittally.

"What would be an educated guess?" I inquired.

Margo looked to Winnie for the response, although she appeared ready and able to field the question herself.

"In Spain?" he contemplated aloud. "I'd think anywhere from ten to twenty years."

"For everybody?" I asked.

"I'm thinking in terms of the ringleader," he replied. "The others would most likely get lesser sentences."

"Or none?" I questioned.

"Not likely here," he responded. "Not with the current spate of terrorism. They might even get significantly longer and more severe sentences in light of that."

"Clemente's status in the country could work to his advantage somewhat, don't you think, Mr. Garrett?" Margo suggested

"Good point," he credited her. "He's some sort of minor nobleman as I recall, in addition to being a large landowner. It could work in his favor, but it might also go against him."

"Will I have to testify?" I asked with sudden apprehension.

"That all depends," he answered. "Let's not worry about that at this stage of the proceedings."

"What time are we due at Interpol?" Margo inquired.

"Directly after lunch," he said. "It's a major case, so there will be media people present after our meeting."

"I was afraid of that," I sighed.

"You're a very prominent person, Christina," Winston

pointed out. "When this breaks, it will be a story of international interest."

"Those Mexican paparazzi are going to make a fortune off those shots of me and Dirk," I remembered.

"No doubt," he agreed. "See all the good you're doing for the poor photographers of the world?"

"I feel I've known Christina for ages just because I always see her picture in every newspaper and magazine I pick up," Margo said.

"It's always a pleasure, too," Winnie added.

I listened to them and thought about how often I had been celebrated. I never claimed to be anything special. I was what I was; I am what I am. It was everybody else imposing roles and fantasy dimensions upon me that made me sometimes appear larger than life.

Winston must have been carried away by the champagne because he continued throwing bouquets at me. "Christina," he went on, "you are a special and very precious person, unique beyond belief. You move among blasé people, and yet you somehow manage never to become blasé yourself. You're always fresh and beautiful, always sweet and considerate . . ."

"I think I'll need Dirk sooner than I realized," I responded. "I'm already being eulogized."

"Not at all, darling girl," he denied, "it's just that we who love you had much time to think about how empty the world was without you during your captivity. There were moments when we silently feared we might never see you again."

"Keep it up and you're going to make me cry," I said.

"Winston's right," Margo joined in, "now that I've really met you, I couldn't bear the thought of not having you around."

"Please, both of you, stop it," I pleaded, "you're embarrassing me."

"The truth should never embarrass you," Winnie said.

I finally got them off the Christina kick and onto the matter of our meeting with Interpol. Margo had prepared the file on the case, and as I glanced over the pages and pages of evidence she had compiled, I realized that she was as good at preparing briefs as she was at taking them off in bed. "I'm really amazed at how much specific evidence you were able to gather without my assistance," I told her. "Some of these things even I didn't know for sure."

"That's why we have our own staff of investigators," she said.

We dallied over coffee and liqueur for almost two hours after finishing breakfast, then went to our rooms to dress for the session with the police. My juices were running at high tide as they always did under stress. "I could use a good, hot fuck right now," I confided to Margo as we confronted each other nakedly once again.

"Your wish is my command," she laughed, grabbing at my crotch.

"That pussy of yours looks like the Biblical burning bush," I noted.

"Put out the fire then," she proposed.

We pretzeled into each other, a tangle of arms, legs, lips, tits, and cunts. "Let me get a vibrator," I suggested. She relaxed her hold instantly.

"That would save us from getting too sweaty and messed up," she agreed.

I got the instrument   a cylindrical device the size of a good cock   and put it between us pussy-to-pussy. "This way we'll both be fucked by the same dick," I said.

"Let me on top," she asked.

"The male role," I teased her.

"I want to fuck you," she said.

I flicked the switch, and the dildo began humming amidst the twin nests of our cunts. Margo moved her lower body provocatively, as though the instrument was her cock.

"Fuck me hot, baby," I urged her, pressing upward against the fleshy mound of her scarlet pussy.

She bent down and sucked on my tits as the vibrator hummed away. I watched the red ribbons of her lips wind about my taut nipples and revel in the friction applied to them. "Move your ass, honey," she told me in a voice reedy with desire.

"Keep fucking me, you sonofabitch," I demanded, lifting her with the arch of my back.

"Bitch baby," she said hoarsely, "I'm going to come and come all over you."

"You fucking whore," I cried as the first response to her fervent fucking coursed through my body. She groaned loudly as it traveled from me through her. From then on we came and came, deep-throating each other with our tongues as the magic repeated itself time after time. It took a reminder call from Winnie Garrett to break us up, or else we might have spent the whole day exchanging climaxes.

"I never met anyone as hot as you," Margo said when we were finally restored to respectability in the elevator to the lobby.

"You're not exactly a native of Antarctica either," I responded.

Dressed in modest but fashionable dress suits, we could not possibly have been suspected of being the torrid sexual combination we really were. It was all part of the game of life, the polite deception we all practiced at times to bewilder the rest of the human race. On occasion I especially enjoyed portraying a very prim and proper young lady, then casually spreading my legs in a somber setting to reveal my naked pussy. What stares of disbelief it always produced! But of course I would do no such thing with the police, even though I knew all police were as susceptible to such enticements as any other males   if not more.

Winston was all business when we met him, some of his natural affability buried in his serious demeanor. It was just another example of why he was such an excellent barrister He knew the fine-line between having fun and being ridiculous.

"Christina," he said in the car en route to headquarters, "I want you to be absolutely truthful and candid about everything that occurred during your kidnapping. Don't try to shade any details to cover up for yourself or any of those involved."

"What about sexual matters?" I asked bluntly.

"Insofar as they relate to how you were treated and how they affected your captivity, you should tell them whatever they need to know," he replied.

"You don't have to tell them how many times you came on a given occasion," Margo injected whimsically, "or the dimensions of anyone's equipment, but short of that they have a right to inquire about your sexual treatment."

"And they will," Winston stated realistically. "It's not often they get an opportunity to intimately interrogate a woman as beautiful as you, Christina."

"I won't have to demonstrate anything, I hope, do I?" I questioned.

"This is a verbal interrogation," Winnie replied, "not a physical one. Remember, you're appearing voluntarily, so there shouldn't be anything but gentlemanly treatment from them."

"I'm beginning to get frightened by it all," I confessed.

"Don't be," he said, patting me on the knee. "It shouldn't take more than two or three hours at most."

The session went comparatively smoothly, though somewhat traumatically for me. It was difficult to relive some of the memories of that long odyssey, and I broke down and cried several times in the process. But I persevered, and when the time came to sign my testimony, my hand was firm and steady.

Winnie took us out afterward to celebrate on champagne and pheasant, after which we drank ourselves dizzy at a flamenco nightclub called Corral de la Moreria. I fell madly and drunkenly in love with one of the slim male dancers named José.

"Take him home with us," Margo whispered to me after

Winnie had left. It was already three A.M., and he had business to attend to in the morning. Besides, it was the drunkest I had ever seen him in all the years I had known him sitting motionless and silent like a portrait of Winston Churchill. Margo and the maitre d' helped him to a cab, then she rejoined me to form a two-member fan club for the tightly trousered dancers. There were several attractive women in the troupe as well, but this was my night for boys. I absolutely had to have a good stiff cock inside me before I could even hope to go to sleep after this trying day.

"I feel the same way," Margo confessed when I told her of my yearning. "Let's invite them all to our suite for a party."

"The women, too?" I asked.

"We can't practice discrimination," she kidded. "Besides, when you wake up later, you just might be in the mood for some sweet Spanish pussy."

I winked at her. "How come you're so smart?" I jibed.

The dancers eagerly accepted our invitation, so Margo called the hotel and arranged for a hasty party in one of the small banquet rooms. There we could make all the noise we wanted since there were no guest rooms near it.

"Perfect," I congratulated her.

"We're going to have tasca-type hors d'oeuvres," she said enthusiastically, "fried mushrooms, padrones, cheese croquettes, baby shrimp, tiny sparrows, meatballs and potatoes in garlic sauce—plus buckets and buckets of booze and champagne . . ."

"How can you think of all that stuff?" I marveled. "I'm too blitzed to think of anything but cock."

"I forgot to add that," she laughed, "and yards and yards of hard cock and sweet pussy."

I ran my tongue over my lips. "Now I'm really getting hungry again," I said.

We spent the rest of the show imagining the sizes of the dancers' tightly compressed pricks. Their bulges were more or less uniform, making any kind of accurate appraisals difficult. But it was fun anyhow, so much so that I completely forgot about the lengthy interrogation I had undergone earlier.

The party was a wild success—or so I think. I was so stoned I had only fleeting remembrances of being fucked and sucked by everybody present, both male and female. Cum flew all over the place like rice at a wedding, and I skidded about in it, doing my own versions of flamenco over the undulating bodies fucking on the floor. Margo took on the entire troupe in succession at one point, blowing and screwing as though there was no tomorrow. Sometime toward noon I slipped away to our suite with José and concentrated all my efforts and attention on his sleek and resilient prick. It rose from the flat of his stomach like a rattlesnake aroused in its nest. He shish kebabed my cunt on it, adding his balls for good measure. Drunk as I was, I could not get enough of him, forcing his cock to revive time after time. Eventually, however, even cocaine could not sustain me any longer, and I simply passed out. Stars were twinkling in the sky by the time I came to hours later. Margo was sprawled on the bed next to me, her naked body bearing a flaming red lipstick scrawl declaring "Super Fuck." The dancers, of course, were gone. It was almost time for another evening's performance.

"Margo," I tried shaking her awake. She did not stir. Then I recalled the old reliable wake-up trick   an ice cube up the cunt.

"Bitch," she groaned as its chill invaded her body.

"We've got to get up," I told her. "We lost a whole day."

"Fuck it," she mumbled, forgetting her professional decorum.

"We were supposed to meet Winnie for lunch," I reminded her. "That was hours ago."

That realization jolted her. She sat up instantly. "Jesus," she gulped.

"There's probably a message at the desk," I suggested.

"I can't call yet," she said. "My mouth feels like somebody defecated in it."

"Try ejaculated," I jested lamely. I was not in great shape myself, but I knew we had to make contact somehow. Neither of us knew exactly what the plans were now that the meeting with Interpol was over.

"What a party," she recalled, holding both sides of her head as though the contents might otherwise spill out.

"Those bastards dance as well horizontally as they do vertically," I agreed.

"Did you try that one kid with the cock like a boomerang?" she asked.

"I tried everybody," I confessed.

"It hurts to laugh," she said, laughing. "He stuck that thing in me, and I thought it was going to come out my ass."

"That one girl with the toe fetish—did she do a tune on your feet?" I inquired.

"Is that what that was?" Margo giggled. "I was so wiped out I thought my feet were bleeding."

We both chortled. "What a fun night," I noted. "I'm surprised we haven't been thrown out of the hotel."

"Maybe we have been," she said, "but nobody could move us. We were dead."

"Now you've made me afraid to call the desk for messages," I said.

"I'll call," she volunteered. "After all, I work for you, not vice versa."

"You work for Winston," I corrected, "you *play* for me."

She smiled in response. "That's sweet of you, Christina," she said.

Winston had indeed called but only once. That was a sure indication that he did not like being stood up. Margo tried reaching him at several numbers but couldn't locate him.

"He'll get over it," I assured her. "He never holds grudges."

"Well," she said philosophically, "we've still got our hotel rooms, but now I'm not sure if I've still got a job."

Neither of us really believed that, but we got dressed in

a mood of solemnity that sharply contrasted with the one of the night before.

"Let's just have a quiet dinner and get to bed early to-night," Margo proposed.

"Amen," I agreed.

CHAPTER TWENTY-SIX

Winston returned to London after informing me that Jan Dvorak had been taken into custody in Malaga along with two other men with whom Winnie had conducted all the negotiations. They were both foreign agents for Miguel's far-flung business interests it turned out, and not the professional terrorists everyone had suspected them to be.

"You keep in constant touch with me now, young lady," he lectured me at the airport. "I'll let Margo stay with you for a few more days, then she'll have to return to London, too."

"I don't want to stay in Madrid if I don't have to," I told him. "It's not really a Christina kind of town."

He looked at me and shook his head, his eyes twinkling with amusement. "Daddy's little girl," he reflected. "Only a few days out of a harrowing ordeal and already she's hell-bent to start kicking up her heels again."

"I don't mean going wild, Win," I defended myself. "It's just that I need clothes. I want to go to Paris and pick up a few new things."

"Margo." He turned to his associate. "This should be an experience in utter monetary abandon for you. Christina can go through money like a shark through a school of fish."

"I can go then?" I seized on his remark.

"I don't see why not," he replied. "Just keep as low a profile as possible under the circumstances."

"You must be kidding," I countered. "After all that media coverage at Interpol?"

"I know it'll be difficult," he said. "In that regard you'd probably be much better off in Madrid than in Paris. The paparazzi are not too well represented here."

"They find me everywhere," I told him. "When that story breaks—which will probably be today, don't you think?— I'll be inundated wherever I am."

"Maybe you should go back to being the dark-haired Nicole Stevens," he suggested.

"Ugh," I reacted, "I'm in love with being Christina van Bell once more."

He nodded and began backing away. "You know how to handle yourself," he said. "Just stay in touch until this whole mess is finalized in one way or another."

"I promise," I pledged.

"Margo," he said with a final wave, "call me in London tomorrow."

"I will," she replied.

We watched as he crossed the runway, climbed the steps, and then disappeared into the belly of the silver jet.

"There goes a man," I declared.

"He is something," Margo agreed.

We were back at Barajas Airport again a few hours later, this time with our own luggage and tickets to Paris. I was glad to have a literate traveling companion for a change after sullen Jan Dvorak and pretty but mostly vacuous Laurinda. At least that was how she now seemed to me in retrospect, especially compared to Margo.

"Christina," Margo said to me once we were aloft, "it bothers me that you never tried to escape in all that time you were being moved from one country to another. You're such a free spirit—as I've seen personally in the past few days—it boggles my imagination to picture you docilely accepting such a fate."

I pondered her statement silently for several moments. "I've tried to explain that to myself, too," I confessed. "I think I was just in some sort of transitional period of my life or something like that. Remember, I wasn't really being mistreated, and I was carrying on a pretty intimate relationship with the girl along the way. . ."

"I didn't know that," she said with a tinge of disappointment, "but it's quite understandable now that I think about it. But still, you weren't free to come and go as you pleased. And then there was that other creature always around. . ."

"Jan? Ugh," I groaned, "don't remind me."

"If you don't want to talk about it, we won't," she said, "but I've become curious now that I know more about the way you really are."

I smiled affectionately at her. "It's sweet of you to be concerned," I said. "Really, it doesn't make complete sense to me either. Maybe I had some sort of lingering love—or more likely sympathy—for Miguel. After all, he was an old friend who'd just gotten himself into a bind and out of desperation resorted to a crazy plot involving me."

Her head bobbed up and down. "Now that sounds somewhat plausible," she said. "You are a warm, giving person, and so you would be capable of making a sacrifice for a friend."

"For a while." I limited my generosity. "I got tired of it all somewhere along the way, and then I did start thinking about escaping."

"Are you still fond of him?" she asked.

"No," I said quickly. "He went beyond the boundaries of friendship as I see them."

"What about her?" she added.

"You'd like her in bed," I replied. "As a person, though, she leaves something to be desired."

"Character?" Margo persisted.

"Something like that," I answered. "I never felt there was anything really lasting between us."

"Do you feel that with anyone?"

"My friends are my friends for life," I stated emphatically.

"And your lovers?" She continued her probing.

I smiled mischievously. "They come and go," I said. "Or should I say after they come, they go?"

"Winston told me you liked to pun and play with words," she told me.

"I like to play with everything," I jibed.

"May I ask you something very personal?" she requested.

"Why not? My life is an open book."

"How old were you when you were first seduced?"

"By a man or a woman?" I asked.

"Either or both," she replied.

"Let's see," I pondered with my index finger to my lips in contemplation, "my governess used to finger my pussy when I was about five, then she really started sucking it seriously when I was about six and a half. . . as for my first legitimate fuck, I guess I was about nine or so. One of my father's friends who was staying at our estate slipped into my room one night and put it to me."

"That's interesting," Margo commented. "You had a fairly early start then, didn't you?"

"And I haven't stopped since," I replied with a lilting laugh. "If I had it to do over again, I'd start even earlier."

"Do you advocate that for everyone?" she wondered.

"Why not?" I responded. "Life is short, and the sooner you get into it, the better."

"I tend to agree with you," she said, "but it might make a shambles of society."

"I disagree," I said. "My mother and father had intercourse in front of me frequently, and I loved it. I'd do the same if I had children."

"You're an exceptionally liberal girl," she noted.

"Libertine might be a better word," I suggested.

"Whichever you prefer," she said. "I think you're just as fascinating as you are beautiful."

"I enjoy being with you, too," I responded.

Our intimate discussion made the brief flight even brief-
er. It seemed we had barely cleared the runway in Madrid
when the seatbelt sign went on signaling our approach to
Orly Airport in Paris.

"We can't be here already," I said.

"We can't be," she laughed, "but we are."

When I emerged from the plane, a blizzard of flashes
streaked across my features. The paparazzi were out en
masse, a sure sign that the story of my kidnapping had hit
the newspapers. Now when I really needed a bodyguard, I
was on my own, except for Margo's formidable presence of
course.

"Don't say anything," she advised me, "I'll handle all the
questions." She took over so naturally and confidently I
imagined that Winston had prepared her for the assignment. But she said later that he had not, that the horde of
reporters and photographers had surprised her as much as
they had me.

"Christina! Christina!" they shouted and cried, urging
me to look first one way and then the other. Thankfully, the
airline rushed several of its public relations people to the
plane to assist me.

"Why didn't you let us know you were coming?" one of
them chastised me. "We had no idea you were arriving."

"I only decided on the spur of the moment," I told him.
"Besides, I had no idea I'd get a reception like this."

"Mademoiselle," he said, "you are the hottest news story
in the entire world at the moment. I really don't know how
we will cope with so many media people."

Television cameras stalked me like evil monoliths as
everyone demanded my attention simultaneously. A bevy
of microphones were thrust in my face like so many cocks
seeking fellatio.

"Tell us how you feel, Christina," one interviewer begged.

"Were you assaulted at any time?" another shouted.

"How could you travel undetected? Were you in disguise?" still another questioned.

"Please, please," I cried out, "I can't talk with so many people all at once."

"Let me have your attention," Margo demanded.

"Who's she?" those closest to me chorused.

"I'm one of her legal advisors," she snapped. "Miss van Bell will make no statements at this time. She's exhausted from the intense interrogation by the authorities, and any information regarding her case will come only from them. As for interviews and the like, your requests must be submitted to her attorneys in London. There will be absolutely no individual interviews granted here at this time."

The groans were long and loud. "Give us something, for crissake," a spokesman called out from the throng. "We do this for a living, lady."

"I'm sorry," Margo stood firm. "There will be no comments whatsoever from Miss van Bell. Now if you would kindly clear a path so we can get through the terminal, it would be most appreciated."

Grumbling and cursing, the small army of newsmen began breaking ranks. With a phalanx of airline PR men leading the way, Margo and I slowly managed to reach the terminal. There we were taken to a private lounge reserved for dignitaries and served welcome cocktails. Even this room was buzzing with media people who had special connections. However, they at least were respectful, contenting themselves with taking pictures and eavesdropping in the hopes of piecing together a story to accompany the photos.

"Whew," Margo whistled, "that was a little hairy there for a while."

"I can't blame them," I said in their defense, "they're sent out on an assignment, and it's tough going back empty-handed."

"We really should have anticipated this," she remarked. "It could have been handled a lot better with some advance planning."

"I suppose Paris wasn't the best choice now that I think of

it," I decided. "It's a city alive with newspapers and magazines, and gossipy ones at that."

"You have to admit it's a pretty tempting story," she said, "an international kidnapping involving the world's most beautiful and celebrated sex goddess, millions of dollars, and a ruined playboy guilty of financing a Latin dictatorship. That's practically the grist for a whole novel, not just a few paragraphs of newsprint."

"You should be a literary agent," I laughed. "That was a very convincing plot synopsis."

I had to sign autographs for the entire crew of our plane. The flight attendants in particular were astonished they had not recognized me before the landing. "We thought you were just another movie star," the cutest of them commented as I signed my name on her handbag.

"No," I replied merrily, "I'm just the kid who got kidnapped, that's all."

"Was it exciting?" another of them inquired breathlessly.

"Oh, very," I exaggerated, "guns, bullets, beatings, and rapes."

"Really?" the cute one gasped in awe.

I would have gone further with my fiction except that I noticed one of the reporters dutifully writing down everything I had just said. "I was only kidding," I told him, tugging on his jacket to get attention. "Nothing like that really happened."

"Sure," he responded cynically, discarding none of it.

I looked over at Margo helplessly. "Tell him it isn't true," I pleaded.

She shrugged. "You said it," she told me, "and he's probably got it on tape. Just don't say any more."

"I won't," I promised. "My mouth is always getting me into trouble."

"You're an oral person," Margo said with a sly look. Whereas earlier she had been my fierce defender, now she seemed to be enjoying all the attention in the VIP lounge, hardly concerned at all with what I said. I decided that I would just have to monitor myself from here on.

"Would you unbutton your blouse a bit?" one of the photographers requested.

"Who do you represent?" I questioned. "Some skin magazine?"

"Hardly," an airline press agent stepped in to answer. "He's with the largest circulation magazine in Europe."

"In that case," I jested, "I'll strip to the waist."

"That would be nice," the photographer said, "but that would be too much   and I wouldn't be able to use it anyway."

"Okay, three buttons then," I volunteered, flicking them open with my thumb and forefinger in short order.

"Beautiful," he said, climbing atop a cocktail table to get an overhead shot of my décolletage.

The confusion and chaos resumed when we tried to venture into the terminal later. Many media representatives were still patiently waiting, determined not to return to their offices empty-handed. We retreated again to the lounge where the director of public relations devised a plan for spiriting us out of the airport.

"We'll go out the cargo exit and take an airport panel truck to the edge of the field," he explained. "There I'll have one of our unmarked airline limos waiting to take you wherever you want to go in Paris."

"I have my own place," I informed him. "The housekeeper's not expecting me, but that's all right."

"Perfect," he said. "You wait here until I give you the signal. Then just get up nonchalantly as though you were going to the ladies' room. The passageway is just beyond it. I'll be waiting for you there."

"Thank you so much," I said.

"It's a pleasure, I assure you," he replied.

Margo waited until he had gone. "I'd like to fuck him," she whispered.

"Our minds are in tune," I responded with a ripple of a smile

The plan worked perfectly except for the fulfillment of Margo's wish. He was so quick and efficient neither of us had a spare moment to steer him into a compromising position.

"How did we let that one get away?" she lamented on the ride into Paris.

"You can't win them all," I laughed. "We're lucky we got out of there alive, let alone oiled and lubricated."

"My chassis could have used it," she quipped.

"I'll let you have my gardener," I proposed.

"Is he young and handsome?" she inquired.

"Not exactly," I replied. "He's seventy-three, and he's got a pot belly."

"I'll take him," she said straight-faced.

We were both lighthearted after surviving the airport siege. Paris had a way of doing that to people. I always felt younger and gayer when I was there.

The town house was in impeccable shape, the way it always was whether I was there or not. I hadn't used it in months and months, yet the bar was fully stocked with all of my favorite potions and the refrigerator filled with fresh delicacies. I loved it there, yet I never stayed more than a few weeks at most. What terrible wanderlust I had, now that I thought about it. Was I destined to be in transit forever? I liked to think not, but the day when I would settle down was still so far off on the horizon, it was invisible to the naked eye.

"What a doll house!" Margo commented approvingly.

"It's cute, isn't it?" I said in response. "Come look at the garden in the back."

"I thought you were going to show me the gardener," she kidded. "Can he still raise his own flower?"

"That you'll have to find out for yourself," I teased her back.

I could tell she was horny, but in this instance primarily for cock. There was a painter several doors down who I once accused of having a cunt for a brain because that was all that was ever on his mind. I decided to give him a ring to invite him over for cocktails and to meet Margo.

"I've got the cock," he accepted cheerily, "and you've got the tail."

"Not me," I notified him before he hung up, "it's my friend I want you to charm with your brush and palate."

"My palette?" he queried me.

"I know what I'm talking about," I said. "I mean the oral version."

"*Touché*," he reacted gleefully. "I'll be over before your receiver hits the cradle."

"Don't forget your jockstrap," I jibed.

Margo took to him instantly. "Marcel and I have so much in common," she gushed to me in the kitchen.

"Uh-huh," I responded, "you've got the hole and he's got the plug for it."

"Must you be so vulgar?" she reacted with mock prudishness.

"I'm sorry." I pretended to apologize. "What I meant to say was you've got the cunt and he's got the cock."

She slapped me playfully on the rump. "You've had him, I know," she said. "How is he?"

"He's got a prick like a horse," I replied, "and a tongue like an anteater."

"I'm hot, I'm hot, I'm hot," she declared as she left the room with a trayful of canapes.

When I returned to the living room just a few minutes later, there they were on the divan, fucking like crazy. Margo's legs were pointing toward the chandelier, her hands gripping her ankles. It opened her pussy to the maximum, which Marcel's fat tool required to gain admission.

"Excuse us," she said to me with a wink, "we're just trying to get to know each other a little better."

"Go right ahead," I replied blithely, "don't mind me. I'll just sit over in the corner by myself and jerk off with a champagne bottle."

"Be careful when you pop the cork," Marcel said, smiling through his beard.

"How do you like British material?" I asked him as he pumped in and out of her.

"That's the prettiest fucking red hair I ever saw on a cunt," he replied, his gaze focused down his body to watch the slippery action.

"She's as hot as fire, too," I said. "You better have a lot of white paint in that tube of yours."

"Gray and white," he responded, "with just a teeny hint of yellow."

"You're a student of cum?" I inquired, feeling myself as I watched.

"I'm a manufacturer," he jested.

"Let's see you produce some then," I challenged him. Margo was in heavenly pain—it was obvious from the strained distortion of her features. I could read every one of her climaxes as they registered on her face.

Marcel responded to my challenge by stabbing her ferociously with his big dick. Ultimately his balls rose with their full load of semen and clung to the base of his cock. With me witnessing, he felt obligated to put on a show, and so he pulled out of her at the moment of orgasm.

"Fuckin' bitch," he cried out as his prick exploded, splattering thick globules of pasty cum all over Margo's tits, stomach, and cunt. She reveled in the generous offering, spreading the warm juice of his cock all over the front of her body.

"Oh, was that good," she moaned, coming again from the act of anointing herself with it.

"How about sucking me off while Christina sits on my face?" he proposed.

"Love to," she replied, immediately kneeling to be close to his still solid organ.

"Don't try to steal any cunt hairs for your beard," I warned him as I squatted over his profile.

"I still say I want to paint this pussy some day," he told me. "It's a classic cunt, and it should be preserved in oils for posterity."

"Suck the fucking thing and stop lecturing," I goaded him.

Margo's mouth seemed to be on the verge of tearing at the corners as she stuffed the filet of Marcel into her gaping lips. "Don't choke on it," I advised her "When he comes, you're liable to be suffocated."

She waved her hand to indicate that she had heard me. But from then on she sucked him with such glassy-eyed devotion, I doubted whether anyone but he could communicate with her   and then only through his cock.

"You've been sucking this whole neighborhood, I'll bet," I said to Marcel. He grunted affirmation as his tongue sloshed about the simmering juices of my pussy.

I let my full weight press the lips of my cunt against his bearded face. He licked away feverishly, pulling my buttocks apart like the halves of a giant peach. I began coming in quick, spastic climaxes as I heard the slurping moans of Margo sucking and stroking his jumbo prong. Then when she sputtered and screamed, I came in a mighty tidal wave that threw me against her just as Marcel's cock erupted with volcanic force. We were both drenched with cum from his glistening, throbbing organ standing up proudly from its nest of eggs and pubic hair atop his strong legs.

"JezuzCrisst!" Margo gasped, licking at the residue sperm on his belly. "JezuzCrisst!"

"Now I have to have at least one good fuck from that weapon of yours," I told Marcel. "I swore I wasn't going to, but this is an emergency."

"I can always get it up one more time for a hole like yours," he said. And he did. We fucked to a fast and furious pair of orgasms, mine surrounded by rings of smaller but still effective climaxes. Margo was out of it for the time being, contenting herself with swigging champagne straight from the bottle.

The party continued into early evening and would have gone on all night if I hadn't called a halt to it. "I've only got a day or two in Paris," I told him, "and I'm determined to shop for a new wardrobe. I can fuck anywhere, but I can only really shop in one place and this is it."

"What do you need clothes for?" he kidded me. "You're always bare-assed and ready to fuck."

"Watch your manners there, van Gogh," I pretended to chastise him, "or you'll never see the inside of this house or the inside of its mistress again."

"Mercy, mercy," he fell to his knees, chanting. But he was generally well-mannered, and he did go as I requested with the promise of a return engagement with Margo the next day.

The next day I assembled a really stunning collection of new outfits chosen from the offerings of Yves St. Laurent, Oscar de la Renta, Pauline Trigere, and Givenchy. Margo was enchanted with one of them, so I presented it to her as a special gift for all that she had done for me. I knew she would be leaving me soon, another day or two at the most. Then I would be on my own again free to go wherever I chose with whomever I desired.

We ducked out of Paris in the middle of the following night to avoid the press. Having learned of my shopping expedition, they traced me to my town house, so there was no peace there for the time being. I decided to fly to London with Margo, then take a train to Bristol. No one would ever find me hanging around the morgue with Dirk Boland, I was quite sure. He was just the right person to help me with my reacclimation to society and to keep me hidden until the furor over my kidnapping had died down.

Winston had good news for me when I called him from Heathrow Airport after saying goodbye to Margo. Miguel and his confederates had confessed in hopes of getting reduced sentences. That meant I would not be subjected to any courtroom grillings, nor would I be forced to face him and Laurinda in person. I was the victim, but in most respects I was now out of it all. There had been no money lost, which would aid in their defense, Winston thought. The entire episode with all its serpentine travels and trials was behind me. I was once again Christina van Bell, heiress and hedonist, lover and lady with all of life's marvelous options open to me once more. As the train roared westward across the countryside toward Bristol, a sense of wellbeing as strong as a thousand orgasms swept through me. How wonderful it was to be young and alive and free! Never would I take any of these things for granted again.

MEET
CHRISTINA
IN AN EXCITING
SERIES OF
ELEGANT EROTICA